MW01201305

SAVAGE GRACE

SYDNEY RYE MYSTERIES, BOOK 12

EMILY KIMELMAN

Savage Grace
Sydney Rye Mysteries, Book 12
Copyright © 2019 by Emily Kimelman

All rights reserved.
No part of this book may be reproduced in any form or by any electronic or mechanical means, including information storage and retrieval systems, without written permission from the author, except for the use of brief quotations in a book review.

Heading illustration: Autumn Whitehurst
Cover Design: Christian Bentulan
Formatting: Jamie Davis

CHAPTER ONE

Sydney

I'm pregnant.

Gripping the pregnancy test in my hand, I can't stop staring at the blue cross in the window.

Tears start to roll, hot and slow, down my cheeks. I crouch, my knees cracking as I huddle in a low ball, emotion bowing me. My dog, Blue, whines and presses against my side, his warm tongue laving my cheek, his musky scent enveloping me. *A familiar comfort.*

Will my child love Blue as I do?

My phone vibrates on the bathroom counter, and I hiccup a sob. Squeezing my eyes shut, pressing more tears free, I hold my breath. Blood rushes in my ears, and my heart throbs in my chest...a tidal wave is washing me away. *I can't do this.*

The soft ping of a voicemail brings my eyes open. I'm staring at the cross again.

Blue shifts closer, leaning his warm weight against me. As tall as a Great Dane, with the elegant snout of a collie, the markings of a wolf, and mismatched eyes—one blue the other brown—Blue means the world to me.

My heart will have to make room for more.

But everyone I love dies.

Fear slices through me, adrenaline flooding my veins and bringing another soft whine from Blue. Standing quickly, the adrenaline demanding action, I glance at my phone.

Robert Maxim.

He can't know. My eyes trace to the trash can of the hotel bathroom. *Wrap up the test and put it in there.*

But my hand won't follow the advice. My fingers grip tighter, refusing to release the small wand of plastic. *The proof. The truth.*

Grabbing my phone off the counter, I step back into the hotel room. Blue stays close to my hip, his nose tapping my waist once, a gentle reminder he is there.

I shove the plastic wand into my bag, pushing it into a zipper interior pocket and closing it up. Locking it away.

Just throw it out.

I can't.

My hand strays to my stomach, and Blue's nose swipes against my fingers. Vision blurred with tears, I stand in the center of the hotel room, my mind reeling. Lightning sizzles across my vision, and thunder ricochets inside my mind.

Oh fuck me.

EK

Robert

Sydney is not picking up.

My hold on the phone tightens. I close my eyes and take in a slow, deep breath, relaxing my shoulders and consciously unclenching my hand. The news anchor on the television sounds gleeful as he predicts the devastation of the coming storm.

South Florida has never seen floods like this before.

Sydney picked a hell of a week to take some alone time. The mansion on Star Island—an enclave for the richest of the rich in Miami—is hollow without her. *Dammit.* I never needed company before.

My three marriages made this house feel overly full—full of clothing and shoes and purses and jewelry. Full of expectations and conversations. They all wanted so much from me.

I'm not a good husband. I don't love and cherish; I procure and protect. Each wife understood the deal before the wedding, yet inevitably found me lacking. Cold, inhuman, cruel even.

My pampered wives never knew cruelty. But they must have understood my capacity for it.

Sydney isn't my wife, but she knows me. *Really knows me.*

Blue's puppies, Nila and Frank, whom Sydney left with me because one giant dog is enough hassle for most hotels, shift at the sound of footsteps approaching my office. Nila's low growl wakes Frank, who rolls over and promptly passes out again. A guard dog he is not.

A light knock. Must be José, my chef. "Come in."

A Cuban immigrant, with a head of hair like Elvis, would envy steps into my home office. "Can I get you anything?" he asks.

I have no appetite for food but a smile turns my lips. José cares about me—worries like a mother hen. "Some toast, please." José nods and turns to leave. "Brock told you the evacuation plans?"

"Yes," José nods. "I'll go with the rest of the staff. Is Sydney back yet?"

My sour mood floods back. "No, I can't get ahold of her."

"You'll reach her, sir."

I wave a hand of dismissal, staring at my computer screen. Glancing at my watch—a gold Rolex I bought back in '98 when I made my first million—I note the time. If I don't hear from her in ten, I'll hunt her down.

A man can only take so much.

Sydney

"A storm is coming," Robert's voice is calm, but his words bolt terror through me. He knows. "Miami is under an evacuation order. Traffic will be hell. We'll take the helicopter. Where are you? I'll send someone to pick you up." I don't respond. "Funny—" He pauses, and I can hear the TV in the background. "They named the hurricane Joy." *My birth name.*

My mother's face flashes across my mind's eye—thin from her recent injuries, her eyes the same startling gray as mine, lit with a similar fervor.

Robert sighs. "I'm not trying to cut your solo time short, Sydney. I can't control the weather." He sounds disappointed in himself for the shortcoming, and that brings a smile to my lips.

All-powerful Robert Maxim can't control the weather. And he hasn't read my mind. My secret is zipped into a pocket of my bag. The storm is not a metaphor but an actual hurricane bearing down on Florida.

"I'm at the Jubilee Hotel," My throat is still raw from the crying I did earlier, and my voice comes out gritty. "I'm surprised you didn't know that; you're usually such a stalker control freak."

Robert huffs out a laugh. "I'm working on those tendencies."

I sit on the edge of the bed, and Blue leans against my leg. "Thanks for calling." I clear my throat, emotion roughening my voice. "For looking out for me."

I've never thanked him. Probably because he's tried to kill me almost as many times as he's saved me. But still...in his own way Robert Maxim cares. We've taken a long and twisted road marred by potholes, fallen trees, and loose electric wires but the journey has cemented a close friendship. We understand each other.

"You're welcome." There is a note of surprise in his voice. He didn't expect my gratitude. I'm not good at thank yous, or goodbyes...or any of that normal, healthy emotional stuff. "Brock will be there soon." Robert references his head of home security.

My next call is Dan. As the phone rings across the thousands of miles between us, I play with one of Blue's velvety ears.

"Hey," Dan's voice is thick with sleep. "Everything okay?"

No! "Sure, sorry if I woke you." I glance at the clock on the side table. It's 2 p.m. here, which means it's 4 a.m. where Dan is, on an island in the middle of the Pacific. It serves as the headquarters for Joyful Justice —the vigilante organization we founded together.

"No worries." He's sounding more awake now. Dan is a computer hacker/genius and often keeps strange hours. If he gets sucked into a project, Dan stays up for days at a time.

"I wanted to check in and see if you had a line on Mulberry…" My voice drifts off into nothingness. Mulberry is another founding member of Joyful Justice and the father of my child. *Holy shit.*

Mulberry is avoiding me for some valid reasons—after almost dying while searching for me in ISIS-controlled territory, Mulberry lost part of his leg and a lot of his memories. He didn't remember me or any of the trauma we'd experienced together. Mulberry reunited with his ex-wife, and I let him. I didn't fight for him. I should have told him the truth. That I loved him…and he loved me.

Instead, I tried to let him have a safe and "normal" life. A laugh gurgles in my chest at how ridiculous that sounds even as a thought in my head, let alone as a sentence spoken out loud. When Mulberry's memories came flooding back, so did a tidal wave of anger…at me. So, yes, he has valid reasons to avoid my calls, but now I've got a life-altering bomb to drop on him.

"He's still in the wind," Dan says. "He knows I'm looking for him. Took out a bunch of cash and either isn't using a phone or has a burner."

I chew on my lip, staring at Blue. His eyes are closed, his dark lashes fanned over his white fur, as he luxuriates in the ear petting. "Okay, thanks."

"Don't worry," Dan says. I hear him shifting in bed, his voice lowering to calm and comfort me. "He'll turn up."

The last time Mulberry and I saw each other. When… my gaze shifts from Blue to my stomach… Mulberry told me he wanted to be a part of Joyful Justice again. But then he ghosted us. And that is difficult to do. "I need to talk to him. Please Dan, find him."

"I'll keep looking." Dan promises.

"Thank you." We hang up, and I watch Blue for another beat before picking myself up. Brock will be here soon. Eventually, I will tell Dan and the rest of the Joyful Justice council that I'm pregnant. But for now I've got a city to escape and a secret to keep.

CHAPTER TWO

Mulberry

The bar smells of sawdust, sweat, and spilled beer. I lock the door behind me and call out. I'm the first one here. Glancing at my watch, I see I'm ten minutes early. *Rather be early than late.*

My boss, Shirley, cares about punctuality.

She inherited the place from her father and has run it since he passed back in '95—dropped dead of a heart attack behind the scarred bar.

With dyed red hair and a sword piercing a heart tattoo on her left shoulder, Shirley doesn't take any crap and holds her employees to a high standard. "Doesn't matter that the bar is a dive and our customers are mostly lowlifes." She punctuated that statement with a laugh made rough by years of smoking. "I run a tight ship. If you want to work behind my bar, you'll be on time, you'll be showered, and you'll smile. Got it?"

I do get it. I like working at the bar. I like Shirley, and the lowlifes, and the cash I take home to my rented room each night. I'm anonymous here, a nobody. Not the only guy in the room using a fake name. *Tyler Dirk.*

I take chairs off tables, their legs scraping on the scratched wooden floor. The main area put to rights, I check behind the bar, removing the plastic wrap over the bottles and checking what I need to bring up from the basement. We're low on well whiskey and Bud cans.

I glimpse myself in the hazy mirror above the booze and pause for a moment to stare at the stranger looking back at me. He looks relaxed. Not happy—too alone for that—but not stressed either. The weight of the world isn't riding on his shoulders.

The beard that coats my jaw has flashes of red in it. My sister's mane of red hair floats across my vision. *I should call her.*

My dark hair, sparkling with hints of silver, curls over my ears. It's grayer than my father's ever was, even though I'm younger...he died before time could take its full toll. In two years I'll be the same age he was when he passed. *He kept all his limbs.* That kind of thing ages a man.

Shaking my head, clearing it, I continue with setup.

The barrel of sawdust is out the back door, and I run into Laura, a cocktail waitress, as I step into the late afternoon sunshine. She gives me a yellow-toothed smile and drops her cigarette onto the alley's broken cement, rubbing it out with the heel of her pink cowboy boot. "Hey, Tyler."

"Hey," I say back, as I take the lid off the barrel, gather a scoop of sawdust and start filling up the two buckets. The briny scent of the Gulf of Mexico barely reaches this spot behind the bar, with its green dumpster and deep shadows, but the beach is only a block and a half away.

"Should be a good night, tonight," Laura says, rummaging in her purse for something.

"Fridays usually are," I agree.

Laura pulls out a pack of gum and folds a stick into her mouth. "You busy later?"

I don't look up at her, just give a shrug. "I'm usually dead tired after my shift." Not a total lie but still a falsehood. After work I go home and read old paperbacks and pretend like this is my life. Like it's all my life has ever been. I spend the hours when I'm not pulling beers and breaking up fights avoiding thinking. I don't think about Sydney Rye or Joyful Justice or how I lost my damn leg.

I just want to be Tyler Dirk, bartender and man of mystery.

"Maybe I could help with that," Laura offers. I glance up. She pops her gum and winks at me.

I give her a half smile. "You're too good for me, Laura." Hefting the buckets now filled with sawdust, I head back into the bar, my leg aching as I take the two steps into the dark space. Laura follows, the scent of cigarettes wafting off her and mixing with the sawdust.

The air conditioner kicks on with a hum, and a cold breeze hits the back of my neck. I spread the sawdust over the floor, throwing it in arcs and then spreading it around with my feet. The front door opens, letting in a flare of orange light from the setting sun. Shirley lets it slam shut behind her, not bothering to lock up. We open in five anyway.

"Tyler," she says in greeting. I nod. Shirley sashays to the bar, and I finish laying the fresh sawdust. "We need well whiskey and Buds," she says.

"Yup. Going to grab them now." I put the buckets back in their spot by the door and head to the basement steps. They're made of plywood and wheeze under my weight. I duck to avoid cracking my head on one of the exposed rafters.

My phone buzzes in my pocket as I'm about to pick up a case of Budweiser. It's a flip phone, a burner, so should be untraceable, but nothing is untraceable for Dan. He and Shirley are the only ones who have the number.

"Hey," I say, straightening between two of the beams. "What's up?"

"Just checking in," Dan says.

"Liar," I smile.

Dan lets out a short laugh. "Sydney asked about you again. She's worried."

Serves her right. I run my free hand through my hair and rub the back of my neck. "I'm just not ready to see her yet." I'll end up kissing her again—falling into her again. It's impossible to stay mad at her when she's right in front of me, looking at me with those eyes of hers, and saying things...sweet, dreamy things I shouldn't believe.

"That's fine, but at least call her, okay?" I don't answer, just stare down at the dusty floor and my scuffed-up work boots. In long pants you can't tell one of my feet is false. "Mulberry?"

"Sorry," I take a deep breath. "I just don't think I'm ready; I can't forgive her yet."

"You don't have to forgive her to talk to her..."

"I'll think about it, okay?"

"That's fine. But I won't keep lying for you. One more week then I'm giving her your number."

"Got it."

"Good."

We hang up, and I put the phone back in my pocket, hefting the case of beer up the steps. I'm shoving the beer into the ice when the front door opens and our first customer of the night steps in. I put on a smile. At least for now I'm still Tyler Dirk. Just a bartender. Nothing more.

And I can always get a new burner phone...

EK

Sydney

Brock takes me directly to the helipad. Robert is standing next to the machine, waiting for me, his gray suit jacket—the same shiny hue as the glinting clouds behind him—flapping in the breeze. Nila and Frank sit beside him, their fur fluttering in the wind. The bay behind them is white capped and angry looking. *A storm is coming.*

Frank lets out a happy yelp when he spots me, while Nila's tail taps rhythmically against the ground. I release Blue with a small hand gesture, and he trots over to his puppies, greeting them with head nuzzles and playful bites. Frank rolls onto his back, feet in the air, instantly surrendering...an alpha he is not.

Robert's matte black sunglasses hide his eyes. *I want to see them.* "We should go," he says, glancing over his shoulder at the waiting helicopter. "My plane is waiting. I want to get out now. Everybody is leaving the city."

"Yeah, traffic will be killer," I say with a smile. Robert turns back to me, a thin smile on his lips. I reach up to his face, and he shies away for a second but then steadies when I take his sunglasses, pulling them off his nose.

His eyes narrow—a blue-green that always reminds me of both the warmth of the Caribbean and the ice of the arctic. Fine lines fan out from them, as if he's spent too many decades squinting with the same suspicious look he's giving me now. "What are you doing?" he asks.

Good question. A rush of warmth spreads a blush over my cheeks and startles me. I don't blush. I'm not that girl.

Fucking hormones!

"Sorry..." I say. His eyes narrow further as he looks at my cheeks, which must be glowing. I turn away, still holding his sunglasses, and he catches my chin. It's forceful and intimate.

"What's going on?" he demands, his voice a low threat. *He will have his answers.*

The pilot, wearing a crisp uniform and mirrored aviator shades, interrupts us. "Mr. Maxim, the luggage is loaded. It's time to go."

We are reflected in the pilot's sunglasses—Robert, his dark hair, silver at the temples, shifting in the breeze as he holds my face; my hair, a sun-streaked blonde, waving in the wind, dancing around my shoulder in small spirals as if it's delighting in the movement. We look almost like lovers—the intense way that Robert is staring into my face, the pink flush of my cheeks.

"Give me a minute, Chris," Robert says, not looking at his employee, keeping his attention laser-focused on me. Chris nods curtly and heads toward the helicopter. "Answer me," Robert says. "What is going on with you?"

I suck my lower lip between my teeth and bite down. He releases my chin and firms his lips into a frown. "Is it Mulberry?" he asks. "Are you worried about him?"

Sort of... "Let's just go," I say, willing myself to meet his eyes. "We can talk about it later. I'm tired." I am suddenly exhausted. I hold out his sunglasses, and Robert takes them, slipping them back on, before gesturing for me to go ahead of him.

We get into the helicopter, the luxury of the private aircraft enclosing us in a bubble of safety as we lift off into the sky. The highways below are crammed with cars, people fleeing the city while we fly above it, headed toward a private airport to board Robert's jet. "Where are we going?" it finally occurs to me to ask.

"Cartagena," Robert answers, glancing up from his phone. "Colombia. I have some business there, and you've never seen the city. It's lovely." Robert, sitting diagonally across from me, returns his attention to his phone long enough to shoot off a text and then takes off his sunglasses, his eyes searching my face. "Brock will meet us there once he has secured the Miami house."

"So many houses, Robert...how do you keep it all straight?"

"I'm very smart," he deadpans.

I laugh. "Yes, you are." Returning my attention to the roads below us, I lean my head against the glass. "Do you ever tire of it?" I ask, my voice low.

Robert doesn't answer me. Probably couldn't hear me over the sounds of the helicopter. Blue rests his chin on my thigh, and I play with one velvety ear.

"No," Robert says.

"Huh?" I turn to him.

"I don't tire of it."

"Of what?"

"Whatever it is you were talking about."

I turn more fully to him, settling back into the seat so my shoulder is against the window. "Then how do you know you don't tire of it?"

He smiles, slow and smug. "I pride myself on my patience."

"Do you?" I raise one brow.

"It's my secret of success."

I laugh. "Your patience is hardly legendary, Robert. I bet if you asked any of your employees, they'd say you're demanding, not patient." I'm grinning now, enjoying how un-self-aware he is.

Robert shrugs and glances out the window. "Demanding, patient... they are not opposed to each other."

"I'm pretty sure they are," I say. "You don't 'demand' something"—I hook my fingers into bunny quotes—"and then wait patiently for it."

He turns back to me. "I do."

"Well, aren't you special," I grin.

"Yes," he agrees. "I am." Robert says it low, just loud enough to be heard over the throbbing of the machine we ride in. The helicopter where he waited patiently for me to arrive...

I swallow and try to keep the grin on my face, but I feel it slipping as his words sink in. Robert holds my gaze, waiting for my response. But I have none, so I cough out a laugh and turn to the window again. The airport appears below us and our descent begins.

Robert will figure out what's going on—he will have his answers. The question isn't if, it's when. Which leads to how...how will he react? What will happen to Robert Maxim's patience when he discovers I'm pregnant with another man's baby? What will he demand then?

CHAPTER THREE

Robert

My house in Cartagena is painted a vibrant blue—like the sky above a Colorado ski slope. It's a walled compound in the center of the old city, a tight network of streets lined with colonial-era architecture.

My Miami mansion is all neutral tones and modern lines, but this four-story townhouse has high ceilings, rich colors and antique furniture. The woman who runs it, Valentina, greets us at the door. Blue's head reaches her breast line, and her housekeeper uniform covers thick curves.

Silvery hair pulled back into a bun gives Valentina an air of dignity, while her smooth skin, flush with excitement as she welcomes me home, gives her an ageless quality.

"How long have you owned this place?" Sydney asks as Valentina leads us through the front hall into a courtyard draped with greenery. The afternoon sun slants across the paving stones and casts a warm yellow glow over a tiered fountain.

"A long time," I answer, my mind drifting back to the first time I saw it...the rain pelting the streets, the clouds turning dusk to night, and the humidity curling my hair around my face. Three days later, I'd know real humidity—the constant oppression of the jungle—but the day I bought this house, I was still naive. A smile drifts across my lips. *How times do change.* "In a lot of ways this country made me who I am," I say, surprised to hear my voice.

"What do you mean?" Sydney asks.

"Nothing." I quickly recover my composure, pushing away the memories of my time in captivity and gesturing toward the stairs, for Sydney to go first, following Valentina.

My house manager grins and speaks in rapid Spanish, telling me about the latest maintenance and offering to stock the bar in the sitting room for cocktail hour. I agree, my eyes watching Sydney as she moves up the steps in front of me.

Blue taps her hip. Nila and Frank follow behind him—as usual, Nila is all elegant control, and Frank is a giant pawed fool still growing into himself. At over a year old, Frank is as tall as his father but not as broad, Nila shorter, sleeker, and possibly even smarter.

Valentina leads us up solid wooden steps to the third floor and my favorite guest bedroom. The canopy bed, made of dark wood and swathed in white, gauzy material, is something for a princess. French doors open to a narrow, wrought iron balcony.

Sydney steps into the room, her expression unreadable. The decor is much more feminine than Sydney would ever acknowledge about herself —yet it suits her. Sydney hides herself, wearing loose clothing and keeping her hair tied back in messy buns, never applying makeup or wearing heels, unless she's traveling incognito as she so often has to do these days.

Sydney opens the door to the balcony, letting heat and humidity into the air-conditioned room. Outside, the spire of a cathedral towers over rooftops dotted with potted plants—terracotta and greenery brilliant under the hot midday sun. Beyond the old town, high rises in white and blue, opaque with distance, hug the shoreline. "It's beautiful," she says.

"I'm glad you like it." And I am glad. *Her opinion means too much to me.* "I'm right down the hall. And Valentina and the other staff are always available to you. Just dial 0." I point toward the phone on the bedside table.

Blue finishes his circuit of the room, the puppies right behind him, Nila's brow knitted with concentration and Frank's tongue flopping out of his mouth. "I'll let you get settled," I say. "Then meet me in the living room for a drink?"

"Sure." She looks over her shoulder at me, her fingers toying with the sheer white curtain as it flutters in the breeze coming through the open door.

I turn to leave and then pop my head back in. "One more thing—there is a pool on the roof if you want to go for a swim."

She laughs. "Of course there is."

"Yes," I agree. I'm not ashamed of my wealth or how I choose to spend it.

After my shower, I change into white linen pants and a pale blue cotton shirt. Rolling up the sleeves, I fasten my watch into place—a simple black band with gold face, subtle and yet expensive. Fastening my knife holster to my ankle, I slip a favorite dagger into the fine leather.

The wood of the hall is warm against my bare feet—the sun heats this interior space. Open to the central atrium, it smells of the greenery and flowers that grow in the courtyard below. The tinkling of the fountain at its center mixes with the twittering of songbirds as I jog down the steps toward the second floor sitting room.

Valentina keeps the place spotless, and I appreciate the effort. Making a mental note to give her a bonus, I enter the living room.

Sydney stands by the open French doors to the balcony, her back to me as she takes in the view. She's changed into linen as well: loose navy blue pants and a matching tunic that reaches mid-thigh. On any other woman it would look like frumpy leisure wear—but on Sydney it comes off as a fighter's practice uniform—easy to move in and lightweight.

Blue sits at Sydney's side, facing me and the door, his mismatched blue and brown eyes missing nothing. He acknowledges my entrance with a low growl of greeting. Frank thumps his tail and wags his way over to me while Nila keeps her gaze fixed on Sydney, waiting for a command. That's a hell of a dog she's got there.

Sydney doesn't turn to me, and I take a moment to admire the length of her neck, which is exposed since her hair is up. Frank gives a small yelp and spins once he reaches me, his big tail whacking into my thigh. Sydney turns quickly, as if she didn't hear my entrance...or Blue's growl. *That's not like her.*

Her eyes meet mine and leap away. Sydney's arms come up and cross over her chest, then she takes a breath before meeting my gaze again. It only takes a moment but is significant. Something is going on inside that head of hers. *Is she missing Mulberry?*

I smile at her, summoning patience and forcing my jealousy away. It won't change anything. "You okay?" I ask. She nods and gives me a weak smile. "Gimlet?" I gesture to the bar on the sideboard.

"Just seltzer, please." She's not drinking? That's strange as well.

She crosses to the worn leather couch and sits as I make our drinks. I pour myself a mescal on the rocks and bring both glasses to the couch. "Has Dan had any luck finding Mulberry?" I ask.

Her eyes jump to meet mine and her lips firm. *I've read her mind.* Of course I have, we are simpatico.

"No," she says. "Have you looked?"

"He's not right for you," I say instead of answering her question. I know where he is, and I'm sure Dan does too. But neither of us wants her to find him. She should just leave him alone. The man left for a reason.

Sydney frowns deeply. "Don't," is all she says.

"Sydney, we're friends, aren't we?" I sip the mezcal, enjoying its smoky spiciness.

She looks at Blue, who's lying next to the couch, head between his giant paws. "I don't know what we are," she says, her voice low and unsure.

I can't help the smile that twists my lips. *She kissed me back. And it was one hell of a kiss.* My gaze falls to her lips, and I am drawn to them, drawn once more to her—a salmon whose instincts force him to swim upstream even though all the herculean effort brings is his death. I stop myself from leaning toward her, from reaching out physically. Sipping my mescal again, I take a moment to steady myself. "Mulberry is out of the game. You could never leave it."

"He said he wanted back in last time I saw him."

Rage bubbles in the back of mind. *When you fucked him. At my house. While I was right down the hall.* "But he hasn't come back." My voice is even, almost offhand. Just the facts here.

"It's been less than two months." But she's not looking at me, she's staring into the bubbles of her untouched seltzer.

Sydney can't see how wrong they are for each other. "He and his wife ended their marriage over a pregnancy," I say, keeping my voice casual. She jolts, her eyes jumping to mine. "You didn't know?" Sydney's jaw clenches. "He wants children someday, I'm sure. Most men do." I give a casual shrug. "But you're not maternal."

Sydney stands so quickly that Blue has to leap out of her way. He and Nila both perk their ears toward her—searching for the source of aggression. "What do you know about what's maternal?" she hisses.

I sit back on the couch, keeping my face neutral, raising just one brow in question at her sudden rage. She turns away from me and stalks to the bar, putting her glass down, then turns and strides back to the window.

She's pacing in front of me like a caged animal, her dogs following closely, Frank managing to stumble on almost every turn—the comic relief to his father's and sister's menacing, stalwart presences. *What is going on with Sydney Rye?*

It hits me like falling into freezing water. Ice courses through my veins, numbing my limbs and making my tongue thick and brain slow. "Are you—?" It comes out hoarse, the voice of a stranger.

Sydney stops. Frank knocks into her leg and then sits onto his butt, tongue lolling out as he stares up at her adoringly. Blue and Nila remain standing, sensing the tensions wafting off Sydney in waves. I lift out of the chair, my legs surprisingly steady considering I feel like the whole world is shifting under me.

Her cheeks are pink and eyes shining. She's about to cry. "Sydney," I keep my voice gentle and my fear leashed. "Are you pregnant?"

Her eyes dart away and land on Blue. A rush of color spreads up her neck and her hand…her right hand splays protectively over her middle. *Dear God.*

A sudden surge of emotion catches me off guard. A lump forms in my throat, and my hands tremble. I close them into fists, staring at Sydney's fingers pressed into the thin shirt over her flat, hard stomach.

There is nothing soft about her now, but there will be.

She pulls in a deep breath, her thin shoulders shuddering. I turn away quickly, giving her my back. The door is right in front of me. I need to leave. Can't let her see me like this, so affected.

I walk slowly down the hall—repressing an urge to run—and push out onto the front deck. *Sydney is pregnant.*

All three of my wives wanted children. They knew I didn't intend to be a father, but as the shine of wealth wore off and their days turned long and lonely, each asked for a child. But I never wanted to be a father —to make myself that vulnerable.

My own father's voice crackles through my memories. I'm huddled close to the fence, listening to the radio—it's usually my mother who calls into "Las Voces del Secuestro"—The Voices of Kidnapping.

"Robert, son—" His voice wavers. Is it the reception or emotion? He clears his throat. "I know how strong you are, and your mother was so proud of you." I sit up, fear slipping down my spine as I strain to hear the radio over the cacophony of insect song. "She passed last night." My vision blurs and I can't breathe. Can't hear over the rushing in my ears.

I tip over, my face scraping on the fence as I slump against it, the pain in my chest overwhelming. A hand lands on my back, and Natalia crouches down next to me. I recognize her small combat boots caked in mud—everything in this hellhole is caked in mud. Natalia doesn't belong here, just as much as I don't.

"Robert?" she says—her voice lessens the pressure in my chest somehow. "Are you okay?"

I pull my gaze up to meet hers, and she raises her dark brows, her sparkling brown eyes sympathetic. She's my captor but...

Shaking my head, I drop my chin to my chest again. Natalia puts her arms around me, pulling me into an awkward embrace. I breathe her in —sweet and earthy. Shifting to better hold her, my lips brush Natalia's neck. She shivers and her fingers dig into my back. *She wants me.*

My grip on the rail of the deck tightens.

I still want Sydney. I want her even more. Impossible, yet true.

My eyes stare out at the city but see Sydney, her hair loose around her face, a smiling infant in her arms, the sun bathing them both in golden light. A strange, disconcerting, new fantasy I can't control.

I can learn to control anything.

I will this dreadful new want away and force the memories of my captivity down.

A movement below catches my attention. Three men are walking down the street—their movements tight and organized. I release the metal railing, hot in the afternoon sun, and move out of their line of sight. They are dressed in dark jeans and T-shirts with baseball caps pulled low over their brows. *These are not tourists.*

I turn and, breaking into a sprint, race back to where I left Sydney in the living room, pulling my phone out of my pocket as I run. "Brock, we've got incoming," I say into the phone as I burst into the room. It's empty.

"Yes, sir, I see them."

Crossing to the TV cabinet I open a drawer and pull out a pistol. "Where is Rye?"

"I don't know." The swish of his clothing carries over the line as he moves. This walled compound is protected but far from impenetrable. There are probably others approaching our back entrance.

"I'll find her and head to the helicopter," I tell him.

"Understood. I'll stop those coming toward the front. I've got men at the back as well. The roof doesn't have coverage at this time. We may have already been penetrated."

"Understood." We hang up, and I take a steadying breath before calling out. "Sydney!"

A floorboard creaks behind me and I duck, spinning around. The low whistle of a bullet flies over my head. There is a woman, clad in black, a ball cap shadowing her face, standing in the doorway. She grips a pistol with a long silencer at its tip. I raise my gun to fire but she dives into the room, sheltering behind the couch.

I lunge behind the matching leather chair, the one I sat in moments ago when I realized Sydney Rye is pregnant. *Don't think about it now.*

Wiping my mind of anything but this present moment, I listen for movement.

My attacker is still, producing no sound except for a quiet, even breathing. An explosion outside shakes the room, making the chandelier tinkle and plaster dust rain from the ceiling. A beam of sunlight catches the drifting motes and time slows. My heart beats. The would-be assassin behind the couch shifts, giving away her position. I rise slowly, silently, and aim at the couch.

The bullet explodes leather and fluff, blasting through the wooden frame. Her body topples onto the carpeting in a quiet jumble.

Keeping my gun up, I stay low as I come around the chair and circle the couch. She is splayed on the floor, her face obscured by the hat, blood pooling around her head. *One down.*

I kick the weapon away from the assassin's limp hand before crouching next to the body. Resting my fingers on her throat, I confirm my initial assessment. Pulling back the hat, I find a pretty face, porcelain skin, and long lashes. There is a radio in her ear, which I take, fitting it into my own. It is quiet, so these are not total morons.

A lot of people want me dead. Almost as many would like to spill Sydney Rye's blood. I pat down the body but find no identification. I'll try to keep the next one alive long enough to ask some questions.

Sydney

There are fresh cut flowers in my room.

Pink and lush, globs of orange pollen flocked to the stamen. I rub one of the delicate, velvety petals between my fingers...it reminds me of Blue's ears.

My father brought my mother flowers every week. She'd smile and kiss him with a breathless thank you. He'd growl low in his chest and tug her close—his strong arms holding her as if he'd never let go.

Her laughter drifted through the house like pollen on a summer breeze...they were happy.

When Dad died, Mom couldn't handle it. Couldn't take care of two kids on her own—couldn't be on her own.

So she drank.

I turn away from the bouquet and look out the window.

I don't expect a man to buy me flowers...I expect him to die. My love is a death sentence. That's why I pushed Mulberry away. That's why I'm best on my own.

I could end this life growing inside me before it really has a chance to get going.

But I won't. I can't. I don't even want to...

Because some part of me does want flowers every week...brought to me by someone who loves me, who thinks of me on their way home from work.

I almost laugh out loud, but the weight on my chest is too heavy. Like I'll ever be with someone who moves to the rhythms of a regular job. It is impossible for me to have a normal life.

I destroyed that option long ago. And I don't want it now.

So what do I want?

Tears blur my view of the city outside my windows. *Damn hormones.*

Blue's teeth graze my clenched fist. The low thrum of Nila's growl raises hairs on the back of my neck as a shock of recognition jolts through me: we are under attack.

I was so damn busy imagining my future that I stopped paying attention to the present.

There's the familiar pop of a gunshot below.

Blue is looking up at me, his mismatched eyes observing. There was a time when I lost his trust. When he became the leader. I refuse to go back there again.

With a jerk of my chin, I send him to the door. His sensitive nose presses to the narrow opening and his tail gives a wag. *The hall is clear of unknowns.*

I pad down it in bare feet, almost silent against the worn wood, Blue trotting in front of me, Nila and Frank on either site.

Blue stops short, his ears perked...his hackles slowly rise. *We've got incoming.*

I flatten myself to the wall—making as slim a target as possible. Knees bent, dogs at attention, I'm ready. There isn't a thought in my head as the quiet of battle descends upon me. This is where I'm meant to be. I'm good at this. At fighting and killing and surviving.

Blue, still in front of me, gives a happy wag of his tail. The sound of bare feet on the steps, inaudible if I wasn't holding my breath listening, stop. Blue's tail goes again. We know this person. Must be Robert.

He steps into the hall, so quick the man is a blur, arms straight, pistol searching for a target. The brutal gaze of a killer shifts—the blue-green warming into the familiar eyes of a friend—when he sees me. We don't speak, don't need to know who's after us or why, not in this moment. All we have to do is make it out alive.

Robert starts down the hall back the way I came. There is blood on the hem of his linen pants. The dogs fan out behind me as I follow him. We are headed for the roof. *I bet he's got a helicopter up there next to his pool.*

We pass my bedroom on the right, the open atrium to our left, the fountain below tinkling. Black ropes drop into the space. The zing of nylon rope passing through a belay has Robert pushing into the next room. They are coming down from the roof.

He closes the door softly behind us, then steps close, listening.

The sounds of the quiet movements of killers pass through the door —the whisper of fabric, the creak of weight on old floorboards.

Our breaths come in long, even, almost-silent-but-not-quite draws. *Life makes noise.*

Robert looks to the French doors and small balcony of this bedroom, the same as mine. We can't climb up or down with the dogs. His lips press tight, and the lines around his eyes deepen. The subtle tells of worry quicken my heartbeat.

He moves deeper into the room, I wait by the door with the dogs. There is no crackle of a radio—no evidence the killers are communicating.

A nearby explosion shakes the house as Robert pulls back the curtains, looking down onto the street. He draws me forward with a small wave of his hand, the way I'd direct my dogs. Clear communication between partners who know each other well.

Blue moves with me, recognizing the command as clearly as me. Nila and Frank stay close, the warmth of their bodies at once a comfort and a weight. *I am responsible for them.*

Shoving that thought aside, I step up to Robert. He looks down at me. We are close enough that I can smell the soap he used in the shower and see the glitter of white stubble among the black along his jaw. His lips turn up into a sly smile as his brows raise. I can't help but return the expression. This is what we live for…what we are meant for.

He leans close, his breath warming the shell of my ear. "We are going to have to fight our way to the roof." I nod. The lobe of my ear brushes against his lips, sending a shiver down my neck. Rapid gunshots echo in the atrium, jerking my head toward the door, and my mouth meets Robert's.

His arm comes around my waist and he tugs me close—so fast and hard that I gasp, opening my lips, and letting him in.

An accident.

He kisses me like it is at once the first and last time…but it's not the first. The heat between us ignites in a terrible ball of furious lust and heart-banging need. *Why does death so close make life so good?*

Robert's mouth tears from mine, his body angling toward the door. He pushes me behind him as the door flies open. The jerk of Robert's gun vibrates through his body—I feel it in his chest where my hand still grips his shirt, and in the fingers he has wrapped around my hip holding me behind him.

But I'm not some damsel in distress.

Blue is already moving, and I step out from behind Robert's protection, following the giant dog into the hall, grabbing the gun off the dead man in the doorway. Lips tingling, body thrumming, I move toward the roof, Robert behind me with Nila and Frank.

A shout, and the wall next to me splinters with a bullet hole. Ducking into the dark, narrow spiral staircase that leads to the roof, I take the steps two at a time, then pause before the sunlight hits me. Robert fires down the stairs behind us. A shadow flickers at the top of the steps, and a bead of sweat breaks free from my hairline, sliding down my nose as the shadow forms into a man.

I fire, the figure falling with a painful yelp. His scream pitches higher as he grabs for his crotch. I aim for his head, firing and ending his suffering.

Robert shoots behind me again. "Two bullets left," he grinds out.

Time slows—taking on that dream-like quality that only happens when my world is in danger of ending. As if time knows there is only precious moments left, so we better enjoy every last one of them.

I move into the sunlight, scanning the roof. At its center is the opening to the atrium—green vines climbing out and black ropes dropping in. The pool, aqua blue water ruffling in the ocean breeze, is just past the atrium, and beyond that sits a helicopter. A four-seater—modest for Robert Maxim. *And I used to think owning helicopters was impractical.*

"We're clear," I say, moving fast now, time speeding up again, heart racing, victory a taste on my tongue.

Blue passes me, his stride longer than mine. He recognizes our escape plan. "Wait," Robert yells as I reach the atrium. I stop, spinning to him. He hands me his almost empty pistol and then pulls a knife from an ankle holster. *I've got to get one of those.* He glances over the edge of the atrium and then begins to cut the ropes.

Nila barks and a figure appears at the top of the steps. I fire a round, and the figure dives back into the safety of the stairwell. "Come on," I say. "The ropes don't matter."

A scream echoes from the atrium, followed by a sickening crunch, and Robert is standing again, shrugging with one shoulder. I try not to smile but fail. Gallows humor takes on a new meaning in these situations.

Robert starts the helicopter while I stand next to it, covering the stairs. The blades thump through the air, blotting out all other sounds. I climb on it but don't belt in, holding onto a strap and hanging out the side of the copter as we lift off, my gun aimed at the stairs.

We rise straight up into the air and then bank toward the ocean. Free and alive.

God, I love this life.

CHAPTER FOUR

Robert

"The compound is ours again, Sir." Brock's voice is gravelly. He's tired.

"Good," I answer. "We are headed to the Panama City apartment." The wind whips Sydney's hair out of her ponytail and ruffles the thick fur of her dogs. We are standing on the tarmac waiting for them to fuel my jet. There is a plush sitting area at this private airport, naturally, but Sydney needed the air. *Because she's pregnant.* An unfamiliar zing of emotion speeds up my spine, settling in my throat and making my jaw tingle.

"I'll clean up here and meet you. I'll send Stevens and Jones ahead with your and Ms. Rye's luggage," Brock says.

"Any idea who they were?"

"Hired mercenaries, Sir, I recognize the woman you killed. We worked together years ago. This was a professional crew."

"Local authorities should be covered." *I pay enough.* I don't want questions being asked about the dead bodies littering my house.

"I've already spoken with our contact. It's taken care of."

"Excellent. See you soon, Brock."

"Yes, Sir."

Slipping the phone back into my pocket, I step up next to Sydney. "I don't believe you've ever been to Panama City. It's fascinating. I think you'll like it."

Her eyes search my face. I keep it totally neutral. We don't have to talk about anything…yet.

"I'll need to speak with the council," she says.

"Of course," I tilt my head in deference to her "council," Joyful Justice's governing body. I'm not a member—they'd never invite into their inner circle a man they consider morally compromised.

Hypocrites. Their justification for killing—protecting the innocent—is no more honorable than my own—surviving at the highest level. I don't just subsist, I revel in life. Something those do-gooders can't quite handle. But they will accept use of my resources, and they will even occasionally take my advice.

I've survived more perilous situations than any of them.

Sydney's eyes narrow. I raise my brows and offer a subtle smile. "What?"

She purses her lips. "Just watching the wheels turn, Bobby."

I bark out a laugh. "You know me so well."

Her eyes narrow further. "Something like that. Do you know who sent them?"

"Not yet." She nods, almost to herself, then looks out at the airport. Surrounded by lush tropical foliage, the tarmac wafts lines of heat into the air. "Do you have any ideas?" I ask.

She shrugs. "Lots of people want us dead," Sydney turns to me, a full wattage smile, so rare, lighting up her face. "We make a hell of a challenge."

"A hell of a team," I say.

The smile falters, a shadow crossing her eyes. She hates to admit how alike we are…how she feels about me. I'd planned on giving her time, unlimited time to realize it for herself. My patience a gift to her. But the pregnancy changes everything.

My timetable must be moved up. I grin at her, and she narrows her eyes again, sensing my shifting plans but powerless to stop them.

EK

Sydney

Robert sets me up in his office for the council meeting. I have my own laptop and hotspot—Dan would never let me use another man's equipment. Far too easy for Robert to spy on us.

My screen is split into four boxes. In one square, Anita and Dan sit next to each other in his office. They are on the private island in the Pacific Ocean that Joyful Justice uses as a headquarters for our strategic operations. Merl is in Costa Rica at our training center, set up in his small office off the dojo with sparring pads piled behind him. Lenox, somewhere in Ireland at the moment, is in the third square, and I can see myself in the fourth.

I tell them about what happened in Cartagena—leaving out my pregnancy and the kiss. "According to Brock, they were professionals. So a hired hit."

Merl nods slowly, his long, tight curls loose and damp, like he just got out of the shower. "Do you think it's Ian?" Merl asks the group.

Ian McCain. Ian and his brothers orchestrated an attack on our island headquarters, blackmailing some of our people into helping them. They created a cabal of criminal organizations to fight back against our justice-seeking ways.

Lenox's dark skin glows in the light of his computer screen, and white headphone wires snake out from his ears. "Ian is pissed, as expected." Lenox's Senegalese accent dances over the words. "He's attacked one of Petra's—" He pauses, his lips firming. "One of our brothels, and I'm sure he plans on more."

We killed Ian's brothers, then Lenox, along with his new partner, Petra, took over the man's prostitution business. But the McCain organization is a many-headed beast, and we've only lopped off two of them.

"Any casualties?" Anita asks, her own accent almost as lyrical as Lenox's. Born in Gujarat, India and educated in the United Kingdom her voice mixes the upper crust of high society from both nations.

"No," Lenox responds, "but one of our guards was injured. He's recovering." Lenox glances to the side, looking at something off screen. He nods slightly and then returns his attention to the council meeting. "Petra is going to visit him in the hospital now."

"Is that safe?" I ask.

"She has guards." Lenox voice stays flat—unemotional. He's not worried about her. Is it because he doesn't care or doesn't believe she is in danger?

Lenox isn't totally comfortable with his new role—he's been in the business of "pleasure"—as he puts it—for decades but only ever sold men. Petra convinced him that he should join with her to create a network of brothels run responsibly. He'd agreed, but I knew it bothered him still.

Dan voices my concern. "Are you worried about Petra's loyalty?" he asks, leaning slightly toward the screen, his pale green eyes narrowed. Petra, a longtime associate of Lenox's, was working with the McCains against Joyful Justice before she switched to our side.

Lenox gives a half smile. "Yes and no. She had me at her mercy— drugged and vulnerable—and she kept me safe. But it could all be a long game...I don't know what she'd do if she felt threatened."

"Bite," I say, the thought escaping out loud.

Lenox raises a brow. "Yes, I suppose any of us would."

"And have," Anita says.

Merl clears his throat. "Would Ian hire mercenaries to go after Sydney, though? The last assassination attempt was the Incels." The Incels are involuntary celibates—a men's rights activist group which recently escaped the confines of internet forums and began taking action in the real world.

"That's right," I say, "and thanks to Declan Doyle, it wasn't a problem."

"Maybe you should reach out to him," Merl suggests. "See if he's heard anything. Dan, didn't you say he's on a new task force?"

Dan nods. "That's right. Doyle joined a task force focused on the Incels and the violent factions following the Her Prophet. The Incels have taken credit for several mass shootings, and it was a follower of the Her Prophet that blew herself up at a recent Incel rally in Savannah, killing five and injuring twenty-five more. Homeland Security sees a link."

The Her Prophet had emerged from the bloodlands of the Syria-Iraq war zone. Initially an inspiration to women abused by Isis to seize control of their destinies, she'd become a global symbol of female empowerment. She'd also saved my life.

"It's a real battle of the sexes," I say. "A war between men who can't get laid and women who are sick of being told all they're good for is fucking."

Merl frowns. "It's a bit more nuanced than that."

"Is it?"

He sighs, his zen-like attitude often tried by my insistence on seeing the world in absolutes. "The Her Prophet calls for the equality of women; that's more than just not being seen as objects of sexual release. She is insisting that women rise up and take their place next to men—as equals. And the fact that she says God is telling her to preach this philosophy makes it a solid argument to a lot of women who've been told by religious texts that they are second-class citizens."

"Okay, so, maybe her message is broader. But what about the Incels? They literally named themselves after the fact that they can't get laid."

"But their complaints are broader as well," Anita says. A former reporter who now heads our public relations and marketing, Anita always likes to nail down facts. "They complain about women automatically getting custody of children. That men's roles in the world have changed too quickly, leaving them and many others behind. That women say they want equality and nice guys but go after macho assholes. Just look at romance books."

Anita waves her hand, almost smacking Dan in the face as she dives into her topic. "The hero is always some alpha a-hole who is slightly softened by a woman's willingness to submit to him." She rolls her eyes.

No one responds. "What?" She looks at Dan, who shrugs, and then back to the screen. "I'm the only one here who read *Fifty Shades*?"

"I did," Lenox answers. "And you're right. Women like men to take control in the bedroom." *And he would know.* "Even my most powerful clients enjoy giving up power once we—"

"I think we've gone off topic," Dan says. "We are trying to figure out who is attempting to kill Sydney, not unravel the mystery of male, female relationships throughout the ages."

"I'll talk with Declan," I say. "But I doubt he'll tell me anything. Last I checked, he hated me."

"He did save your life," Anita points out.

I shrug. "Worth a try."

"I'm still in his computer," Dan says, his attention drifting to another screen. He hacked in after Doyle saved my life—he was following me, hoping to catch me in one of my more vengeful moments. The man has had a hard on for taking me down since I escaped New York. But when an Incel member attempted to assassinate me, Doyle stepped in. Dan never trusts a knight in shining armor, one of the many things we have in common. "I can dig around. But he's smartened up and doesn't put much work stuff on there anymore."

"I think Ian is concentrating on Petra and me at the moment," Lenox says. "He's not exactly a big thinker. His brother, Michael, was the brains. I think Ian will take his revenge before anything else. I'm not saying the threat to Joyful Justice is over, just delayed."

Comforting.

"Ian was working with the Incels," Dan says. "Providing them with sex slaves. It's possible the two are still working together to try to kill Sydney."

More comfort.

"Yes," Lenox agrees.

"Maybe they weren't even after me," I say. "Maybe they were trying to kill Robert." Everybody nods. Robert does piss a lot of people off. "I'll talk with Declan," I say. "Dan, you check out his computer. Lenox, you'll continue to monitor the situation there. What's next on the agenda?"

We go over details about an addition Merl wants for the Costa Rica compound. Dan and Anita catch us up on the ongoing missions and a few that might become active soon. I try to pay attention, but it feels like all I'm doing is *not* telling them about my pregnancy. I want a chance to speak with Mulberry first...that's the excuse I'm using at the moment to justify my silence.

But eventually I will have to tell them. Not today, though. No, not today.

Robert comes in as I'm putting away my computer. "Everything to your satisfaction?" he asks.

"Yes, thank you for letting me use your office." I can play the polite friendship game. I stand up and heft my backpack onto one shoulder. "I'll get out of your hair."

I come around the desk and start for the door. Robert watches me go, a shock of electric something leaping between us as I step past him.

"Mulberry isn't right for you," he says as I reach the door.

I turn back to him. Sunlight spills in the windows, filling the office, and melting into the fine wool of Robert's suit, tailored to every sharp line of him.

"He's the father of my child," I say, the first time I've spoken the truth out loud.

"But he doesn't see you the way I see you." Robert's voice is low, almost stern, his fists clenched by his side as if he's struggling not to do something with them. *Grab me? Punch the wall?*

I'm staring at his hands now. At the blue veins running over the tops, the corded tendons, the whitening knuckles. *He plays piano beautifully.*

"No," I admit. "He doesn't see me the way you do."

The fingers relax just a little, my acknowledgment giving him some kind of peace. "He can't make you happy." Robert's voice is a low thrum, a deep bass.

"No one can make another person happy." I bring my eyes up to meet Robert's, and he's waiting there for me. Those blue-green eyes that reflect the warmth of the Caribbean and the ice of the Arctic holding my gaze the way those two bodies of water cradle a ship. *I must be careful not to drown in them.*

"You don't think people affect each other?" His lips twitch into a half smile—mocking and victorious.

My back straightens, and his half smile turns into a full one. "We are all responsible for our actions."

He nods slowly, his gaze dropping to my stomach. "Yes."

I expect him to go on, but his lips close into a tight line instead.

"What?" I ask, knowing there is more he wants to say.

He gives a small shake of his head and turns away, walking to the far side of his desk, putting the glass and metal between us. *I don't want anything between us.* The thought is quick, cracking and illuminating as a bolt of lightning.

My hand rises to my belly, the fingers splaying protectively across it in a new gesture that is foreign and yet so natural. My mother did this, and her mother. I am struck suddenly by the magnitude and yet mundanity of this…of being an expectant mother. So many women have done this, and yet to each of us, it feels as if we are the first. *The only.*

It is as if I can see the line of women behind me who labored my bloodline into existence—and a spidery filament of women who will come into existence because of my own labor. Because of this hand across my belly. Because I will do anything to protect this child and make sure that it, too, can one day parent.

The urge for survival is a taste in my mouth, a scent on my skin, a sensation in my chest—it is everything.

And Robert Maxim is a man who can help me survive.

CHAPTER FIVE

Sydney

I wake up gasping in terror, wrapped in a bundle of sweaty sheets. *I'm scared.*

Blue's teeth nip at my heel, grounding me.

The last five years I've invited danger, but now...I want safety. I want to stay alive. Even as the thrill and calm of battle gives me comfort, apparently it also gives me nightmares. *Thanks, hormones.*

Lightning cracks outside, blaring white light through the strange bedroom, illuminating the modern lines of the furniture and washing out the bold colors of the art on the walls. Rain pelts the windows in a rat-tat rhythm of impatience.

Responsibility for my unborn, unformed child chokes me—fear tightening my chest.

This spark inside me is not more important than the lives I've saved...or the ones I've taken. But it's mine. Mine even more than my life.

A sickening sensation in my stomach blooms. I owe my mother a phone call. I owe her the chance to reconcile. For both of us to find peace.

I don't have her phone number. But Robert will have it. God, he looks after me—a trait that has rankled me in the past and that I've come to accept, without grace, in the present.

I'm an asshole.

A soft knock on the door...think of the devil. Blue gives a wag of his tail, confirming that it is someone we know.

"Yes?" I say, pulling the sheets straight.

The door eases open, and Robert's trim shadow enters. "I heard screaming. A bad dream?"

"Yes."

"Do you want to talk about it?"

"No." The word comes out curt. I suck in a breath. "Thank you." I try to recover some class.

He nods and goes to leave. "Robert?"

"Yes, Sydney?" He turns back into the room. Another crack of lightning throws the room into sharp relief, catching Robert in the doorway, his bed clothes pressed and hair rumpled, eyebrows raised, waiting for me to speak...always waiting for me.

"Do you know where my mother is?"

"Yes."

I swallow the lump trying to form in my throat—trying to keep the words contained, the request at bay. "Can I have her number? I think I owe her a phone call."

"You don't owe anyone anything." His words rumble along with the distant thunder.

"Thank you, but I want to—"

"Her phone is bugged. Homeland Security suspects she is involved in the bombing of the Incel group in Savannah."

"Was she?" I ask.

"I don't believe so."

I sigh. "So I can't reach her."

"Of course you can." Robert sounds insulted. He takes a step into the room. "We can drop her a burner phone. We can go see her. Whatever you want. We can make it happen." This is a man who built an empire from nothing, designs his own weapons, does whatever he wants whenever he wants.

"Do you know where Mulberry is?" I blurt out. Robert doesn't flinch. *He knows.* "Don't lie to me."

"Yes," Robert says quietly.

I can't see his face in the darkness. "You know I need to talk to him."

"I suppose."

"You suppose?" My voice rises with anger. A fresh wave of rain slaps at the glass, seeming to back me up.

"He abandoned you."

"I'm not going down this road with you again. He has a right to know I'm—" My voice cuts off. I still can't finish that sentence. *Not yet.*

"Pregnant," Robert finishes for me. He doesn't sound afraid of it. There is almost something possessive in his voice.

"Right. I need to tell him. You know that."

Robert shrugs, all casual about this shitshow. "If you want. Which contact should I make for you first. Your mother or…"

"The father of my child," I finish for him this time.

"Yes." Curt, cold…bordering on cruel.

"Where is he?" Silence stretches between us. "Dammit, Robert. Tell me!" I stand up, the sheets falling to the floor. Blue leaps to his feet, Nila rising next to him, while Frank continues to snore peacefully.

Robert doesn't flinch. I stalk over to him, anger making me brave and reckless. I want to punch someone. Fear is gone, replaced by my near constant companion over the last half decade—righteous rage.

Lightning flashes, illuminating Robert's smug smile and blazing eyes. "You're gorgeous like this," he says, reaching out and snagging me, using my forward momentum to pull me close.

"Screw you," I growl, stepping into him, placing a foot behind his ankle and pushing him into it. He goes down, dragging me with him. We hit the floor, his hands on my waist, mine on his shoulders. My hair falls around us, creating a shadowed, intimate world between just the two of us as thunder rolls through the room in thrumming waves.

Blue and Nila watch, hackles raised, waiting for my command. Frank stirs, his collar jangling.

"Please do," Robert says.

Stupid, arrogant bastard. My hands bunch into fists, gripping his soft pajamas. "Why are you like this? You have to hold everything over me. You can't ever just…" I run out of words.

Robert's body tightens under me and his eyes shutter, but the man doesn't speak.

"Well?" I shake him a little. "Why? Why can't you just help me without there being some strings attached? Something in it for you."

His eyes narrow now, anger sparking. *Good.* I hate being the only angry asshole in the room.

"What more could I do for you?" Robert asks, his voice even, void of the emotion in his gaze. "How much more could one man offer a woman? I saved your life."

"You've tried to kill me."

He ignores my point and goes on. "Provided protection, luxury, and a place to heal. You were broken, Sydney, I stayed with you. Fought for you. I am the one who is by your side. No one else." He blinks. "Except Blue."

"Selfless martyr doesn't suit you."

"No. It doesn't." He grabs my hair and pulls me in, crushing his lips to mine. But I'm not falling for this again. I rear back, open my fist, and slap his fucking face. The crack of skin against skin is louder than the lightning. His head jerks, and when he looks back at me, there is blood on his lip.

Fuck.

Robert slowly smiles, his split lip oozing. He explores the wound with his tongue. "Nothing great was ever easy to obtain."

"Obtain this, jackass." I go to slap him again but he catches my wrist this time.

"I plan to."

"Tell me where Mulberry is."

His eyes narrow and his fingers tighten on my wrist. "Florida."

"Florida?"

"Gulf coast. Dan knows too, I'm sure."

They both lied to me. But Dan doesn't know why I need to speak to

Mulberry, and Robert does. "Dan was protecting his friend's privacy; you've been protecting your own interests."

"And you, I've been protecting you." Robert says. My jaw tightens at his words. I can't count on him to survive. I need to be on my own. Take care of myself for a while. "I keep telling you Mulberry is wrong for you. I honestly believe that. He's not nearly strong enough to handle you. All your darkness…all your passion."

I shake my head and go to stand, but Robert still has my wrist. He sits up, pulling it close so that I'm sitting on his freaking lap now. I twist my hand, breaking his hold and rise, standing over him. "I'm leaving," I say.

It's too dark for me to see his face clearly but I hear a soft intake of breath. He doesn't try to stop me when I step away from him and move toward my backpack. Blue and Nila follow me. *They have my back.*

"I will take you to Mulberry," Robert says.

"I need to do this alone." I start grabbing my clothing off the floor and shove it into my bag with my laptop and hot spot. Frank stands up and shakes, sleepy eyes searching out his sister for some direction. I can't keep leaning on Robert Maxim. He's dangerous. And so am I. Two dangerous people don't make a safe place.

"As you wish," Robert says.

He closes the door when he leaves, and I let out a long, slow breath. Blue's wet nose taps my closed fist. We don't need Robert freaking Maxim.

EK

Robert

If you love them let them go. If they return…

The advice of losers. I let Sydney walk out of my apartment. Even gave her Mulberry's location. But I'm not letting her go. No, this is all a part of the plan. Show her what it's like to move through the world without me.

Getting to Florida is going to be a challenge with three giant dogs and no access to my private aircrafts.

When she does get there, she'll realize that Mulberry can't handle her. I'm the only man who can last that particular storm. I'll go see Mulberry myself and talk to him...*talk.*

"Sir." I glance up from the tablet in my lap at the secretary interrupting my train of thought. Dowdy and efficient, her eyes meet mine with just the right amount of fear in them. "The Frangellicas are here."

"I'll meet them in the conference room. You've offered them refreshments?"

"Of course, Mr. Maxim."

She leaves to escort our guests, and I lock the tablet in my desk drawer before heading to the conference room. The Panama City office is not as large as the one in Colombia, but we needed to evacuate. *Not the first time I've fled that nation.*

Josh and Amy Frangellica sit with their backs to the wall of glass windows, pale blue eyes trained on the door—a healthy suspicion in their gaze.

We were cast in the same crucible.

They rise as I enter. "Thank you for coming to Panama City," I say. "Sorry we didn't get to see each other in Colombia."

Amy steps forward and we embrace. She wears the years well. Only a few months younger than me, her hair has maintained its rich chestnut tone, and the wrinkles that line her face are elegant, giving her an air of sophistication. The scar on her neck is faded—but my eyes are drawn to it anyway. If you didn't know it was there, you might not notice it. But I was there when it happened and will never forget.

Her brother, Josh, clasps my hand, pulling me into a hug. "Good to see you, Robert." Five years my junior, Josh could barely grow a beard when we met. Now, his whiskers are peppered with silver.

There are few men I let hug me. But when you've survived captivity and escaped together through a jungle rife with danger, an embrace is appropriate.

We take our seats. "Tell me," I say. "What can I do for you?"

Josh and Amy glance at each other before Amy speaks. "We've got a problem."

"I assumed as much," I say with a shrug. "Usually we meet for dinner and drink too much fine wine." I smile. "Wanting to meet in my offices clued me in that this wasn't a social call."

Josh nods and sits back in the chair, his lips tight. Amy goes on. "We've gotten a packet from Joyful Justice."

Damn. I shake my head, putting on an expression of regret. "I'm sorry to hear that."

"We know you've protected clients from them."

"I got out of that business. But I'm happy to help you comply, help you negotiate."

Josh snorts. "Nothing is the same since the FARC made peace." He shakes his head, nostalgia for the past thick in his words. The Revolutionary Armed Forces of Colombia funded their revolution with kidnap ransoms and drug trafficking—it's dirty work trying to create a utopian society.

"Lots has changed," I agree.

"And you're totally legitimate now?" Amy asks, her tone doubtful.

"Yes," I answer. *One of my many gifts to Sydney Rye.*

"I never thought I'd see the day," Josh shakes his head, more of that regretful nostalgia...but he gives me a warm smile. "You took Fortress Global public, must have made a bundle."

"The details are not important," I brush off the billion I netted on that move. The SEC is still investigating, after all. Though that toothless organization doesn't worry me. "Tell me what Joyful Justice is going after you for?"

"Same as always," Amy says, shifting in her seat. "Drugs."

I cock my head. "I've never heard of them making threats against an organization *just* running drugs. What does the packet say?"

Amy leans over and picks up a briefcase by her feet, placing it on the table. She pulls out the packet and slides it across the table to me. The logo of Joyful Justice is printed on the cover, a red heart with "Be Brave" written on undulating ribbon across it. I suppress the smile that pulls at my lips. *Such sentimentalists.*

"We've been approached by another organization that wants to destroy Joyful Justice," Josh says.

I raise a brow as I open the packet. "How do they plan to do that?"

"Apparently they have a few people on the inside."

Glancing up from the packet, my fingers playing with the paper, I nod slowly. "That's useful but hardly a full plan."

Amy sighs. "I agree, Robert. I think these men are underestimating the loyalty of the Joyful Justice members. This isn't the FARC. They don't treat their soldiers poorly."

"The FARC lasted over fifty years," I point out.

"Exactly. Joyful Justice has a similar fervor but with better conditions. They've got deep pockets and high ideals," Amy says. "The philosophy of the FARC kept it intact, but the kidnapping and drug running took its toll."

"Greed took its toll," Josh says.

I sit back in my chair and eye my old friends. "So what exactly are you asking for?"

"We want your help," Amy says. "Destroying Joyful Justice."

I spread my hands on the table and look down at them. "Who is the group that approached you?"

Amy snorts. "Some Irish brothers running a sex trafficking operation. They're aligned with a couple of other groups including men's rights activists." She shakes her head. "Not a crew I have any interest in being associated with. But—" She smiles at me. "The three of us...we make a good team."

"That we do," I agree. Or at least we did, decades ago. "I have no interest in joining with a men's rights group though," I say.

"They call themselves Incels," Josh says, shaking himself. "Involuntary celibates. Pathetic."

"The one thing I agree with them about," Amy says, "is that Joyful Justice needs to be stopped."

I return my attention to the packet. Very organized. The table of contents lists several infractions. I flip to the first one: rape and murder perpetrated by contractors. Scanning the first few paragraphs, I return my gaze to the siblings. "Your men at the border are raping and killing innocent women?"

"I don't see how we are responsible for that," Josh says. "It's how they celebrate. What are we supposed to do about it? It's part of their culture."

Amy frowns and rolls her eyes at her brother. "You come off like a real ass when you say things like that. But, the fact is we don't have control over the Federales. We pay them to move product, and they celebrate successful deliveries. No one can get drugs across the US/Mexican border without them. It's impossible."

"I'm impressed you're still moving product over land. With all the changes within the cartels, you've managed to keep good business relationships."

"Our US distribution is unparalleled," Amy says with pride.

They bought mine off me almost two decades ago, and combined with their existing efforts, they must control most of the flow of cocaine in the United States.

"What about air transport? I thought you were using planes."

"You know how complicated that became after 9/11," Amy sighs, as if the negative impact on moving drugs through the air was one of the biggest tragedies of that day. Her chagrin brings a smile to my lips.

Josh sits forward. "Robert, you can't seriously suggest we try to comply with this nonsense."

I shrug. "Some of it isn't too taxing," I wave a hand at the packet. "Containing the Federales'," I pause, searching for the right word, *"celebratory* practices would be good for business, right? It would take heat off the border."

"I don't think it makes a big difference," Amy says. "It's been going on forever, and no one cares—well, people *care*, but no one with power has done a thing about it until these busybodies," she points to the packet. "Business is business and this is...well, it's about morality." She smiles at me. "You know the two don't mix well."

No, they don't.

"I'm sorry," I say, "But I don't think I can help you, unless it's to mitigate some of these infractions. I'm totally legitimate now. There is no dog in this fight for me."

"That's disappointing," Josh says.

"Why don't you two get out of the game?" I ask, leaning back in my seat. "Retire. You must have all the money you'll ever need. Why not enjoy yourselves?"

"We like what we do," Amy says, her voice tight. "Just because you've gone soft—"

"Hey," Josh interrupts her. Amy's cheeks flush. "That's not fair. Robert worked hard for his success. He deserves his retirement."

"He's hardly retired," Amy says, waving her hand around the office.

"I'm not getting packets like this." I tap the papers.

Amy sighs. "Robert." She leans over and pulls the papers back to her. "We've been through a lot together." She lets that sentence hang in the air, as if I owe her something.

We carried you through the jungle. You wouldn't have made it out alive without us, her silence accuses.

And it's true. But I sacrificed the woman I loved to free us from the cages. If Natalia hadn't fallen for me so hard, and so true, we would be dead—rotted in the jungle, bones picked clean by that harsh environment. Instead she died, and we survived.

I owe them nothing.

I smile, my eyes communicating as much.

We are even.

Amy puts the papers back in the briefcase. "Is there nothing we can do to change your mind?" she asks.

Warning bells chime in the tone of her voice.

"No," I say. "But please—" I stand, rebuttoning my suit jacket. "Let me know if you want help with negotiations."

I walk them through the office and to the elevator. We say our final goodbyes. Josh leans into Amy, speaking into her ear, as the doors shut.

Did they hire the mercenaries to scare me into helping?

Or am I getting paranoid in my old age?

Back in my office, I pull up the surveillance from the elevator and watch Amy and Josh enter. I turn up the volume, trying to make out what Josh is saying, but it's unclear. She hushes him, and they are silent for the rest of the ride.

I rewind and play it again, putting on headphones. I think he says the name *Natalia*, but can't be sure.

I call my surveillance department and ask them for a transcript—rushing the order.

They get back to me in fifteen minutes. "It's not totally clear, sir, but this is what I have." The tech clears his throat. "Inaudible. Natalia wouldn't…and then she says, quiet."

I hang up the phone and sit back, steepling my fingers. Why would they be talking about Natalia? The woman's been dead for decades. Are they hoping to use sentimentality or guilt to persuade me to help them?

I stare at the paused video footage on my computer. *What are those two plotting?*

CHAPTER SIX

Sydney

Getting from Panama City to Florida isn't difficult...unless you're traveling with three giant dogs. Oh, and are an international fugitive. Not to mention the hurricane ravaging the eastern coast of the state.

Of course, I've got multiple IDs, so I can travel incognito. The bad weather and three big-ass dogs are the larger problems.

Not even Robert Maxim can change the weather, but flying around in his private jets solved the dog issue for me in the past. Now I've either got to travel over land, convince a commercial airline I need three emotional support animals, or hire my own private jet.

I go with the jet.

Time solves the hurricane issue for me. Miami still faces record flooding, but the air is clearing, and I'm headed well to the north.

The plane is a rental, so not as fancy as Robert's but still... it is a private freaking jet. The flight attendant who brings me my soda water with a slice of lemon grins at the dogs. "They are so cute," she coos. Frank eats it up, sitting on her foot and making a fool of himself. The disdain on Nila's face is practically human. Blue sighs and leans against me. *Will Frank ever learn?*

I hope not. Let him maintain his innocence for as long as possible.

Tallahassee is low-slung strip malls and flat pavement scented of rain and ozone. I drive south toward the gulf, wind buffering the outside of the rental SUV. The town that Mulberry has made home is small and tacky, with neon signs, T-shirt shops, and brightly painted buildings. A motel on the outskirts has vacancies, and the man behind the counter—bulging belly and gold chain nestled in graying chest hair—accepts the dogs for an additional nonrefundable deposit. "If it's nonrefundable then isn't it just a fee?" I ask, leaning on the counter.

He holds out a key with a seashell dangling from it, the number three painted on it. "You want the room or not?"

I accept the shell in exchange for a wad of cash. It's off season, so I don't see any other guests as I make my way to the room. It is decorated in seaside motif, with fish nets and loops of thick rope hanging from the walls. The bed creaks under my weight when I sit down on the quilt printed with blue anchors.

Blue and Nila perform a perimeter check, ears swiveling, nose to the floor, while Frank goes to drink water out of the toilet. I sigh. "There's water right here." I point to the bowl I've put out for them. Frank looks up at me, his jowls dripping on the toilet seat.

Nila goes into the bathroom and nips his heel, chasing him out. "Thanks, girl," I say. She comes over for a pet and rests her chin on my thigh, looking up at me with her ice blue eyes. Her snout is shorter than Blue's—her mother is a white Kangal Mastiff, so her face is in between the squared-off structure of her mom's and the long, elegant collie snout of her dad. I rub between Nila's eyes, and she closes them, sighing appreciatively.

"You're such a good girl," I tell her. "Look after your brother for a while. Blue and I have to go see someone."

EK

My heart slowly climbs into my throat as I navigate to the bar where Mulberry is working. It's got dark wood siding, the windows thick with neon signs for beer and booze.

I park across the street, the engine still running, and stare at the door, a lump in my throat keeping me from swallowing. Blue, sitting in the passenger seat, his ears brushing the ceiling, whines softly.

"Mulberry is in there," I say. "Or maybe he's not working today." A small blip of hope. Maybe I can hold off on this conversation a little longer. But dread follows just as quickly. I have to get this over with.

How in the hell is he going to react? Will his anger evaporate in the face of his impending fatherhood? Or will it seem like one more betrayal in a slew of them?

I wet my lips and then bite down, trying to ground myself. *Shit.*

Blue and I start across the street toward the bar, and I stop in the middle of the road as if my feet have morphed into cement and joined with the paved surface.

Blue noses my hand, questioning what's going on. My vision tunnels onto the bar door, and my heart hammers. I can't do this.

I *have* to do this.

A horn honks, breaking the spell, and I jerk my gaze to the driver. He's got a greasy ponytail and is gesturing at me to move the fuck out of the way. *Friendly town.*

I back up, returning to my SUV, and the car pulls forward, turning into the bar's parking lot.

I close my eyes. The briny sea breeze plays across my face, and I turn to look down the block. The beach is close. "How about a quick walk?" I say to Blue. He wags his tail, always up for a stroll, especially when the ocean is involved. "Come on," I turn away from the bar and toward the beach.

I'm going to tell him—but not right now. Not this exact moment. *Soon...*

Mulberry

It's Saturday, so we're open earlier than normal, catching day drinkers who work during the week. Shirley stopped opening at noon on weekdays in the off season because it got "too damn depressing". And the bar's rocking night business makes her plenty of cash. Maybe I'll buy a bar someday. Yeah, open a margarita shop in paradise somewhere. I'm smiling to myself at the fantasy when the bell above the door jingles.

I glance up and see a figure silhouetted in the sunlight. *Oh, shit.*

Robert Maxim steps into the bar, the door swinging shut behind him. His eyes find mine, and he gives me a subtle nod before crossing to a stool at the far end. I let him get settled, elbows on the wood, hands clasped in front of him, eyes trained on me.

I make my way slowly to him, scanning the almost empty room as I go. "What can I get you?" I ask.

"Do you have any decent whiskey?"

"Johnnie Walker Black."

He gives a nod. "Neat." I take a step backward, keeping my eyes on Robert as I pull the bottle from the shelf. He smirks at me. I place a glass on the bar in front of him. "Make it a double."

"What are you doing here?" I ask once his drink is poured.

Robert wraps his long fingers around the squat glass but doesn't lift it. "What are *you* doing here?" he asks back, meeting my gaze and holding it. My lips tighten, and I don't respond. He's living with Sydney Rye. They're probably more than friends by now. *Fuck, I should have dragged her out of there. No, she—* I cut myself off, refusing to run around that maze again.

"I'm working." The bell above the door jangles, as if to prove my point, and a small man with a greasy ponytail comes in out of the sunshine.

Robert lifts the glass and gives it a subtle sniff before taking a sip. He puts it back on the bar and lifts a brow. "You need money?"

"You think money is what motivates me?" I can't help the huff of a laugh that escapes me. "For a smart guy, you're pretty dumb sometimes, Bobby."

"What do you want, then?"

"Who said I wanted anything?"

"Hey, bartender, can I get a beer over here? Jesus!" Greasy Ponytail wants my attention. I grab a Bud from the ice bucket and turn my back on Maxim—a dangerous move, but I like to live dangerously.

"Sorry about that," I say, popping the top and putting it on a fresh napkin. "This one's on me."

Greasy Ponytail gives me a smile as he grabs the beer. I take in a fortifying breath before returning to Robert.

The bar is mostly empty and dusk dark. Sunlight ekes through the windows, tinted and littered with neon signs provided by beer and liquor companies.

Robert's spinning his glass on the bar. "You know Sydney's been looking for you."

"Well aren't you a supportive friend, coming to find me." My voice is thick with sarcasm. He wants her to be his. But she's mine. Hard to say that when you're hiding behind a bar and haven't called her since you left in the middle of the—*stop thinking.*

Robert is watching me, probably reading my damn mind. His eyes drop to the bar. "You're no good for her." He says it as if it's a fact. One I'd agree with. But I don't.

The bell above the door jangles again, drawing my attention. I squint against the sun. *Speak of the devil.*

Sydney walks in, Blue by her side—his nose grazing her hip as the door swings shut behind them. "Damn!" Greasy ponytail blurts out. "That's one hell of a dog."

Sydney doesn't look at him. Those storm-gray eyes are on me, shimmering in the low light. Her brows raise, asking an unspoken question.

Robert stands, drawing her attention, and surprise flits across her features, quickly replaced by anger. She's pissed at him. *Excellent.*

The smug smile I'm sporting doesn't last long as Sydney returns her attention to me. She crosses the near empty room, Blue's nails clicking on the floor.

"Hi," she says, giving me a weak smile.

"Hi." *So lame.*

Sydney glances over at Robert. He is staring at her with those eyes of his, that strange blue-green—the heat of the jungle and the frozen recess of an iceberg. He raises his brows and shrugs. Not repentant.

"I need to speak to you," Sydney says, returning her attention to me. "In private."

"I'm alone here today," I say, gesturing to my few customers. *Jesus, so lame!*

Shirley comes in the back door at that moment in a swirl of heavy perfume and thumping boots. "Tyler," she says, slapping me on the back.

"Yeah," I answer, not taking my eyes off Sydney. It's like I can't. She's different somehow. As mesmerizing as ever but something... My mind flashes back to the last time we saw each other... the heat and the anger and the...love. "I need a break," I say to Shirley, still staring at Sydney. She's staring back. Not running. Not hiding. My heart gives a loud, pathetic thump of hope.

No. I won't let her break me again. Sydney Rye is dangerous. Our whole relationship, she's warned me off her. *My love is a death sentence.* Well, Sydney, I'm not gonna let you kill me slowly anymore.

"Sure, take fifteen," Shirley says, giving my back another slap.

"Want to walk down to the beach?" Sydney asks, her voice low, gentle—like she's afraid of my answer.

"Okay." I take off my apron and come around the bar—hardening my heart against her. It doesn't matter what she has to say. I can't love her anymore. Not if I want to live.

CHAPTER SEVEN

Sydney

Wind tugs strands of hair free from my ponytail, lashing it across my cheeks. The beach is deserted, the dark clouds threatening rain and rough surf keeping the few tourists in town away. "I've been looking for you," I say. Mulberry's lips press together as if he is trying not to speak. "I have something important to tell you." I yell a little to be heard over the crashing waves.

He gives a small shake of his head and looks back over his shoulder; the main street dead ends at the beach, and his bar is only a block away. "Well, spit it out. I'm working."

"I'm pregnant." His head snaps back to me. Mulberry's mouth opens...closes. Opens again. Dread is spinning my insides, chewing them up. I might puke. "It's yours," I say, just so we're totally clear.

"Mine?" His voice is so low I barely hear it over the pounding surf.

I nod, my eyes narrowing against a blast of sand carried by a strong gust of wind. It stings my face and grits my lips. I press them together, my turn to keep words from spilling out.

Mulberry's eyes, sharp green and sparkling gold, drop to my stomach. I resist the urge to cover it. Blue pushes his nose against my hand,

and I rest my palm on the back of his head, pushing my fingers into his fur instead.

"How?" Mulberry asks.

A laugh escapes from my chest, loosening something in there. "You want me to draw you a picture?"

Mulberry flinches, and his face hardens. "How do I know it's mine?"

The crack of my open palm slapping his cheek is louder than the waves and the wind. His head rocks to the side, and he stumbles a step back. "Fuck you," I spit at him before turning on my heel. Blue gives a low growl as he joins me, his nose tapping my hip in solidarity as we stride down the beach.

"Wait, I'm sorry." Mulberry runs up next to me. He's smart enough not to grab me. That's what Robert would do—he'd grab me and make me stop—but Mulberry doesn't; he falls into step with me. "That was a dick thing to say." My jaw is clenched so tight I can't answer him. "Please, I'm sorry." Focusing on the length of beach in front of me, I pick up my pace.

Mulberry's limp is more pronounced in the sand. He's struggling to keep up. His awkward gait wrenches at my heart hard enough to stop me. "You know what?" I say. Mulberry steps in front of me as if to block my path. *I could knock him on his ass.*

"I'm sorry, I wasn't expecting..." He thrusts a hand through his hair, making it stand on end.

"Robert told me not to tell you. He said I'd never get what I need from you."

Mulberry growls and steps closer, so that we are barely inches apart, his big body blocking the wind. "And you listen to him now?"

I meet his eyes, narrow mine. "Was he wrong? You just asked how I knew it was yours." My voice cracks on the last word, and I clench my jaw, refusing to get emotional. Absolutely refusing to care about him.

A fool's errand.

His whole body seems to soften, the tension in his broad chest easing as he reaches a hand up and cups my cheek. His lips curl into this private, tiny smile—one he seems to save just for me. *Just to melt me.* "Don't," I say. But I don't mean it. My body trembles with the need to be melted. To have him say he loves me, and that he wants me, the baby —that he wants this whole impossible thing that is happening between us.

When he remembered me—and our life—Mulberry came to Robert's house to confront me. To yell at me for pretending like we'd never known each other. We ended up falling into bed. But when I woke up he was gone—too angry to forgive me no matter what we whispered to each other in the dark. No matter how we really felt about each other.

I can't wrap my mind around this, not any of it. *How did we get here?*

Mulberry closes the distance between us, folding his arms around me and pulling me into his chest. Tears burn my eyes, but I don't let them free. I breathe him in. The detergent he's using is different, and the lingering scent of the bar clings to him, but still, under all that, is his smell. I close my eyes and lean in, let him buffer me from the wind and warm me. Slowly, I bring my arm around his waist and squeeze back.

We will be parents together. If there wasn't anything else between us but the bundle of cells growing inside of me, we'd be connected, but there is so much more. A terrible, exhilarating history that binds us together.

"I'm sorry," he says again, his breath warm on the top of my head.

"You should be." It comes out like I forgive him. "I'm sorry too. I should've fought for you."

His arms squeeze tighter. And when I pull back, and look up into his face, his eyes are wet. I reach up to try and brush away a tear, but he shies away, roughly wiping his cheek on his shoulder.

"What do you need?" he asks, his gaze on the ocean but his arms still tight around me, his chin right in line with my lips.

"I don't know. I don't know what to do." His jaw clenches. "What?"

He lets out a long breath and slowly looks at me. His eyes are flashing green, the sunlight peeking through the clouds catching glints of gold in there. "Marry me."

"What?" My voice is high. "Are you insane?"

He frowns deeply and pulls me tighter against him. "Marry me." It comes out like a demand this time—not that it ever sounded like a request.

I push against his chest, trying to get some space. "Why would we get married?"

"We're having a baby." He's almost yelling now.

"So? That doesn't mean we have to get married." His arms are like vices.

"I don't want my child to be a bastard."

I stop struggling and look up into his eyes. "Wow," I say. "Being a Catholic kind of fucked you up."

That gets him to drop his arms. "Fucked me up? If anyone here is fucked up it's you!" And now he is yelling.

"I'm worried about how I'm going to keep this baby alive, not whether it's going to hell or not."

He shakes his head and blows out a breath. He's trying to calm down. "Why won't you marry me?" he asks, his voice low, almost sounding hurt.

"You've been hiding from me for weeks and now you want to commit to being with me for the rest of your life. Really?"

"I always wanted to be a husband and father."

The sadness in his voice rips my chest open, leaving my heart just pumping away in the sand and the salt. *It hurts.* I don't speak. Can't think of what to say. I don't make dreams come true; I am a fucking angel of death.

We stare at each other, the wind blustering around us. Blue leans against my leg, warming my side. I look down at him. He's staring up at me in that way he has—pure adoration and faith. A big breath in and I return my gaze to Mulberry. "I never thought I'd be a mother. And I'd make a terrible wife."

"No you wouldn't."

I laugh. "It's like you don't know me at all or something."

"Or that I know you better than you know yourself." He steps close again, that private, shy smile slipping loose. "Robert wants you to think that you're like him: a cold, calculating killer out to get what you think you deserve. But that's not true. You want to help people, Sydney. You always have."

"Everybody I love dies." It slips out so quietly Mulberry leans closer, like he couldn't hear me.

"What?"

I have to be brave. Meeting his eyes, I say it again. "Everybody I love dies."

"I'm not dead," he points out.

"Because I left you alone; I saved you by abandoning you."

He lets out a huff of a laugh. "And you say I'm the fucked up one."

"This from the guy who wants to commit a lifetime to a woman he wasn't even talking to an hour ago, because he's got some antiquated notion about bastards." *That sounded better in my head.*

His smile grows. "I'm not going to die." His arm comes around my waist again, a subtle promise.

"You have no control over that. I'm a curse. Only a cockroach can survive me."

"A cockroach like Robert Maxim?"

I wince. "I don't know."

"You've never been willing to trust me," Mulberry says, his fingers curling around my hip in a protective hold.

"That's not true; I did trust you. And then you lied to me and basically sold me out to Robert Maxim."

Back in New York, I told Mulberry I planned to kill my brother's murderer—the act of vengeance that spawned Joyful Justice. But when I arrived at Kurt Jessup's office, he was already dead... at the hands of Robert Maxim. Not only did Robert steal my revenge but he framed me. I later learned it was Mulberry who convinced Robert to kill Kurt... trying to save me from becoming a murderer. *Another fool's errand.*

After I failed at killing my brother's murderer, I hated Robert Maxim, myself and basically the whole human race. Mulberry found me drowning my anger and guilt in a bottle of tequila on a beach in Mexico and convinced me to work for him...but it turned out I wasn't working for *just* him. Robert Maxim was a silent owner of the detective agency he'd started. Mulberry threw the wool over my eyes while Robert sank his claws into me.

"I was trying to protect you." Mulberry's voice is low. He knows that excuse is dead between us. "We keep hurting each other by trying to protect each other." *He's right.* "Let's try something new. I'll love you and you love me, and that's all we'll do."

Tears burn again, and I can't look at him. Can't even breathe. "I don't know if I can do that." I'm whispering again.

"Why not?" His voice stays soft.

"Because I'm confused and uneasy, and I don't know..."

"You don't love me?" A dull edge roughens the quiet tone.

"I do."

"But?" The edge sharpens.

Forcing my eyes open, I stare at the sand, at my sneakers sinking into it. "I don't think I can explain it."

"Try."

"I might..."

"Do you have feelings for Robert?" The edge is cutting now.

I shake my head, a denial on my tongue but unable to escape my mouth. Because Mulberry might be right.

Blue gives a sharp bark. Mulberry and I both look back the way we came and see Robert running down the sand at us, his suit jacket open and flapping in the wind. "Run!" He yells, the sound of his voice barely reaching us over the rev of a powerful engine as a quad spins off the main road and onto the beach, sand spitting out behind it.

There are two men on the quad, one aims a long and powerful rifle at Robert's back.

No!

Mulberry bends to his ankle, rising with a pistol in his grip, and steps forward, steadying the small weapon with both hands and squinting to aim.

Gunshots ring out—louder than the surf, louder than my fear—and Robert falls forward, arms out, eyes wide, sailing through the air.

Not even cockroaches can survive me.

EK

Robert

Sand grits my teeth. Sharp pain bites my knee. Sydney's scream assaults my ears. I grip the rough handle of my pistol and pull it free from the shoulder holster, rolling onto my back.

The quad bears down on me. The driver's head jerks back—Mulberry must have shot him. I take aim at a tire and blow it, throwing the vehicle off course. The driver's body falls off and the survivor bails, rolling in the sand about twenty yards away.

I aim at that second figure and pump two bullets into it. It slumps, lifeless. Mulberry passes me, running toward the downed men. "No time," I yell. "Help me up, we need to move!"

The thwapping of a helicopter racing over the waves toward the beach makes my point.

Sydney grabs my bicep and hauls me to my feet. I sling an arm across her shoulders, wincing as I inadvertently put weight on my knee. Damn weak thing—twisted years ago and never quite came back.

Memories of that injury pound through my brain: Amy's eyes, those pale blue spheres boring into my own, her voice, barely audible through the ringing in my ears as she yelled for me to keep going. Josh dipping under my arm the way Sydney is under it now, the brother and sister dragging me through the thick jungle, fleeing from our captors. *They could have left me to die.*

Mulberry slips under my other arm, and they half carry me over the sand as I hobble along. "Who the fuck are they?" Mulberry yells over the sound of the helicopter.

"There is a culvert up ahead," Sydney points, ignoring Mulberry's question. Who they are doesn't matter right now.

We veer up the beach toward the large metal tube that drains storm water onto the beach—a stream bed created by years of runoff cuts through the beach to the ocean.

Bullets pound into the sand, shooting it up in front of us, stinging my eyes. Shit, this will not go unnoticed.

We dive into the culvert—it reeks of brine and street filth. Crouched low, splashing through puddles left from the last rainfall, we move into the shadows and out of range of the helicopter's gun. The far side of the tunnel is twenty yards ahead of us, the opening we fled into, ten yards behind. We stop, the rank water soaking our feet.

Mulberry steps out from under my arm to face me. "What the fuck is going on?" he demands.

I smirk at him, leaning on Sydney, keeping her close. I'm injured, after all. Mulberry's eyes narrow as his gaze drifts to my hand clutching her shoulder. "I don't know," I answer, making it sound like I do know but just won't share with him.

Mulberry snarls and steps into my face. I straighten and glance down at the gun still in my hand before slipping it into the holster under my jacket. I'm not going to shoot him. Lifting my eyes to meet Mulberry's, I raise one brow.

"Would you two stop it?" Sydney says, shifting away, leaving me balancing on my good leg. I test weight on my knee and find it painful but bearable. She moves back toward the entrance, crouching to peer out at the helicopter. "They are hovering over the culvert," she says. "Waiting for us."

"He brought this here," Mulberry grinds out.

"Who cares?" Sydney snaps, keeping her attention on the beach. "We need to get the fuck out of here." She splashes back toward us. "The police are going to get called. Or those fuckers are going to land."

Mulberry returns his attention to me. "What are you even doing here?" he asks.

"I came for the fine whiskey at your shithole establishment."

"Fuck you." He pushes me, and I let him.

The difference between this man and me: I am ruthless and he is honorable. You know who wins that fight? Hint: me.

I pretend to stumble, and he comes at me, fists clenched. Mulberry is shorter than me but broader, a veritable pile of boulders to my more sinewy strength. Younger, dumber, and desperate for a fight, he's lost before we even begin.

Bending my knees, I get under him in the cramped space, coming up hard and fast. My fist barrels into his chin. Mulberry arches back, falters as his head hits the top of the culvert, but doesn't go down. Instead he heaves forward, launching himself at me. Bear arms come around my shoulders, holding me as we fall into the shallow water. My face goes under, and I press my mouth closed.

Lashing out with my feet, I kick at his bad leg. Mulberry groans, and his grip loosens enough for me to get my hands between us and push him off. Gasping for air, I roll away from him. He grabs for something—a tree limb?—and turns back to me, on his knees, holding it out like a weapon.

It's not a tree limb; it's his fucking prosthetic leg.

Standing, I stay low, circling him. He's soaking wet, water dripping into his eyes, soaked through his long sleeve shirt, the cotton molding to his skin. It drips off my jacket, making it heavy. It won't be easy for him to get up with just one leg.

Mulberry starts to smile, then a laugh breaks free and he shakes his head. "What?" I ask.

"You," he says. "First person I've fought since losing my leg who showed no pity."

"Pity you?" I shake my head. "No."

"I appreciate that."

He looks past me then turns to look behind him. I take a step forward, preparing to kick him in the chest and send him back into that stinking water, when I realize Sydney isn't here. "Where is she?" Mulberry asks, voicing my question.

I turn in a circle—it's just the two of us. The helicopter sound is fading.

Mulberry struggles to rise. I do not offer help. Pushing my wet hair back, I check the way we came in…the helicopter is out over the waves, returning from where it came. The distant singing of sirens reaches me.

Mulberry approaches, and as I turn to tell him, his fist connects with my jaw. I stumble into the side of the tunnel. "You're trying to keep her from me. I'm the father of her child!"

I rub my jaw, tasting blood. "You left her."

"You are incapable of loving anyone but yourself." Even bent over, Mulberry is steady on one foot, holding his fake leg in both hands now, waiting for me to come at him again rather than take advantage of his position. *What an idiot.*

"You are incapable of protecting Sydney. You're not strong enough, Mulberry, and you know it. That's why you ran away. Because you're weak." I spit the blood gathered in my mouth into the water. His frown deepens. "I can keep her and the baby safe."

"She can keep herself and the baby safe." Mulberry's frown tilts into something like a smile. "You underestimate her, Robert. Most people do."

I straighten, rubbing my jaw again—nothing broken. "We should move. The police are on the way."

"Where is she?" he asks me.

"I don't know," I answer. "But I'll find her."

"Not if I find her first," Mulberry says, bending over to reattach his leg. Once again, I do not offer to help.

"You're not a bad man," I say, staring down the length of the culvert as he struggles with his wet, flopping pant leg.

"You are," he grumbles, and I huff out a laugh. The leg clicks back into place.

"She will come back to me," I say, confident in my words.

He straightens up and smiles. "You never had her, Robert. There is nothing to come back to. Sydney Rye isn't a prize or a pet."

"No," I agree. *But she is mine.*

CHAPTER EIGHT

Mulberry

"What happened to you?" Shirley asks when I come in the back door. "And what the hell was going on out there on the beach?"

I can't even.

One look around the bar tells me Sydney isn't here—isn't looking for me anymore, huh? So like her. She loves dropping bombs and running away. Bitterness grips my throat, and I head to my tip jar, emptying it, and stuffing the bills into my wet pockets. I need to move fast before the police show up.

"Where are you going?" Shirley asks as I start back toward the door. I don't answer her. "Tyler!" she yells. I keep walking. She follows me out the back. "Hey! You at least owe me a goodbye."

I turn to her, rage and disgust at myself, at Robert, at Sydney eating my guts. *What kind of father could I possibly make?* "Good bye Shirley. I'm sorry," I grind out.

Shirley deflates but juts her chin out. "Good luck."

I'll need it.

Back in my room, I shower and change into clean clothing before packing the rest of my belongings into a duffle. I pry up the loose floorboard where I stash my tip money and fill my wallet, then hide the rest in my socks and waistband.

Ready to go, I sit on the unmade bed and call Dan. "She found me."

"I didn't tell her." He pauses. "Everything okay?"

"No." I close my eyes, tilting my head back. Should I tell him? Dan loved her once...maybe he still does. Sydney is like a freaking cancer; you can be cured but are never truly free.

"What happened?"

"Robert showed up first and then Sydney came. She wanted to talk." I take a deep breath. "She's pregnant, Dan."

"Oh," Dan says.

He doesn't sound surprised enough. "Did she tell you?"

"No. No." *Why did he say it twice?*

"Well, Robert knew. And then someone tried to kill us, so we got interrupted."

"Oh shit," Dan says.

"Once again, Dan, you do not sound surprised."

"This is the second assassination attempt this week."

"On Sydney?" My heart beats faster and I stand, clenching my free hand into a fist.

"We don't know if it's Robert or Sydney. We are trying to figure it out."

"Well..." I pace toward the door. "She ghosted us."

"What do you mean?"

This is embarrassing. "Robert and I started to"—I clear my throat—"fight, and while we were trying to drown each other, she left."

He huffs a laugh. "Sorry," he coughs.

"It's not funny."

"No." His voice is overly serious. He's mocking me. And I deserve it. Bile burns my throat. I need to beat the crap out of something.

"Do you know where she is?" I ask.

He doesn't answer right away. "I'd have to check that she wants you to find her."

"She's pregnant with my child." My voice comes out choked.

"I kept your location secret. I owe her the same." There is compassion in his tone—he gets I'm wrecked.

"Well, at least let her know she needs to get out of this town. The police will be swarming. Two bullet-ridden bodies on the beach will do that. Even in the off season."

"Tell me what happened."

I do, Dan typing the whole time. "Hmmm," he mutters. "Doesn't look like they've got any bodies. Just a report of a helicopter firing bullets at three people. They've got vague descriptions of the people." He types some more.

"No bodies? Maybe the helicopter went back for them."

"Their strongest lead is the helicopter."

"What about it?"

"Came from a yacht off the coast. They are trying to track down who owns the boat. Bound to be a shell company," Dan says. "I'll look into it. Where are you headed?"

I take a deep breath. "I don't know."

"Let me call Sydney. Maybe you two can leave together. Any idea where Robert went?"

"He had a car, and last I saw him he was headed for the highway."

"I'll call you back."

We hang up, and I heft my duffel bag onto my shoulder, check my ankle holster, and then leave, not bothering to look back. Either Dan will call back with her location, or I'll find Sydney myself. This running away from each other has to stop. We are going to have a baby. Sydney and I must learn to work together, even if we can't figure out how to love each other without almost getting ourselves killed.

What kind of parents are we going to make?

Robert

The beacon pulses on my screen—the tracking device is in Sydney Rye's phone.

Her motel is a short drive from the bar on a busy road. It's a two-story building with peeling paint and a red vacancy sign glowing in the gloomy day.

She takes a private jet here and then decides to stay in a shithole. It's not penny pinching. Sydney Rye has plenty of money—not as much as me, but Dan is a savvy investor and has helped make her a very wealthy woman.

She stays in crappy places because she does not want to draw attention to herself. But you can't fully hide the sun behind even the darkest of clouds.

I press the ignition button and the Mercedes purrs back to life. She left Mulberry and me in that tunnel. My body vibrates with the need to go and shout at her—to make her see my point of view. *I should let her go so that she can realize the truth for herself.* I just want to take care of her. She hasn't even been to a doctor yet.

I'm out of the car and striding toward her room before I fully realize what I'm doing. Stopping under the eaves of the motel, I stand in a cloud of uncertainty. *I hate this.*

Then I'm knocking on her door. No sound on the other side and no response. But the beacon pulses inside. I knock again. Would she leave her phone behind?

A motorcycle engine pulls my attention to the lot. *Mulberry.* He climbs off the bike and removes his helmet, his eyes landing on me. We frown at each other across the almost empty parking lot.

He strides over, holding the helmet under one arm—his prosthetic leg barely slows him down. I tense but don't draw a weapon. "You shouldn't be here," Mulberry says.

"You either," I point out.

"The cops got called."

"Obviously."

"She's not opening the door?" he gestures toward the hotel room.

"Captain Obvious strikes again."

"You are such an ass." He turns and starts back toward his bike.

"Where are you headed?" I ask.

He pauses and looks over his shoulder, eyes narrowed. "Why?"

"It doesn't do me any good if the police find you. I've got a plane, come with me."

"Where are you going?"

"I'd like to find Sydney and get us all back to Miami. You two can talk."

He turns fully toward me. "Now you want us to talk? A few hours ago you were trying to make me disappear."

I shrug. "A wise man can change tactics. That is no longer going to work. You're invested."

"Invested?" He shakes his head. "That's hardly the word."

He's right; you can walk away from an investment.

I step off the curb, heading back to my car. "Meet me at the airport. Or don't. Just avoid getting picked up by the police."

The screeching of tires jerks my attention forward. Marked police cars and black sedans flood into the lot, shaking on their shocks as they brake hard. Doors fly open, and police pour out, using the vehicles as shields, their guns aimed at us.

"Hands in the air!"

Mulberry's helmet hits the ground with a thump as he raises his arms. I lift my own toward the sky.

The clouds part and the sun sneaks out, casting a ray of gold onto the scene. *Sydney motherfucking Rye.*

EK

"I want to call my lawyer," I say again, my voice even. I pull my shirt sleeves straight, taking a moment to finger the cufflinks—emeralds mounted in brushed gold, so that the stone's brilliance is the focal point. The gold isn't even important.

I bring my eyes up to meet the detective's, keeping my expression neutral. "We can get this all cleared up without involving attorneys," she suggests, again. The woman, who introduced herself as Detective Phelps, is about my age, her suit off the rack. It might have been pressed at the beginning of her shift but is wrinkled now. Phelps doesn't bother dying her gray hair and just pulls the whole curly mop back into a pony-tail. I am way out of her league. And she knows it.

"You have not arrested me," I point out.

She nods, keeping her face blank. Not a total fool, but pretty close. "We just want to know what happened on the beach today."

"Attorney," I say, not bothering with the whole sentence this time. "Or release me." I check my watch—I'm wearing the Patek Philippe Grand Complications Perpetual Calendar Chronograph manual-wind today. A white gold case surrounds a silver opaline dial on a black alligator strap with an 18k white gold Calatrava Cross deployment buckle. It costs more than this woman makes in a year.

There is a knock at the door and another detective enters—this one male and younger. He hands her a tablet. "The footage you asked for."

"Yes. Thank you." She takes the slim device and he leaves. Phelps turns the screen toward me and starts a video. Taken from the board-walk above the beach, it shows three blurry figures, one being carried between the other two, as a helicopter chases them, firing bullets into the sand.

The videographer's attention is more focused on the helicopter than the fleeing victims, but I can tell it's me. Wouldn't hold up in court though—not that it's against the law to be shot at by a helicopter.

"That's you," she says, pointing to the figure in the middle.

"Attorney," I say again.

"This is Tyler Dirk." She points to Mulberry. *She doesn't know his real name.* "A local bartender." She meets my gaze. Her eyes are a soft brown with long lashes, her best feature. "Why would a billionaire, CEO of a private security firm, even be within 100 miles of this town, much less getting shot at from the air, and then hanging out with a bartender in a motel parking lot?"

I don't respond, but I do wonder why she is so focused on the helicopter and hasn't even asked about the two men we shot.

She lays the tablet down on the table.

"Attorney." I cross my arms over my chest and glance down at my watch again. She made me wait over twenty minutes and has been questioning me for ten. I'll give her another ten, then I'm leaving. I'm not going to waste a full hour on this nonsense.

"You must wonder how we knew you were in that parking lot. How we know it's you in this video." She raises one brow. I keep my face still —maintaining a bored expression.

"Do you recognize the helicopter?" she asks. Not waiting for a reply she continues. "Belongs to a yacht that was anchored off the coast." She wakes the tablet and looks down at the still of the helicopter. I glance at it. There is no name on the bird.

"Someone is trying to kill you," she says. "Or maybe it's this woman they are after," she points to Sydney's form. "Witnesses say they saw the bartender shoot a man on a quad. And you shoot another. But we didn't find any bodies on the beach." I sigh and roll my shoulders. *I'm so bored.* "The helicopter must have picked them up. Leave no man behind." She watches me closely but I give nothing away. "You were never in the military...unusual for your line of work."

I check my watch. Three more minutes. "Tyler Dirk doesn't have a military record either," she goes on. A one-woman show, this gal. "Doesn't have any kind of record." She shrugs. "Missing part of a leg though. That's the kind of wound you might sustain in the army...or security."

"Detective," I act like I've forgotten her name. "I'm going to leave now. You can arrest me, though I'm not sure for what."

"How about shooting a man on the beach?"

"Sure, if you have any evidence of such a crime. But you don't because it didn't happen. So..." I stand up, the chair scraping on the floor as I rise. "I'll be going now." She stands as well, her lips pressed tight. She's got nothing, and we both know it. "Enjoy the rest of your afternoon," I suggest as I open the door.

A uniformed officer waits outside the interrogation room, and after a nod from Phelps, he escorts me through the station. Pulling my phone out, I call for a car to pick me up. I walk with my shoulders back, arms loose at my side, as if I am totally unconcerned and completely innocent.

While Phelps isn't much of a detective, she was right about one thing—I am curious about who told them to go looking for me in that motel parking lot. Somebody gave my name to the police. They didn't mention Sydney Rye. So it seems that I am the intended victim in these attacks.

I love when someone who hopes to gain from me gives instead.

But who, I wonder, is trying to kill me?

CHAPTER NINE

Mulberry

It's grown still, and a light rain has started as I step out of the police station. The sky is low and gray, air thick with the scent of garbage. This is a gross part of town.

Police cars line the street, glistening in the drizzle. No traffic moves down the block. My bike is back at the motel. I finger my phone in my pocket. It is a simple flip phone, so I can't look up a taxi number or use an app for a ride.

There is a sticky note next to the cash register at work with four taxi companies' numbers printed on it. I close my eyes, trying to remember the digits.

The rumble of an engine and the wet thrum of tires on the road pull my eyes open. A sleek black town car slows as it approaches the entrance to the police station. The station door just behind me opens and Robert Maxim steps out.

His mouth is pulled down, and his brow furrowed.

He catches sight of me and relaxes his face, hiding away the concern.

What's got him so upset? So upset he let emotion control his features, even if for only a moment. Robert pulls down his sleeves, the gold and emerald cufflinks flashing before he rolls his shoulders and steps to where I'm waiting under the overhang.

The rain picks up, pinging off the parked cop cars.

The black town car, exhaust pluming from its tailpipe, purrs at the curb. The driver gets out and opens an umbrella before starting toward us. Robert holds up a hand to keep him at a distance.

"Can I offer you a lift?" he asks me.

"No, thanks." I'm holding onto my pride like it's an umbrella and a ride-sharing app.

"We need to talk."

"I've got nothing to say to you."

Robert shakes his head. "You're an idiot." He steps out from under the overhang, droplets of water darkening his light gray suit. The driver rushes forward and covers him with the umbrella.

I pull out my phone as the black car pulls away from the curb. While I'm trying to remember the numbers on the post it, Detective Phelps comes out and stands next to me. "Want me to give you a ride back to your bike?"

"It's the least you could do," I say. "After dragging me over here for no reason."

She frowns, sticking out her lower lip. "You're the one who made it useless. We could use your help on this."

"I told you—it has nothing to do with me."

"That's not what Robert Maxim said."

I laugh and shake my head. "Nice try. Which one of these is yours?" I gesture toward the line of police vehicles.

She points to an unmarked sedan, and we step out into the rain, jogging toward it. Inside smells like stale coffee and the pine tree-shaped air freshener swinging from the mirror.

It reminds me of the car I drove when working as a detective in New York City. A lifetime ago... when I first met Sydney Rye. I stare into the gloom outside the car window and picture her the way she was back then. Young, bright, fearless...unscathed. Losing her brother and her own injuries changed her. How could they not?

And then she changed me.

"Tyler?" I turn to Phelps, realizing it's not the first time she's said my name. "You okay?"

I give her a half smile. "Lost in memories for a moment."

Her eyes light, hearing the truth in my words. She's going to try to get more out of me. "What memories?"

"Rainy days and romantic interludes." Murder, revenge, and a woman I later fell for hard enough to blow myself up over…repeatedly.

Phelps peppers me with questions on the ten-minute drive back to the motel but I answer in monosyllables and grunts. She doesn't get frustrated, just stays doggedly determined to wring information out of me. She's a decent cop.

"Look," she says, putting the car into park next to my bike. "I can see this isn't your first time talking with law enforcement." She dangles the worm at the end of her hook. "And I can see you don't want to tell me about what happened on that beach, but we will find the woman who was there with you and Maxim." She turns in her seat fully to face me—so I can get a good look at her eyes and she can watch every muscle of me. "We will figure this out, Tyler, and if you talk with me now, it will go better for you." She is waving the worm in my face, threatening to dig the hook through my lip if I won't bite it.

"Sorry," I say. "You've really got the wrong guy."

A tight smile crosses her lips. "Have it your way."

She leaves me next to my bike. The rain has stopped, and the setting sun is glowering over the gulf a few blocks away, throwing up sprays of pink into the dissipating clouds.

The Mercedes Robert was driving earlier is gone. He probably got dropped off here and then headed to the airport. I'm guessing Sydney did too. So I climb on my bike and start toward Tallahassee.

It's dark when I pull into the private airport parking lot, parking near the terminal.

An employee waits at the entrance with a luggage cart. I smile at him, and he nods, offering a smile in return. I might be a local bartender who has no place at this high-end airport, or I could be a billionaire. He's gonna play it safe.

"Can I help you?" he asks. Probably in his forties with thinning pale hair, he's wearing fingerless gloves and a name tag that reads Nate.

"Maybe." I pull out my wallet and extract one hundred dollars in twenties. "Did you see a woman come through here with a really big dog?"

He eyes the money and then looks up at my face. "Who wants to know?"

This does make me look like a stalker.

"I'm a private eye. My client just wants to make sure his wife is where she said she'd be." I give him a knowing smile. *Women, and the men they drive crazy.*

Nate purses his lips. I pull out a few more twenties, doubling the amount I'm offering.

He takes it, counting it once before looking up at me and raising one brow. I lay two more twenties on the pile. "Saw a woman this morning with three big dogs."

"Did they look like wolves?"

He nods. "One of them sure did." *Blue and his puppies.* "Has she come back?" He shakes his head. "You've been on this whole time?"

"I work a double today."

I smile. "That's lucky for me. Did you see what kind of car she left in?"

"An SUV thing—with that many dogs she'd need it, right?" He grins.

"A rental, you figure?"

He nods, "Yup, used one of those services where they drop the car off for you."

"Do you know which one?"

Nate puts the cash in his pocket and then holds up his empty hand. I take out a few more twenties, leaving my wallet empty. "Enterprise," he says, pushing the new bills into his pocket to join their brethren.

"That office close by?" I ask. He gives me the address.

I'm heading back to my bike when Robert's Mercedes turns into the lot. I stop next to my bike and he pulls up, rolling down his window. "Fancy seeing you here," I say.

"We need to talk in private. Get in the car."

"I already told you I have nothing to say to you."

His jaw ticks with annoyance. "Someone gave our names to the police."

"They gave my fake name to the cops."

He raises one brow. "And isn't that interesting? Get in. Don't be an asshole."

"Like you?"

He sighs, and I relent, going around to climb in the passenger seat. Robert pulls into a parking spot and turns off the ignition. "The helicopter came from an off-shore yacht. We need to figure out who owns it. I spoke with Dan and he is working on it, but that is an easy thing to hide."

"I'm sure you know all about it."

He doesn't take the bait. "Whoever is trying to kill us—"

"You," I point out. "They don't even know my name."

"Sydney and me."

"How do you know they are after her?"

Robert turns to me, his eyes bright in the car's dark interior. "What makes you think they're not? You do not understand what's going on. She is in danger. Don't you want to protect her?" There is an edge to his voice—he's angry and upset.

"You can't figure out where she went, can you?"

Robert shakes his head. "If you love her, let her go. She'll come back if it's meant to be."

"When did you start working for Hallmark?"

"Watch your back," he responds.

"I'll be watching Sydney's too. Not that she needs either of us."

Robert's jaw ticks again. Ah, he thinks she needs him. He opens his door and gets out of the car, leaving me alone in the luxurious interior. *That's one way to end a conversation.*

I join him in the misty evening. "I'm going to check on that yacht. In person," Robert says as I join him on the sidewalk.

"Great. Good luck with that."

He shakes his head in that you're-an-idiot way he's got down pat and walks away from me. The car beeps and flashes that it's locked. "Asshole," I mutter to myself as I head back to my bike.

The Enterprise office is in a strip mall sandwiched between a pizza parlor and a nail salon. A bell jingles as I enter the space. It's small, with a few waiting chairs, gray indoor–outdoor carpeting and a white Formica counter, behind which sits a young woman with giant glasses that make her look like an innocent owl.

She smiles and pushes the glasses up her nose. "Welcome," she says with what sounds like genuine warmth.

I've restocked my wallet with cash, but I get the sense greed will not motivate her. Let's see if I can make her feel bad for me. I play up my limp as I approach the desk.

"Good evening," I say with a weak smile. "I'm hoping you can help me. I've lost my phone."

"I'm so sorry," she says, her voice high and distressed, the way only a millennial can be at the loss of a phone.

"I appreciate that," I smile, putting a twinkle into my eyes. She blushes just a little. "I'm hoping you can help me, because my wife rented a car here, and it's our anniversary. I wanted to surprise her." I shake my head. "But of course, all the information is in my phone." She nods, totally understanding how one might lose all knowledge when their phone goes missing. "I'm hoping you have some information that might help."

"I'm so sorry, sir." She looks it, too. "But I can't share any information about our clients." She bites her lip.

"Nothing?" I raise my brows in distress. "We've been married for ten years tomorrow. And she had to work, and I pretended I couldn't join her." I bow my head. "She's actually kind of pissed at me. God, she will think I don't care." Looking up at Owl Eyes from under my lashes, I give her my most pathetic look.

She sighs but doesn't relent. *Policy is policy.* I nod, understanding. I'm a reasonable man. Totally normal. "Can I use your bathroom before I go?"

She jumps off her stool, excited that she can help in any way, and points to the rest room. It's past the desk, down a narrow, poorly lit hall, the end of which is a back exit with a push bar door. On the wall by the bathroom is the familiar square pull of a fire alarm.

In the bathroom, I wad up paper towels. Before heading to the front, I ease open the back door and then put it back into place but with the paper between the lock and the catch.

Owl Eyes apologizes again, and I leave with my head hanging, noting the hours on the door as I go. They close in forty-five minutes.

Back on my bike, I pull out into the street and circle around to the back of the mall. Cutting the engine before I reach the rear entrance, I park it just out of sight behind the nail salon, the scent of which burns my nose.

I still have twenty minutes before they close. There are two options —wait for Owl Eyes to leave and then sneak in or go in now and pull the fire alarm to get her away from her computer... hopefully leaving it unlocked. My gut tells me there is an alarm system which will alert Owl Eyes that the back entrance is unsecured when she goes to set it at closing. And I'd bet money that she follows protocol to a T.

Taking a deep breath I slowly push open the door. Stepping into the familiar hall, I let the door slip back into place, being sure that the wadded paper towel prevents any clicking sounds.

The phone rings once before Owl Eye picks it up, her voice high and eager. The clacking of the keyboard starts up as I reach the alarm. I bring down the T-shaped handle, and the alarm screeches, accompanied by flashing white strobes.

Owl Eyes screams. The handset clatters to the floor, and I dip into the bathroom, waiting a full sixty seconds before slipping back out into the hall.

Through the tinted front windows, I can see Owl Eyes standing on the sidewalk, her purse clutched against her chest, a man in a white apron smeared with red sauce next to her. Must be one of the pizza chefs from next door.

Staying low, I sneak in behind the counter—I can't see them anymore, but neither can they see me, unless they come back in. Owl

Eyes is too much of a stickler to return to a building where the alarm is still sounding.

As I'd hoped, she's left the computer unlocked. The system is simple, and I only have to go through three of Sydney's aliases before landing on Grace Smith. Her license pops up—red curly hair, dark eye makeup, and brown contacts.

I write down the license plate number and click through until I find the LoJack key, writing that down too. Return location: Washington D.C.

The wail of sirens rises over the blaring alarm, and I peek over the desk to see a fire engine pulling up.

Time to go.

I'm out the back door before firefighters enter the building and merge onto the highway minutes later. Weaving through traffic, I head north for twenty minutes before I pull into a rest stop and call Dan.

"She left her phone behind," he says.

"I know, but I've got her LoJack number. And she's returning her car to D.C."

"Well that's useful," Dan says, a smile in his voice. I give him the LoJack as an SUV pulls into the parking spot next to me. A woman leaps out of the passenger side and rips open the back door where an infant is wailing. "It's okay, baby," she coos, struggling to free the flailing baby from its car seat.

"Yup," Dan says. "She's headed north."

"Any idea why she's going to D.C.?"

"I do, but that's Joyful Justice business."

"Okay." The woman has the infant free and sits back into the passenger seat, bringing the red faced baby to her breast. I turn away, giving her privacy—though I doubt she's noticed me. That baby is her entire world. "You can't tell me why Sydney is in D.C. But can you tell me where?"

"She may be going to see Declan Doyle," Dan says. He sounds sympathetic...like I'm pathetic.

"Thanks," I say, and we hang up.

A man gets out of the driver's seat, his eyes shadowed by dark circles, his stare miles long. "I'm going to go get a coffee," he says. The woman either ignores him or doesn't hear.

Slipping my phone back into my pocket, I watch him walk away.

Could that be Sydney and me in nine months? Exhausted, confused...struggling at the hands of a helpless, demanding baby?

Only if I'm very lucky.

CHAPTER TEN

Robert

Sunrise is just a slight brightening of the clouds. No sprays of pink, blushes of peach, or twinkling blue. The clouds are too heavy for the sun to play any games this morning.

Our research in the night didn't turn up any information about the ship that the helicopter left. But Dan tracked it over satellite, and we know it's off the coast of Naples now. Though the clouds are hiding it, Dan has a projected path based on its course over the last twelve hours.

He's helping me, because he still thinks they may be after Sydney. But I believe they gave my name to the police because this is a game they are playing with me. And me alone.

"That's a storm ahead, and it looks pretty rough, buddy," the pilot, who introduced himself as Willy, says.

What about me suggests that I'm anyone's buddy?

"I don't care."

Willy glances over at me, his pale green eyes ringed in dark circles. His breath reeks of coffee, and his bulging stomach and stained shirt affirm his slovenly lifestyle.

Willy returns his attention to the sky in front of us. The clouds have thickened, and the helicopter bumps in the choppy air. I glance down at my phone, where I have the map Dan sent me with the projected course of the yacht.

We're thirty miles off the coast. "Go lower," I say. "The clouds are too thick, we can't see the surface."

"This cover is low; it's dangerous to go closer to the surface."

"Do it." I don't bother looking at him—just use the force of my will and the weight of my expectations to make him follow my commands. The sea appears beneath us. The surface is riled, white caps peaking on silver-gray waves—the color of Sydney Rye's eyes.

"Is that what you're looking for?" Willy asks.

In the distance, I can just make out a ship. It's a large yacht, over 100 feet long, with a helicopter pad on the stern, and, from what we could see in the satellite images, a mounted machine gun on the bow.

Through binoculars I can see that the ship is bursting through the waves, white spray flying on either side of her—the wake wide and turbulent. I try to make out the name on the stern but can't—we are still too far, and the helicopter is bumping too much.

"We need to get closer," I say. The pilot nods, continuing on course. The yacht slows, its wake subsiding. They must've spotted us. Through the binoculars I see figures running to the stern. They are holding machine guns.

"They have guns!" Willy yells.

"Keep going," I command. The ship begins to turn. "I need to see the name." Willy doesn't respond. I glance over at him. His eyes widen as the ship comes fully about—he sees the mounted gun. "Move, you asshole!" I yell at him.

My voice jerks Willy from his stupor, and he starts to turn the helicopter fully around, returning the way we came.

"No! I need to see the name on the back of that ship. Circle around now!"

"I'm not going to die for you, Mister. All the money in the world can't bring a dead man back."

"I'll kill you myself. Now go." He looks over at me, sees the truth in my eyes, and with shaking hands, lifts us into the clouds. The bird shakes and shudders as he moves through the rough air. We descend again, right above the ship.

The men below scramble to aim the weapon at our underside. Willy veers quickly to the stern. And I see it. I see the name of the yacht.

The Escape Plan.

I can't breathe. The past swamps me.

The fire lit up the dark night, throwing wild shadows around the jungle. The explosion from the storage area sent the camp into chaos—soldiers running through the thick mud, their boots making loud sucking noises with each step. Commanders yelled for "Agua", their prisoners forgotten in the clutch of survival.

My hands shook as I fit the key into the metal cuff around Amy's neck. It came off, leaving a red welt in its place. *She's lucky she didn't die of infection.* The cutters clipping through the fence made an audible ting. Amy, a rock clutched in her hands, smashed at the padlock holding her lover's cage door shut.

Antonio Marguezes, a political prisoner, pressed against the back of the small crate until the lock finally gave way. He burst from the cage, the promise of freedom lending his weakened body strength. *Antonio didn't make it out of that jungle alive, though.*

Josh held the cut fence piece down, and we climbed through, staying low, as though if we made ourselves small enough the soldiers running to extinguish the blaze wouldn't see us. *Natalia saw us, though.*

She stood outside her tent, hair down, wearing just a T-shirt and underpants. *She'd been asleep.* Men ran between us, smoke—the wet jungle wood steaming—fogged the air, but still I could see her face. The hard set of her mouth, the narrowed eyes...you betrayed me, she accused.

The keys still gripped in my hand, the roaring flames all around us, told the truth. *I used her.* But I planned to take her with me.

When I started forward, Amy grabbed my arm. "What are you doing?" she hissed. Antonio and Josh stood behind her, the dark, thick jungle just beyond them. If we wanted to escape, we had to do it now.

"I'm not leaving her," I said.

Amy gave a small shake of her head. "There is no time."

I broke free of her grip and started toward Natalia, whose commander appeared out of the night. He grabbed her arm, hauling her up against him—his mouth moving. Making threats.

I broke into a run, but my leg sucked into the deep mud, my knee twisted and I fell, pain vibrating through my body. Amy's small hand grabbed at my arm again. Warm wetness seeped from my thigh. I'd been shot.

Another explosion shook the camp, and I blinked against the heat, sweat blinding me, the bright flash leaving an aura in my vision. Natalia's tent was on fire—the flames licking at the night sky, sputtering at the moisture it met there.

Her body lay on the ground, the fire's light dancing over her naked legs. "She's gone!" Amy yelled, hauling me up. Josh got on the other side, and together they pulled me free of the mud. They dragged me into the jungle, into the night, toward freedom.

I'd told Natalia she needed to have an escape plan—hinted that we would not be captives for much longer. She didn't listen. *Why?* The thoughts tore at me for all the days we fought our way out of that jungle.

My knee recovered, though my bullet-grazed thigh continued to weep through the makeshift dressing. I took my turn carrying Antonio. He died on my back, his cheeks hollow and skin yellow—as Amy wept, her face red, splattered in mud, the wound at her neck festering—all I could think was...*why didn't Natalia have an escape plan?*

Now, as the helicopter banks hard toward shore, the safety belt biting into my chest, I realize that she did have a plan—Natalia made it out of that jungle alive. And now she wants me dead.

EK

Sydney

The front door opens, and hard leather soles clack on the wood floor. The hall light goes on. Keys jingle as they get hung on the hook. Declan appears as a dark shadow in the entryway to the living room. He flicks on the light and jerks, his eyes going wide when they land on me.

Recovering quickly, he starts to reach into his suit jacket. "Don't," I say, the pistol in my hand stilling him. "Sit." I gesture with the barrel at the armchair across from me. He puts his hands up and smiles, moving into the room.

Declan is wearing a suit way more expensive than a man in his position should be able to afford—he comes from money, and it's written all over him, from the confidence in his gait to the gold watch glowing on his wrist. His wealth is a bubble that protects him from almost everything.

"You've made yourself at home," he says, eyes tracing the dogs around me as he sits in the leather armchair. Frank wags his way over to Declan.

"That's Frank," I say. Frank makes himself at home on Declan's foot, giant tail thumping on the floor. "He's friendly."

"I see that." Declan frowns as Frank rests his massive head on the man's lap.

"Sorry to just show up like this," I say.

Declan settles back into the chair, laying a long, well-muscled arm across the back of it, ignoring Frank's plaintive whine for pets. "You could have called first...or knocked." He smiles, his brown eyes glinting with amusement.

"Yes, but then you could have called law enforcement."

"I am law enforcement."

I shrug. "I hardly think of you that way." When we first met Declan was a mounted police officer in New York City, he was promoted to detective soon after I fled the country, then joined Homeland Security. We dated in New York, when I became a fugitive he hunted me, and since he saved my life we've had an unspoken truce between us.

Declan laughs. "So what are you doing here?"

"I've got a few questions."

Declan raises one brow. "Me too."

"Maybe we can help each other out."

"I'll show you mine if you show me yours." His grin widens. He's having fun.

It's my turn to laugh. "Excellent. I understand you're on a new task force focused on the Incels and the Her Prophet followers." He nods slightly, his smile fading. "The man who tried to kill me is in prison awaiting trial." An Incel working with the McCains to traffic Isis prisoners as sex slaves, my would be assassin was a zealot hell bent on punishing women for his celibacy.

"That's right."

"Has he shared any information with you?" I know the answer to this question—the man confirmed that Ian and his brothers were the source for the sex slaves that the Incels were importing. And he gave up several men who had bought girls. But, I want to see how genuine Declan is about sharing information.

"Yes," Declan's gaze darkens. He tells me what I already know and ends his summary with, "Creeps."

"It's nice when we can agree," I say. "They are real creeps."

"My turn." Declan sits forward and Frank shifts so that Declan is forced to pet him or lean back again. One of Declan's hands lands on the dog's head and stays there. Frank wriggles, the motion creating the petting session he so desperately wants. *The dog is persistent.*

Nila lets out a quiet sigh, and I control the smile trying to twist my lips. She's totally embarrassed by her brother.

"Is Joyful Justice working with Her Prophet followers?" Declan's eyes are intense.

"Not officially, but I'm sure some of our members believe in her...divinity."

His lips pinch. "That's not an answer."

"It is, just not super detailed." Declan shakes his head and sits back again, leaving his hand on Frank's head. "Have you heard any rumblings about Incel hiring mercenaries?" I ask.

He frowns and shakes his head. "No, why?"

"Because I've got mercenaries after me. They've made two attempts on my life in as many weeks. And that's over my quota." I smile.

Declan's eyes drop to my body and back up. "You seem to have survived unscathed."

"I usually do."

"My turn—"

I cut him off. "Actually, you just asked me one."

He smirks. "Fine, your turn."

"Is Joyful Justice a part of your investigation?"

"Not a focus." I open my mouth to ask a follow up but he waggles his brows. "My turn. Is your mother working with the Fellowship of the Blood?"

"I have no idea what that is. Or if my mom is involved. But it does sound like her crowd—I'm guessing the blood has something to do with Christ." He goes to answer, but I hold up a hand. "That's not one of my questions. Don't answer it."

He laughs. "Your mom's been making a lot of waves since heading back out on the road."

"She's known for wave making." A devout follower of the Her Prophet, mommy dearest is largely responsible for her growing popularity in the Western world. An Incel shot her a few months ago, but she's made a full recovery and is back on the road preaching her truth. After years of marriage to a televangelist preacher, proselytizing comes naturally to her.

"Are you worried about your mom?" Declan asks.

"She's a survivor."

"Like mother like daughter."

"Something like that. My turn again."

"I think it's mine."

"You asked if I was worried about my mom. I'm not. Moving on. This new task force—you're looking at Incels and Her Prophet followers. Why combine the two? They're pretty much opposites."

He cocks his head. "Because a Her Prophet follower blew up an Incel gathering. And an Incel follower shot your mother." He says it like it's obvious, and he's pretty sure I know it.

"So you think the two groups are equivalent?"

He shakes his head. "No, but I think they're going to war with each other. Now I get two questions."

"Shoot."

"What is Joyful Justice doing about Ian McCain?"

"Ian?" I say, acting confused. "I don't know who you mean."

"I thought we were scratching each other's backs here. Do you think he might be the guy behind your mercenaries?" I don't respond. Declan rubs the top of Frank's head, causing his left leg to thump with appreciation. "Or do you think he's too busy trying to get revenge on his old partner, Petra Bokan?"

"I don't know, Declan, like I said, I spent the last few weeks dodging bullets. I have not had much time to think about anything else." My pregnancy flashes across my thoughts, and I shove it back down, but Declan saw something.

His eyes narrow. "What's going on?" he asks.

"What aren't you telling me?" I say, ignoring his question and rising to stand. Declan stays seated, Frank's head still on his thigh. "You've been following the Incels and have not heard any chatter about me?"

"Nope. I think it's my turn though. Please sit." He gestures with the hand not petting Frank.

"What about my mom?" I persist. He doesn't answer. "You have someone watching her." Again, no answer. "Someone undercover or just surveillance?" His face stays neutral, but that tells me something nonetheless. *They have her covered.*

"Sydney, it's my turn to ask a question."

"I'm done with this game." I start to move toward the door, Blue and Nila at my heel, Frank tripping over himself to follow.

Declan stands. "Hey, wait a second." I turn back to him. "Let me see what I can find out about these mercenaries. If I hear anything, how should I contact you?"

"What do you want in return?"

He shrugs. "Anything you can get on the Fellowship of the Blood would be very helpful." Declan gives me a sheepish smile—which, even with all his arrogance and machismo, works for him somehow.

I take a deep breath, reminding myself that Declan saved my life.

That even if he is investigating Joyful Justice, my mom, or me, he's actually kind of a good guy.

"I have no plans to see my mother, but if I hear anything I'll let you know."

"And I should reach you...?" He leaves the rest of the question unasked.

Just send an email to yourself and Dan will see it... "I'll call you," I say.

"Fine," he relents. "Give me a few days."

"Will do, boss."

He laughs as I step out his front door.

EK

Mulberry

I watch Sydney leave Declan's apartment building and follow at a safe distance as she heads down the block. The rain has stopped, and the streets smell like wet cement. Water beads on the parked cars, glistening under the streetlights. People are out, heading home from work, or to happy hour.

A brief pang of longing for my old anonymous life tightens my chest —my biggest concerns were being on time to the bar and making sure the register came out right at the end of the night. But those memories, and the facade of simplicity they embody, drift away as I pick up my pace when Sydney rounds a corner.

She's wearing a black fedora with her hair up underneath it and a long raincoat that hides her body. The dogs are on loose leashes, staying tight to her sides.

People eye her, their heads turning to follow Sydney's progress. A dangerous flash of possessiveness rumbles in my gut. *She should be all mine.* Anger clenches my fists. How could she just disappear after telling me she was pregnant and turning down my marriage proposal? What kind of person does that?

A selfish person.

Or a selfless one who thinks everyone she loves dies.

Shit.

Sydney ducks down an alley, and I stop at the entrance, waiting for her and the dogs to reach the other end before following. The rancid scent of garbage mixes with the stink of urine. What a lovely capital we have. Sydney turns the corner and disappears from sight.

As I reach the end of the alley, Sydney steps out in front of me, a knife glinting in the streetlight a millisecond before it's pressed to my throat. She's got me pushed up against the building next to a dumpster before she recognizes me. Her eyes narrow. "You're following me now?"

"What did you expect?" I ask, clearing my throat.

She lowers the knife and takes a step back. "I could have killed you."

I nod my agreement. "But you didn't. Silver lining." She lets out a small laugh and backs up, giving me space to move off the wall. "We were in the middle of a conversation."

"How did you find me? Was it Dan?"

"Good old-fashioned detective work."

"Sure, right." She bends down, slipping the knife into an ankle holster.

"Can we go somewhere and talk?"

Sydney stands up and meets my gaze. "So me running off didn't deliver the message that I don't want to talk?" Her voice is as cold as the steel she just pressed to my jugular.

"I asked you to marry me."

She sighs and looks out of the alley to the residential street beyond. "My rental is close."

We walk in silence, Sydney leading the way to a brownstone. She goes through the gate and around to the basement entrance, unlocking the door with a key code. Slipping off her coat and hat, she hangs them in the entryway next to a sign that reads *Welcome Guests!*

I follow behind her dogs down the narrow hall to a small living room-kitchen combination. A door offers access to a tiny backyard. There are three dog beds next to the door and another sign. This one says *Welcome Furry Friends!*

The dogs settle onto the beds, all three of them curled up together— like a family. My chest aches watching them.

Sydney goes over to the stove and puts on a pot of water. "Want tea?"

"Sure." I sit on the futon, the only piece of human furniture in the small space.

She pulls down two mugs. "All they have here is mint, that okay?"

"Anything is fine. I just want to talk."

Without her coat and hat, she looks smaller. She drops a mug, and it clatters across the counter. She catches it before it falls off the edge. "You're tired," I say.

"I drove here."

"Me too."

Nerves force me to stand. Sydney doesn't look over at me, but Blue raises his head, watching as I cross the small space to stand behind her. "You can lean on me," I say, quiet and true.

Her body tenses when I place my hands on her shoulders, but then she sighs and rests against me. Her back on my chest is warm and welcome. We stay like that, quiet and together, until the kettle whistles and she moves to grab it, pouring boiling water into the mugs.

Steam rises, bringing the scent of mint with it. She's an arm's length away, and I don't move to close the distance, fighting against every instinct to grab her and throw her over my shoulder and just make her mine.

"I'm sorry," she says, surprising me. I bite my tongue, trying to be patient, to let her talk. "You guys were just acting like such macho assholes." She looks up and gives me a tired smile. "I had to bail."

I give her a half smile. "Okay."

Her lower lip trembles, tears welling in her eyes, and I can't hold myself back from reaching out to her. "Come here," I whisper, pulling her into my arms, holding her against my chest again, petting her hair. "Everything is okay," I say.

"No, it's not." Her voice is muffled by being pressed against me. "Someone is trying to kill me. And I'm crying about it. I don't cry about this stuff."

"That's okay, you can cry when people try to kill you." I can't help the smile that turns my lips. She's so funny, in her own morbid way.

Sydney pushes back just enough to see me. Her eyes are red rimmed, and she looks so tired it actually hurts me a little. "No," she says, firming her voice. "It is not okay to cry when someone is trying to kill you. I don't have time for this. I need to find them. And destroy them." Her voice vibrates with conviction.

"Okay, but how about a good night's sleep first?" She starts to protest, but I keep talking. "Merl always says that sleep is paramount. You'll be able to think better in the morning. Besides, Sydney"—I lower my voice just a little, as if I'm talking to a skittish animal—"You're pregnant. You need more rest."

She sighs and drops her head against my chest. I swell with hope. *Maybe she will listen to me.*

"Okay," she says.

"I'll stay, if you want. No funny business, I swear." I say quickly, before she can protest.

Sydney nods her head. "Is that the only bed?" I ask, looking over at the futon.

"No, there is a bedroom." She steps out of my arms. Sydney doesn't look at me as she heads back down the hall. I follow her into a small bedroom with a double in it. She goes into the bathroom and closes the door. I find extra sheets and pillows in the closet and am making up the futon for myself when she comes back into the living room.

She's in an oversized T-shirt that comes to mid-thigh and hangs off one shoulder. It's a pale cream silk, and I grit my teeth, guessing it belongs to Robert Maxim. Sydney's hair is down, the tips brushing her shoulders as she walks to her cup of tea. "Can we talk in the morning?" she asks, leaning her back against the counter, her mug in both hands.

"Sure."

I lay awake, staring out the barred window up at the sky—it's bright, the city lights reflecting off the low cloud cover. Frank climbed into my bed the second I laid down and refused to decamp. He is snoring like a locomotive and occasionally whimpering, his legs shaking—probably burying bones in his dreams and losing them.

This dog is kind of an idiot, but I can't help but like him.

Blue and Nila are in with Sydney, and I hear them stir, their collars jangling, then the bedroom door opening.

I sit up as Sydney comes in. She stands in the entryway. "Everything okay?"

She doesn't answer, just comes over to the bed and pulls back the blanket, climbing in next to me. She rolls over, facing away from me. I lie back down and tentatively put an arm around her waist. She takes my hand and pulls it up to her chest. I take a deep inhalation of her scent and sigh.

Blue nips at Frank, who rolls over and tries to climb up the bed, escaping his dad's condemnation and getting ready to spoon me. I elbow him away, and he jumps off the futon, going over to where Nila has settled on one of the dog beds. She bites his ear when he tries to cuddle her, which does not faze him, and soon he's snoring on her.

Sydney's breathing grows deeper, and I close my eyes, just enjoying this moment, ignoring all the unspoken words and all the ones that have been hurled.

Sydney's grip on my hand relaxes, and I move it slowly down to her stomach, splaying my fingers over it. *My child is growing in there.*

My heart gives a hard thud, and a painful joy swells in me.

I'm going to be a father.

CHAPTER ELEVEN

Sydney

I go to sneak out from under Mulberry's arm, but he pulls me closer, nuzzling my neck—still asleep and yet still possessive. Like a dog with its bone.

When I pull free this time he lets me go, curling up onto himself. I tiptoe away, heading to the bathroom, Blue's eyes watching me, something reproachful in them. Or maybe that is just my imagination.

I dress in the bedroom, and when I come out, Blue and Nila are sitting up, waiting for me by the back door. Frank has climbed onto the futon and is splayed out at the foot of the bed, snoring. Mulberry's on his back, his chest rising and falling with each deep breath.

I trace the outline of him under the covers. My stomach shudders when I reach his left leg… what's left of it.

His prosthetic leans against the end of the futon. I didn't even notice it last night. Because it doesn't matter. Our bodies are not what make us whole.

But it does matter! He lost a part of himself searching for me in Isis's doomed caliphate, one of the most dangerous places in the world. What will he lose if I stay with him?

I tap my thigh quietly. Blue and Nila move with me toward the front door, Frank stays snoring at Mulberry's feet...foot.

The morning is crisp, the rain last night ushering in fresh air. We go around the block, hitting up a coffee shop. I buy two cups. *If you're going to tell a man you refuse to marry him despite being pregnant with his baby, you really ought to buy him a coffee first.*

When I come back in, Mulberry is on the edge of the bed, his hair sticking out every which way, his eyes puffy with sleep. Frank sits on Mulberry's foot and thumps his tail, staring up into his sleepy face with adoration. They are adorable.

I have this moment, this flash of what it would be like to stay here in this basement apartment—or one like it—with Mulberry and live together as if we were normal people. As if all the fighting and striving for justice was just something we read about in a book. I could get a job as a barista at that coffee shop and he could go back to bartending, and we could fight about money and bathroom habits and whose turn it was to empty the dishwasher.

"You brought me coffee?" Mulberry asks, scratching his head.

I nod, my throat tight with the vision of us as regular folks. People who don't worry about mercenary assassins and are not willing to die for the greater good. Couldn't we just be selfish for a little while? Cocoon ourselves in a fantasy?

Mulberry reaches for his false leg, and I walk to the counter, putting the coffees down and grabbing the bag of dog food I've got in the cabinet. Mulberry comes up behind me and reaches around for one of the cups. "That one's mine," I say. He puts it back.

"Cinnamon in coffee is gross," he says before grabbing his cup—black and strong, just the way he likes it.

"You're just saying that because you have no taste."

He laughs and takes a sip. I feed the dogs, and Mulberry makes the futon back into a couch. I open the back door, and Frank goes out to do his business then settles in a patch of sun.

I stand in the doorway and watch him. "That guy is a real doofus," Mulberry says from behind my shoulder.

"Yes," I agree. "He is. I hope he stays one forever."

"Doofuses usually stay doofuses."

I laugh and turn to him. "They do?"

He's got his jeans back on and the green T-shirt he slept in, just a few shades darker than the glints of emerald in his eyes. "Yup." He sips his coffee, watching me. "You ready to talk?"

I wet my lips and take a deep breath. "We are not getting married."

"Okay."

"Okay?"

He gives me a half smile. "I hear that you're not ready."

"You think you are?" Annoyance rises up my throat. "Remember how you weren't even talking to me a few days ago?"

"I was angry."

"And you're not now."

"I am. But about different stuff."

I shake my head. "That I won't marry you?"

"No." He grimaces and looks down at his feet. "I'm angry at myself for being such a dumbass." *Well, that takes the wind right out of my rage sails.* "I shouldn't have left that morning without saying goodbye. I can't help how I felt then. Or how I feel now. I want you to be mine. All mine."

His gaze rises. I can't look away. "But I will be patient. Wait for you to realize what I already know." I swallow, a tickle of anger itching the back of my mind. *Another man who thinks he knows more about me than I know about myself.* "That we belong together." His eyes drop to my stomach.

"You're starting to sound like Robert."

Clouds storm Mulberry's eyes, and he takes a step toward me before pulling himself up short. "Is that why you're sleeping in his T-shirt?" He clenches his jaw, as if immediately regretting the words. "Sorry," he says, dropping his gaze back down to the floor. "It's none of my business. But the baby *is* my business. And I want to help."

"Can you leave me alone?"

He doesn't look up at me. "You think that would help?"

I don't know if there is any help for me. "I've got some stuff I need to do, alone."

"Will you tell me what?"

I squeeze my coffee cup too hard and spill some over the edge. It burns my hand and Mulberry turns to the counter, grabbing a cloth. He crosses to me and holds it out.

"I need to go see my mom." I pass him the coffee and wipe at myself.

"Your mom? That sounds dangerous. I'm sure she's under surveillance."

"I know how to hide."

He huffs out a laugh as I take my coffee back. "You certainly do."

"You told me you wanted back into Joyful Justice then you disappeared," I point out.

He stiffens but nods. "That's right."

"So why don't you get back into it? Rejoin the council."

His lips twist into a smile. "Are you trying to keep me busy? Distracted." I shrug. "I told Dan."

My stomach drops. "You what?" It comes out a harsh whisper.

His lips tighten into a straight line before he answers. "I needed his help to find you."

"So you told him I'm pregnant?" My voice is rising all on its own.

Mulberry takes a step back. "It's not only yours, you know!" He's yelling back. Great. Just freaking great. I take a deep breath and try to calm myself. "Are you even supposed to be drinking coffee?"

My right hand clenches into a fist, and he takes a big step back. "Sorry," He hits the kitchen counter. "I just read you're not supposed to have caffeine."

"You can have one cup a day," I say, my voice low and dangerous. "I really don't think my caffeine intake is the biggest danger here, do you?"

"I—"

"It's probably the mercenaries trying to kill me, right?"

"They could be after Robert," he points out. "You seem to be doing fine without him."

"I do just fine on my own, period." I look over at Blue and give him an apologetic nod. Obviously, he knows I need him.

Mulberry puts his coffee down on the counter and runs a hand through his hair. "I didn't come here to fight with you. I just want to help. And if you want to go see your mom, then let me help you do that."

"But you think it's a bad idea."

"Of course I do."

"Robert said I should go."

"Well, bully for him."

I laugh. "Did you just say bully for him?"

Mulberry's face is getting red. "Can we not talk about him right now?"

"I need to go see her. She's on tour in Louisiana. I'm going to head there today."

"Can I come with?"

"No."

"Well, that answers that."

"Just give me some time, okay?"

"How much?"

"I don't know."

"We have a bit of a ticking clock here," Mulberry says, gesturing toward my stomach. I cock my head and give him a look. He sighs. "Can you please just call me? Tell me how you are…stay in touch. Can we do that? Can we stay in touch?"

That seems reasonable and fair, so it will probably get us both killed somehow.

"Okay," I agree, unease slipping down my spine. "I'll stay in touch. Will you rejoin the council?"

He nods. "Yes."

"Good."

"Good."

Then why do I feel so bad?

Robert

I sit at my desk, my feet on the floor, one hand resting on the glass surface, the other holding the phone—it rings on the other end twice. "Robert," Amy answers. She doesn't sound surprised to hear from me.

"Amy," I say, my voice even, warm almost. "How are you?"

"Good, and you?"

"I'd like to meet again."

"Would you?" *She knows.*

"I'm coming back to Cartagena. Let's have dinner, at my place." My fingers tap on the desk, and I still them. Still everything.

"Sure." She says it all light and breezy. "When?"

"Tomorrow night."

"Perfect, should I see if Josh can join us?"

"I'd love to see you both."

We hang up, and I wake up my computer, looking at the records again. There is no death record for Natalia Rojas, though a death in the jungle could easily go unrecorded. Born in 1972 in a rural village outside Medellin, she lost her parents at fifteen and joined the FARC that same year.

We met in 1990; we were both so young.

I saw her die. It was my fault. I used her.

We weren't the only people who looked for privacy in the storage area—butts of cigarettes littered the dirt floor. It was the only solid structure in the camp, with walls of knotted wood. On the day Natalia pulled me in, rain pinged off the metal roof and the metal chains that bound my wrists clanked. Light piercing through holes in the walls revealed propane tanks lined up like sentries and shelves stacked with cans.

Natalia unlocked my cuffs, her breath fast, rainwater beading on her skin...her gorgeous, soft, kissable skin. The chains dropped to the ground, the keys following, and I filled my hands with her as she wrapped herself around me. *We were starving for each other, desperate to be one.*

"I love you," I whispered against her neck, my fingers pulling at her clothing.

"Te amo," she responded, unleashing a fresh wave of desire inside me.

We made love, furious and fierce, her legs wrapped around me, my mouth covering hers, promises of a future lingering in the air.

We'd been at the camp for almost two weeks, and I didn't know how much longer we would stay; they moved us almost constantly. In the months since my mother's death, Natalia had become the center of my world. We'd fallen in love. But I still needed to get out—and I needed to take her with me.

After, she locked my cuffs on again, her mouth—swollen from my kisses—pulled into a sad frown. "I'm sorry," she said, slipping the keys into her back pocket. I put my arms over her head, my chained wrists at her back, and pulled her into a kiss. She went weak against me, my fingers digging into her, slipping the keys from her pocket and palming them. When I let her go, Natalia's eyes were glassy, and a dewy smile turned her wet lips.

She went out first and I followed, pausing for just a moment to open the valve on one of the propane tanks, the low hiss of the gas escaping quieter than the rain...

My hand closes into a fist on the desk. We—Amy, Josh and I—would never have escaped without her.

EK

The house in Cartagena is all put back together. The rug in the living room replaced, the fountain repaired, the bloodstains scrubbed away. Valentina greets me with the same welcoming smile she's always used. "Welcome back, Mr. Maxim."

"Good to be back," I say.

Amy and Josh arrive on time, and we start with cocktails on the roof. A warm breeze stirs the surface of the pool, and the sun sets in the distance, splashing the sky with pastels. All so gentle. A smooth transition from day to night.

In the jungle, twilight arrived in a crescendo of wailing insects, the setting sun piercing through the foliage—a bright orange warning: the heat of the day is over, and the cold and wet of night is about to begin. The bugs were always bad, but at night it felt like their feasting on us was more personal. As if, though the FARC were our captors, the bugs were our tormentors.

"I hope you've changed your mind," Josh says, swirling ice in his drink, bringing me back to the present moment. "You'll help us destroy Joyful Justice?"

"Well," I say, calm as ever, "I am more open to your request. I'd like to make an exchange."

"You want to know about Natalia," Amy says.

I nod slowly, as if her words didn't just send my heart skittering around in my chest looking for something to hold on to. "She's alive," I say.

Josh leans forward, his hair flopping over onto his forehead. He pushes it back—he still seems so young, even if only five years my junior. But that is just old memories clouding my vision. *He is dangerous.* "We will need your help on Joyful Justice."

It's my turn to swirl ice, clinking it against the crystal. I take a sip of the rum before answering. "I think we can work out an arrangement. How long have you known...that she survived?"

Amy and Josh exchange a look. "She's been our contact since the beginning."

I take a sip of the rum. *Since the beginning!* The liquor burns my throat but I don't cough—I give no outward signal of the turmoil inside me.

"Is she well?" I offer a gentle smile, as if I'm asking after an old friend rather than the first woman I loved...who I thought died because of me but turns out didn't.

Amy stands and paces to the edge of the roof, the wind playing with her loose hair. *There are more secrets here.* "We need your help, Robert. Natalia does too."

"With Joyful Justice. She received a packet too?" My mind leaps to asking Dan about her—though she must be using a different name. She could not have operated for decades without my hearing her name. *Natalia Rojas.* How many times did I whisper her name in that horrible, freezing darkness made warm and beautiful by her presence? My grip tightens on the glass, and I consciously relax it, pushing those memories away. I can't think about her now.

I've spent decades hiding those memories. I can certainly keep them at bay through cocktails.

"No, she has not been contacted by Joyful Justice," Amy turns back to me, her hands clasped together. Behind her the church glows in the sunset. "But she is intimately involved in our business."

"And you never told me." My voice is low, the thrum of a threat lingering below the surface.

Amy stiffens, her chin rising. "She asked us not to."

I sit back in the chair, forcing nonchalance to ooze out of me. "She didn't want me to know she was alive. Thought I deserved the guilt?"

"What guilt?" Josh asks, his cheeks red. His glass is empty. He's getting drunk. Still a boy in so many ways. My gaze returns to Amy. She's protected him too much.

"She never shared her reasons with me," Amy says, her voice tight. "But I imagine she felt betrayed."

I should have gone back for her. "I did get shot." I say it like I'm joking around, as if my reasons are ironclad. "And I thought she was dead. Why would I go back for a dead body?"

"That's in the past now, Robert."

Anger tries to dig its claws into my gut, but I pry the talons loose, clinging to detachment. "Yes," I smile. "It's in the past. But here she is," I open the palm of my free hand to indicate the present, "trying to kill me. Now."

"She's not trying to kill you." Josh waves it off, standing and heading to the bar. Amy watches him, her lips pressed tight. She wants to tell him to stop drinking but won't do it in front of me.

"Isn't she?" I ask, raising a brow.

"No," Amy says. "Despite everything, I believe she still cares for you."

My heart is skittering around again, and I struggle for a brief moment to maintain my composure. "So, who then is trying to kill me?"

"It's not her," Josh says.

"Who then?" I ask again. "Someone is using her yacht." I wave my glass through the air. "Her resources." They glance at each other again. "What?"

"It's not for us to say," Amy answers. "If you help us, we can put you in touch with Natalia and she can answer all your questions."

"If I survive."

Amy smiles. "Robert, you always survive." I sip my rum, trying to cover the bitter taste her words leave in my mouth. "Do you agree?" she asks, pushing me. "You'll help us destroy Joyful Justice in exchange for a meeting with Natalia?"

"Yes," I answer, the taste of betrayal curling my tongue. Amy's right —I always survive.

CHAPTER TWELVE

Mulberry

Birds sing in the tree canopy, monkeys hoot, and grass tickles my exposed skin. The sun warms my bare chest and beats down on my closed eyelids, making the darkness behind them glow orange.

I'm lying in the open field used for combat practice. But it's the hottest part of the day, so everyone is grabbing food or resting, waiting out the sun.

Footsteps approach, and I peek between my lashes. "Hard at work?" Merl asks.

I raise a hand to shield my face from the sun. "Just taking a break." I force a smile. The aerosol line-striping machine lies next to me. I'd offered to freshen the lines around the fighting circles, but the heat of the day and the weight of my worries dragged me to the ground.

Merl sits next to me on the grass, wrapping his arms around his knees. His three dobermans fan out around him, like sentries. "Nice spot."

"Yup." I close my eyes again, hiding the view of the jungle. Merl shifts, his exercise shorts scraping against the grass. "How are you?"

I huff a laugh. "Awesome."

"Do you want to talk about it?"

"What is there to say?"

Merl doesn't answer. He's like a zen master, just sits silently waiting for people to spill their guts—it's a classic detective trade tool. But I'm not planning on spilling anything. Nope. I'm staying quiet. Keeping all my raging emotions shut down tight where they belong.

The wind carries a sweet flora scent to me and I sigh, some of that bubbling emotion welling up into the sound.

"Did Dan tell you?" I ask.

"He tells me lots of things."

I crack an eyelid and look up at Merl. He's staring straight ahead, his chocolate brown eyes with their long black lashes focused on the jungle in front of us. He's wearing a white T-shirt and black, shiny exercise shorts. His skin, browned from all his time down here in the sun, glistens with sweat. Merl isn't a big guy, but he is a martial arts master, and his corded muscles speak to the hours of practice he puts into his craft.

"Do you want to spar?" Merl asks, turning to look down at me.

"I don't think that's a fair fight."

Merl grins, showing off the gap between his front teeth. "I think I can hold my own."

I laugh. "I'm sure, but you have a leg up on me."

Merl shrugs. "Our perceived weaknesses are often our greatest strengths."

"You should put that on a T-shirt."

Merl stands, all balanced strength, and holds out his hand to help me up. The sun behind him means I'm squinting up at him. His hair is down, in long, tight curls, the same slick black as his dobermans.

I release another sigh and take his hand, letting him haul me up.

"You're not in bad shape," Merl says, being kind.

I give him a half smile. "Sure. I've been going to the gym but...I don't have awesome balance." An understatement if there ever was one.

"We can work on that. But right now, I'm guessing you may need to just get some anger out."

I laugh. "What about a man napping shirtless in the sun says rage machine to you?"

"It's your jaw. If you keep clenching it that tight you'll ruin your teeth. We can't have that."

Merl steps into one of the circles painted on the lawn and sinks into a fighting stance. Another sigh escapes as I follow him into the ring. "I haven't beat you yet, Mulberry. Let's keep the sighing until after I've made you tap out." Merl grins at me.

"Fine."

I mimic his stance but know that I look nothing like him. I'm much wider...fatter, some might say. He gives a small nod, and the game is on. We circle each other, my misery and angsty feelings wrapping themselves around my brain until Merl strikes out fast and hard, hitting me right in the chin. My head snaps back, and I stumble away with a grunt. "Stop thinking and pay attention," Merl admonishes.

I shake it off, and we circle again. I test our distance with a jab, and Merl lets me. I jab again, stepping closer this time. He shifts back. I keep going, following my jab with a cross punch that he easily avoids, spinning away from me and landing a blow on my kidney. I turn to face him but he's already gone, having continued around the circle. I spin again and lash out inelegantly at him. Merl is a shadow, dancing in my peripheral vision, and it's starting to piss me off.

I kick back with my good leg, almost losing my balance when I actually hit him.

It's his turn to grunt, and I pivot, planning to punch him right in his zen-filled face but he comes up underneath me, rocking my head back with an uppercut.

He's gone by the time my eyes can focus again. Merl stands outside the circle, drinking from a bottle of water. He holds it out to me, and I accept the cool drink.

"Well, this is fun. Just what I needed instead of a nap, getting my ass kicked."

He shrugs and grins.

The sun is so hot it feels like a weight on my shoulders. Sweat drips into my eyes as we circle again, the grass prickly under my bare foot. I miss having two feet. Sometimes I still feel it. Often in the morning, when I'm just waking up, I'll go to scratch an itch and find there is nothing there.

Merl gets close, and I lash out, anger at my missing limb mixing with the already simmering rage at my impotence in the face of my impending fatherhood.

I can't do jack shit about fuck all. I should put *that* on a T-shirt.

Merl takes the punch and pivots away, dropping down and swiping at my feet, sending me onto my back and knocking the air out of me.

Laying on the ground, staring up at the sun, I suck air like a fish. Merl waits for me to get my breath and then offers his hand again. "I thought this was supposed to help me get out my aggression, not humiliate me."

"Am I supposed to let you win?"

"No," I grumble, refusing his help and standing on my own. "But I wouldn't complain."

He offers the water again, and I drain the bottle. "It's hot as hell," I say.

Merl nods, lifting his hair and wrapping it into a bun using a tie from his wrist. "Want to get a bite to eat?" When I don't answer, he gives a short nod. "How about a beer?"

I grin at the idea of a freezing, bitter, bubbly beer. "Yes, please."

We sit on Merl's balcony, his three dobermans curled up in the shade, a fan ticking back and forth, drinking from ice-cold bottles. "This is what the doctor ordered," I say.

"Do you want to tell me what's going on?" Merl asks.

I sigh as memories of Sydney's face flood back, when she asked me to leave her alone—the exhaustion in her eyes, and the determination to keep me at bay. Why can't we just be with each other?

"I'm going to be a dad," I answer.

Merl swallows a mouthful of beer and licks his lips. "Congratulations," he says.

"Sydney." I answer his unasked question.

His eyes widen. I look out over the compound. Merl's apartment is in the main building, and we can see the rooftops of the villas dotted around the property. A former luxury eco-resort deep in the Costa Rican jungle, the training center for Joyful Justice can house around a hundred people, but there are only sixty on the grounds now.

"I asked her to marry me, and she said no," I continue, spilling my secrets all over the floor. Merl makes a sound, and I turn to him. "What?"

His face is flushed from the heat, and he takes another sip of beer before answering me. "She's never struck me as someone who wanted to get married. And...weren't you avoiding her?"

I sit forward in the chair and rest my elbows on my knees. "She's not the marrying kind, no. But I am."

Merl doesn't respond to that. I hear him swallowing more beer and sip from my own. Insects buzz in the trees, their music coming in waves.

"Shouldn't a kid grow up with both parents? Together."

"There are lots of ways to grow up. Some of us don't do it until we're way past childhood."

I slant a glance at him. "Are you saying I'm acting like a child?" He sips his beer and watches me over the top of the bottle. "What? I have some kind of childish fantasy about what life should be like? Come on, man." I wave at the compound. "We all have a fantasy about what the world should be like. Justice for all. Protect the weak. Rise up against oppressors. Be brave. You can want all that, and I can't want the woman pregnant with my baby to marry me?"

"You can want whatever you want."

"What is that supposed to mean?" I stand, and Merl's female dog, Lucy, sits up, sensing my anger. She cocks her head at me in the same way Merl is doing. *Why are you getting your panties in a twist?*

Because I'm going to be a father, and there is nothing I can do about anything!

"You want her to commit to you?" Merl says.

"Is that asking so much?"

"Yes, a lifelong commitment is a lot to ask." Merl sips his beer and nods to himself. Is he thinking about his girlfriend, Mo Ping? "Especially when she's just learned that she has inadvertently made a lifetime commitment to a child growing inside her. How far along is she?"

"I don't know exactly. But..." that night floods back, the memories of us together more powerful than the ones of Sydney pushing us apart. I'm lost for a moment, back in that bedroom, the curtains waving in the breeze, the sheets whispering against our skin...the words we said to each other. No promises made, only declarations. But love does not conquer all, no matter what the movies will have you believe.

And when I woke up in the darkness, lying next to her, I couldn't stay. Couldn't live up to the declaration. Anger stole my will and replaced it with instinct. She'd left me. Lied to me. And I'd die for her. If I stayed, I would perish.

"You're clenching your jaw again," Merl says, snapping me out of my thoughts.

"About two months," I say, the distance between that night and this moment expanding and shrinking all at once. I finish off the last sip of my beer and sit down again, exhaustion crashing over me.

"She went to go see her mother," I grumble.

Merl nods. Of course he knew. Sydney wouldn't pull a stunt like that without informing the council. "She's matured." Merl says. "When you sent me to her, I knew right away that she could be a powerful fighter. But I worried that her anger would weaken her."

I grunt, looking around, wondering if another beer might magically appear on the deck.

"And it did, for a long time." Merl is staring off into the distance, his beer still mostly full. "Motherhood will be good for her." He turns to look at me. "And fatherhood will be good for you."

I shake my head. "I can't even imagine what kind of parents we will be."

Merl smiles, quick and broad. "You'll figure it out."

"But what if we don't?" The fear that's been gripping my heart since Sydney told me voices itself for the first time. "What if we fuck it up? Or worse..." I force myself to say it. Say it all. "What if we get it killed?"

"I'm sure Sydney is afraid of the same things."

"So don't we have a better chance of keeping it alive together?" My voice is rising, fear morphing into anger as quickly as ice melts into water.

"I don't know," Merl answers. "You two have a large community that loves you and will do whatever it takes to keep your child safe."

I sit back in the chair. "I hadn't thought of that," I admit.

"What?"

I let out a strange laugh that comes straight from my belly. "We have good friends. People who will protect us. Safe places to be."

"That's right," Merl says. "Are you ready to get back to work? To rejoin the council and do what you need to do, to keep not only Sydney and the baby safe, but fight for justice around the world?" Merl's eyes are bright, but his voice is even. He says it like it isn't crazy. Like what we are, what we fight for, isn't nonsense. That it's normal. Somehow Merl makes it sound like...home.

"Yes," I answer, sitting forward. "I am."

Merl nods. "Good." He stands. "Let's get to work. You have a lot of catching up to do."

I follow him into his apartment, the dogs filing in after us. I can do something about some shit. And I'm going to do it.

CHAPTER THIRTEEN

Sydney

My mother, her eyes focused on the stage where she's being introduced, wiggles her fingers and rolls her thin shoulders. She licks her lips and circles her jaw.

Mom's tailored suit speaks of professionalism and feminism with a touch of fashion—certainly not too much, though. This is a woman of God—not a politician. She's not applying for a job, *she was chosen for it.*

The crowd noise swells. Thousands of people all here for her...for Her.

A big breath, chest expanding, smile growing, and Mom steps out into the lights. I move out of the shadows, my dogs trailing close, stepping to the edge of the stage. She approaches the podium, her hair glowing in the lights. It's shorter than the last time I saw her. She's gained some weight, and the circles under her eyes are diminished. She is healthy, recovered from the bullet wounds inflicted by a shooter—a men's rights activist who considered my mother a threat to his way of life—a threat to all men.

And maybe she is...

"Good evening," Mom says, her voice booming over the crowd. They cheer and clap. Mom releases the microphone from its stand and paces away from the podium. "Thank you for coming, for listening." She sounds genuine.

"I want to tell you a story." A hush falls over the theater. "Last year I spent several months in ISIS-controlled territory in northern Syria. There I witnessed unspeakable horrors." My mind flashes to that land where I almost died...where I *hoped* to die. Blue nuzzles my hand as if he can read my mind. He helped keep me alive, his plaintive whining holding me here.

Mom raises a hand toward the roof and closes it into a fist, letting her head bow, chin toward her chest, mouth close to the microphone. "But let me start with this message: Women have an equal place in this world." She lifts her gaze to the crowd. "And we must fight for it. Release the wolf!"

Clapping and cheers echo beyond the lights.

They are selling T-shirts in the lobby with the silhouette of woman's face set into the snarling profile of a wolf. It's Blue and me...the miracle woman come back from the dead. Proof of the Her Prophet's divinity. The story is so much more twisted than that...so much more complicated.

Rida, the woman who they now call the Her Prophet...#IAmHer, found me bleeding to death. She took me back to her cave. A skilled surgeon caught behind ISIS lines, Rida fled her family's village with her dogs, a herd of goats, and all the medical supplies she could carry. Was it God who sent her to help me or a random event spun out of nothingness in an unknowing, chaotic universe?

"You've all heard the words of our prophet." Mom paces back toward the podium. "Have seen evidence of her divinity—the videos of her bringing people back from the dead."

I cringe at her words. Those videos were my idea...I wasn't myself. For months I remembered nothing from my recovery. I went from dying on a mountaintop to racing into a battle, Blue by my side, Rida's mastiffs, giant, fearless, and terrifying, backing me up.

The video of my rampage that day has over twenty million views. That's why I'm wearing brown contact lenses, glasses, and a wig of curly red hair. It's my Orphan-Annie-grown-up-to-become-a-librarian look.

Robert says it's sexy. I say it's ridiculous. Everyone is entitled to their opinions in this world. And my mother's opinion—though I'm sure she'd call it a belief—is that Rida is a divine prophet who brought me back from the dead to prove the equality of women.

Mom's sermon lasts over an hour and a half. There is a chorus who joins her, and they sway and swing, moved by the spirit. After her final exhortation to follow the prophet in the fight for female equality, I head back to her dressing room and close the door behind me. The applause as she leaves the stage is still booming when the door opens and she walks in.

She is smiling, sweat shining her face. Her head cocks in confusion when she catches sight of me and then recognition blooms. "Joy," she whispers.

An assistant tries to follow Mom into the room, but she turns quickly and dismisses her, closing the door behind the woman and slowly turning to face me.

I clear my throat and try on a smile—it feels forced and uncomfortable. "It's so good to see you," she says, taking a half step toward me and then stopping, her movements unsure. She doesn't want to scare me off.

"I..." Words fail me. I don't know how to do this.

Her eyes dart around the room, as if looking for a way to make this not awkward. She lands on Blue and takes a deep breath, giving him a weak smile before looking at me again. "Do you want something to eat or drink?" she asks, gesturing to a table laden with options.

Hunger roars to life and I stare at the bowl of M&M's as if they may be my salvation. "Okay, thanks," I approach the table. She steps up next to me. I take a handful of M&M's while eyeing the fruit basket.

"How are you?" she asks, standing to my left, both of us staring at the bounty before us.

"I'm pregnant," I say, the words garbled by the massive amount of candy in my mouth.

Mom stills. "Pregnant," she whispers.

I nod, still staring at the bananas, but I can feel her looking at me. Feel the force of her emotions. I swallow and take a breath before meeting her gaze. Her eyes are filled with tears, and a smile splits her face. It makes her look younger, reminding me of the woman my father loved...*that I loved* with the fierce innocence of a child.

"That's so wonderful," she says.

A little laugh eeks past the lump in my throat. She's the first person to have that reaction. Robert freaked and left the room; Mulberry questioned his parentage...I experienced fear like I've never known. But my mom—she's happy. She thinks it's wonderful. A thought blooms, unleashed by her joy...maybe it *is* wonderful.

"I'm scared, Mom." I sound like a child. Maybe I still am one.

"Oh honey." She puts her hand on my shoulder, and it's the most natural thing in the world. "Of course you are," she smiles. "All moms are scared."

"They are?"

She laughs. "Terrified."

"But I have good reasons to be scared. My life..."

"It's a miracle. It's important." Her hand squeezes my shoulder. "You're a very special person. And your child will be too. You were gravely injured." Her voice dips on the word gravely, just like a preacher's should. "The fact that you can even get pregnant is a miracle."

"Mom, can we not talk about miracles?"

"How can we talk about new life without talking about miracles?" She sounds genuinely confused.

"Let's try."

"Okay." She moves her hand from my shoulder around to my back, pulling me into a hug. "I'm so glad you came to see me."

"Me too." And I actually mean it.

Frank takes that moment to press between us, his whole body wagging. Mom laughs and steps back. "He's grown," she says, bending down to pet him.

An impulse throbs through me. "Do you want him?" I ask.

She looks up. "What?"

"He's so sweet," I say. "And I'm afraid if he stays with me, he'll get ruined." Frank wriggles onto her foot, leaning the length of his body against her leg. "He likes you."

"I bet he likes everyone," she says with a smile.

"True," I admit.

Her eyes find Nila behind me. "But she is not so quick to trust."

I shake my head. "No."

"No," Mom agrees with a nod.

Blue lets out a low growl moments before a knock at the door. "Just a minute," Mom says, disrupting Frank from his perch as she moves toward the door. She opens it a crack, shielding the room with her body.

"You've got that meeting with the Fellowship of the Blood," a woman's voice reminds my mother.

"Oh, right. Give me a few minutes. Please apologize for me."

She closes the door and turns back to me. "The Fellowship of the Blood?" I ask. *The group Declan asked about.*

"Yes, they are a wonderful new church that is bringing the word of the Her Prophet to this area. I'm meeting with their pastor and several members to discuss putting together a text."

"A text?"

"Yes, a written document for followers to refer back to." She clasps her hands in front of her, twining the fingers.

"Like a bible?"

"No, no." She shakes her head. "The Bible is the word of God. This is the word of a prophet. It's different."

"This is another subject I'm thinking we should avoid."

"If you want." She steps away from the door. "Can you stay?"

"I didn't plan on it."

"Where are you headed?"

"That's probably another topic to avoid." I give her a sad smile.

She chews on her lip for a moment. "I'll cancel with the Fellowship. I want to spend as much time with you as I can."

"You don't need to do that."

"But we have so much to discuss," Mom steps forward, grabbing up my hands in hers. "When is your due date? Where are you going to have the baby? And"—she clears her throat—"if you wouldn't mind sharing who the father is?" My brain is stuck back on my due date...and stuttering toward where I'm going to have the baby. "Joy?"

I blink my mom into focus. "I don't know."

Her lips pinch with disapproval but she nods. "Well, how many men is it between?"

I cough out a laugh. "No, Mom, I know who the father is."

She lets out a breath, a blush spreading over her cheeks. "And it would be fine if you didn't. It's your body." She pats my hand.

I laugh, taken aback. "Wow. I never expected to hear that from you."

"I've given up a lot of my old beliefs, Joy."

But still define your morals from an outside source. Add that to the list of topics not to discuss. "I don't know my due date. I haven't been to a doctor."

"Oh." She glances down at my flat stomach. "How far along do you think you are?"

"Almost two months."

"How have you been feeling?" She squeezes my hands. "I had the worse morning sickness with your brother." Her words steal my breath. *James.* Are we talking about him now? Is this a safe topic? "He was an easy baby, not like you." She shakes her head, eyes unfocused, obviously seeing that long ago time when she was a young mother...and my brother a new life. *A miracle.* "James was always smiling. And boy could he make you laugh."

Tears well in her eyes and she sucks in a breath, shaking her head and closing her eyes. *Her baby is gone.* It's a fresh stab wound in my heart. I've mourned my brother's loss and resented my mother for the way she acted after his death—as if his life was wrong, a sin, as if his love for another man made him evil. My hand covers my stomach as the reality of her loss sinks into me, touching some deep place in me...a new place.

"I miss him," I say, grief welling. *James won't meet my child.* Another dagger of pain. My grief has dulled over the years, worn by time as sharp glass is smoothed by the sea. This is a new pain, a fresh wound. A loss I never recognized before.

"Me too," Mom says, her eyes meeting mine—magnetic gray, the silver of mercury and the slate of a brewing storm, the same as mine. For so long I've thought we were such different people.

But I didn't always feel that way—when I was little, I wanted to grow up to be just like her. Since my father's death, I've believed her to be weak. But maybe it was the strength of the love she had for him that made her so weak. Love can destroy us as easily as it lifts us.

I pull back, but her grip tightens on my hands. "Let me help you, please."

Tears escape, warm and slow, easing down my cheeks. "Okay," I whisper.

She embraces me, her smell saturating me, pulling me back to my childhood, the girl I was and the woman she was and all the fierce love that we shared seems to blossom anew between us.

CHAPTER FOURTEEN

Sydney

The air in the parking garage is cold and wet, tainted with the scent of gasoline. Mom links her arm through mine, our feet echoing in the space. The dogs trail behind us, Blue's nose rhythmically tapping my hip.

The sound of an engine comes up from the first floor, and headlights flash around the corner. We pause to let the van pass. It slows and Blue lets out a low growl. I back up a step, pulling Mom with me. The navy blue van stops, the door sliding open, and two men wearing ski masks leap out, followed by two more.

They move fast, coming at us in a wall of black garb and muscle. Blue and Nila launch themselves at the two in front. They go down, scrambling on the ground.

The next two stop, their eyes going wide, as their friends struggle against my dogs. "Get her in the van!" a voice from inside the vehicle commands. As if emboldened by that voice, the two men advance toward Mom and me, where I've positioned us between parked cars. Mom stands behind me, her fingers digging into my shoulder. "Let me handle this," I say under my breath as I sink into a fighting stance, adrenaline rushing through me, a smile curving my lips.

One of the men on the ground screams. Frank's bark echoes in the space as he hops around.

"April Madden, you're coming with us," the one in front says, his voice gravelly and low. The other man spares a glance back at where his friends are getting mauled.

"No, she's not, Bozo," I say. His eyes narrow and his lips tighten.

"You dumb bitches." He steps forward and I kick out, catching him under the chin, he stumbles back into his friend who oofs out air but neither goes down.

I take advantage of their momentary unbalance and throw a jab at Bozo's chin, following it up with a hook to his gut, then power into an uppercut. His eyes lose focus before he drops.

Bozo's accomplice catches him but let's go as I step forward. Wearing a black T-shirt and cargo pants, pale blond hair curling from under his mask, he puts up his fist just in time to block my jab.

Blondie's green eyes light with success. They flick around my face, and his right shoulder tenses, telegraphing his counter punch. I catch his wrist between my own and twist until a sickening crunch sounds. He lets out a high-pitched scream that makes the hairs on the back of my neck rise.

"Freeze or I'll shoot." A fifth black figure steps around the front of the van. He must have been in the passenger seat. His lips are glistening with spittle and surrounded by a bronze beard. He's holding a shotgun, barrels aimed at me. I put my hands up and smile.

At my feet, Bozo lays still, and Blondie has dropped to his knees, cradling his injured wrist. "I think she broke it," he mews to no one in particular. Blue and Nila each hold a man by his neck, razor-sharp teeth pressed against pulsing arteries. The scent of piss floats on the air. *Not professionals.*

Behind me, my mom is whispering...probably praying.

"Get in the van," Shotgun says.

Blondie glances back at the man and starts to stand. "Take Gunther with you." *Gunther?*

"But my wrist—"

Shotgun cuts him off. "All of you get in the van!" His voice goes high, and a flush breaks out over his neck. Blondie struggles to drag Bozo aka Gunther toward the open van door, past the two prone figures held on the ground by my dogs. Shotgun swings his weapon toward Blue. "Come," I say sharply, bringing both Blue and Nila to my side and releasing two more would-be kidnappers.

Shotgun swings the barrels back toward me. "I said, get in the van," he says, all macho dumbass.

"Leave now, and I'll let you all live," I respond.

"Wait," Mom says, stepping out from behind me. "I'll come with you." She slides past me, her shoes scraping on the dirty cement floor.

Shotgun smiles and nods to himself. His focus stays on Mom as she walks toward the open van door and the four men waiting inside. I grab her arm. "No," I growl.

"Shut up!" Shotgun yells, his eyes wide and glittering with emotion.

Mom turns back to me, laying her hand over mine. "It's okay; I'll be fine." She smiles at me and nods. *God is watching over me.* But I don't believe in that. If she gets in that van, she's dead. I'm not losing her. Not today. Not when I just got her back.

She pulls away, and I follow her. "Mom, stop."

She steps up to the van and hands reach out, sucking her into the shadowed interior. Blue growls, warning me not to follow, but I step closer, letting them haul me in after her. The door slides shut and the dogs go crazy—barking, growling, their nails scraping on the cement as the van lurches forward.

They've got Mom and me on the floor, Bozo propped up against the back doors, Blondie curled up behind the passenger seat, holding his wrist like it's an injured puppy.

A mask comes off, exposing a young man, his neck bleeding from teeth marks, his eyes glinting in the near darkness. "Pass me the tape," he says.

Duct tape—these guys are real original.

He grabs my ankles, pulling the tape to wrap it around, but I kick out, hitting him once in the gut, then bringing my knee up to my chest,

I kick out again, striking his throat. His eyes go wide, his mouth working like a fish out of water as he falls back onto Bozo, his throat crushed, his life over.

The tape rolls across the van floor. I snatch it up as a body slams into my back, hunching me over the tape. The scent of cheap aftershave and cheese puffs envelops me, along with flabby arms. I twine the length of tape meant to bind my ankles into a cord before elbowing Aftershave in the ribs.

He expels rancid breath but holds tight, his lips close to my ear, his weight bending me over my legs, the rope of tape trapped in my lap.

"Get her under control!" Shotgun yells from the passenger seat. "Hey, no! Get off him or I'll shoot!"

Aftershave rears back, and the clank of a body hitting the side of the van vibrates through the cramped space. *Must be Mom.* Pivoting, I'm on my knees, the twine of tape around Aftershave's thick neck, cutting off his air supply before he can come back at me.

"Let him go!" Shotgun screams. He's hanging over the passenger seat, the shotgun aimed at me...but the gun is not so maneuverable in that cramped space, and I've got Aftershave in front of my body. Blondie has pressed himself up against the back of Shotgun's seat and squeezed his eyes shut. *A real hero, that one.* My mom is behind the driver's seat, holding the side of her head, blood trickling from between her fingers, gray eyes bright and powerful, watching me and smiling, like she's proud.

Aftershave struggles harder, tearing at the tape with dull nails as I pull it taut, sinking it into the folds of fat. His body shudders, and Shotgun's eyes go wide, realization dawning that I'm strangling his friend to death.

"Dennis!" Shotgun screams. Blondie shakes his head, squeezing his eyes even tighter. Guess his name is Dennis...like the menace but without the gumption.

Aftershave kicks wildly, his long legs flailing. He connects with the door, sending another loud clang through the space. He tries to heave himself forward, but I've got him tight against my body, legs wrapped around his waist—he is a fly in my spider web.

With one more awful spasm, Aftershave goes limp. Shotgun swings his weapon to aim at Mom. She keeps her eyes on me. I push Aftershave forward, bringing my legs behind him, and Shotgun looks over at me.

"Tape yourself and her"—his chin juts toward mom—"or I'll shoot her."

I slip the knife from the ankle holster I bought in D.C.—it's not as fancy as Robert's but does the trick—and keep it hidden behind Aftershave. Dennis opens one eye then slowly lifts his head to look at Shotgun.

The van swerves wildly, throwing everyone off balance. Aftershave slumps to the side as we slide into the side of the van, exposing me. Shotgun falls onto the driver, the barrel of the gun aiming at the ceiling. Dennis collides with my mother, crying out in pain.

The van swerves the other way, overcorrecting. We all tumble to the other side, my mom landing on top of Dennis, Shotgun slamming into the passenger side door, Aftershave rolling onto me.

I push him off, scramble over his body and grab onto the passenger seat headrest. Shotgun struggles to bring his gun up. I step on Dennis, propelling myself over the seat and driving my knife into Shotgun's neck.

His eyes go wide behind the mask. His weapon drops into the footwell. I dive for it, my feet kicking off the headrest. As my fingers close around the weapon, I twist, aiming it back up my body at the driver.

He's another masked man, his seatbelt crossing a large pot belly, his hands gripping the wheel, foot pressing onto the accelerator. His eyes dart to me for a moment, then return to the road. The van's tires throb over the rough surface.

"Pull over," I say. His foot presses harder, his lips firm. "Stop the fucking van."

He shakes his head, speeding up even more.

Fuck me, he's going to crash this thing.

CHAPTER FIFTEEN

Robert

Amy lives in one of the modern apartments overlooking the ocean. The penthouse has a private pool on the balcony, a helipad on the roof, and marble floors that click under her low heels as she leads me to the office.

Josh waits for us, standing next to a large touch screen monitor. The curtains are drawn against the sun, leaving the room in half shadow, the monitor glowing softly.

I can smell the booze on Josh—his eyes are red-rimmed but sober, so the alcohol is sweating out of him from last night. Amy stands next to him, her wide-legged pants and white button-down shirt crisp. The gold necklace at her throat looks almost like a collar. *She is no one's pet, though.*

Amy's effortless elegance contrasts with her brother's rumpled sports jacket and jeans as she brushes a finger across the touch screen, bringing up the Joyful Justice logo. Another swipe of the hand and the emblem of the Her Prophet appears next to it—the silhouette of a woman's face set into the snarling profile of a wolf.

Josh steps aside, ceding the monitor to Amy, and she opens a file of photographs that spread out across the screen—images from the bombing of a Men's Rights rally in Savannah from weeks ago. "I'm sure you know about this," Amy says, not turning to me.

"The bombing, yes."

"And the shootings," she pulls up more photographs, including one of Sydney's mother, bleeding on a stage, along with a mug shot of the shooter.

"Yes," I say, again. "I'm aware of the two groups. What do they have to do with Joyful Justice?"

Amy turns to me, leaving the images on the screen, her smile small and knowing. "I'm sure you're aware that while Joyful Justice is pursued by international law enforcement, there is a tentative peace based on the fact that they are both going after—" She raises her fingers into air quotes. "Bad people."

"To a degree, yes," I say. "But there are more reasons than that."

She raises one brow. "Such as?"

"While Joyful Justice has a central command, the missions are always brought to them by the"—I wave a hand of dismissal—"injured parties. And often those parties are then trained to deal with the issue themselves. Even when given more concrete support, it still remains a community-led action. So, law enforcement can go after members of Joyful Justice for conspiracy, but it is very hard to prove, and those committing the violent acts are so often victims who are defending themselves that it wouldn't look good to have international enforcers of justice, in effect, acting to protect the oppressors."

"You sound like you admire them," Josh says. He's taken an armchair by the window slightly behind me.

I'm standing in front of the monitor and have to look over my shoulder to address him. "Joyful Justice is well organized. Smart. Determined. Keeps the players at the top protected. Much like we've always run our businesses." I smile at him. *We are on the same side.* "It's one of the reasons they are so hard to beat."

"Exactly," Amy says, drawing my attention back to her. "One of our biggest hurdles is their reputation for protecting the innocent. Of being 'the good guys.'" I nod my agreement. "So, we plan to tie them to the Her Prophet's most violent factions."

"Interesting approach. You believe this will entice law enforcement to take a harder look at them?"

"Yes, and turn the public against them."

"Tell me more." I glance at my watch to imply that while interested, I also am important, and have other tasks to attend to this afternoon.

"A mass shooting," Amy says, her voice quiet, as if she's just dropped a bomb and is eager to hear the explosion.

I look up and raise a brow. "A mass shooting?"

"Yes." She's slightly breathless, excited by her plan. "A mass shooter who claims allegiance to Joyful Justice."

"Like the shooters in Paris did to ISIS," I say.

She grins. "Exactly."

"But the target would have to be innocents for your plan to work. Hard to make it believable. It would be like Robin Hood and his merry men massacring the good folks of Nottingham." I shrug. "You might be able to fool the public into hating them, but those tasked with watching Joyful Justice know their M.O. and won't fall for a false flag event."

Amy turns back to her screen and opens another folder, a photograph of Declan Doyle and me appears on the screen. It's from when we were friendly back in New York, and I was trying to woo him to work for me. "We want you to convince Declan Doyle that the mass shooting threat is for real. In fact, we want you to warn him it's going to happen."

I offer a suppressed smile—one that says, *oh honey, I'm so sorry your plan is so silly.* "There are several problems with that." I keep my voice sympathetic—I don't want to be ruining all her hard work, but some-one's got to tell her. "Besides my earlier points, Declan does not trust me. And, it would be out of character for me to go to such a low-level operative with important information. I dine with the head of Homeland Security. Why would I warn an investigator?"

Amy steps toward me, her eyes holding mine. "Do you want to see Natalia again?"

"Of course, and if you want me to speak with Doyle I will, but it won't advance your plan." I raise my hands, palms up. "This is your play, though. I'll do as you ask."

"Yes," she agrees. "It is my play. And you will do as I ask." Her voice goes hard. Amy is a formidable woman who has used her brother as a front for decades—I am one of the few people who knows where the power really sits in their organization.

Josh shifts in the seat behind me, and I glance back at him. He gets up and, catching my eyes, mutters something about going to the bathroom. Once the door shuts behind him, I turn my attention to Amy. "How long has the drinking been this out of control?" I ask, the way any good friend would.

She may be blackmailing me into cooperating with her, but that doesn't mean we are not old, dear friends. It does not negate our history.

Her eyes shutter and she turns away, then returns to the previous subject. "I have my reasons for wanting the message delivered to Declan rather than a higher up."

"Okay, give me more details, and I'll deliver whatever message you want."

Her back to me, she opens another file on the monitor and brings up a map of Miami. "I'm sure you're aware of the massive storm damage in Miami."

"Obviously. The city may never be the same." Where is she going with this?

"There are refugee centers set up here and here." She points to higher ground outside the city. "We have a woman who claims that she was raped at one of them and ignored by officials. She appealed to Joyful Justice, and they arranged to get her a gun."

Amy doesn't turn around, so I can't see her expression, but her voice is flat. "She'll kill as many people in the center as she can before being taken down. Men, women, children…she'll claim they were all complicit in her rape. Nobody stopped him."

Her voice is too flat. For all the horrors that Josh and I endured, Amy endured more. Worse.

"This will have a powerful effect on public opinion. While the woman's rage is understandable, her slaughter of so many innocent people—people already traumatized by the hurricane's damage—will create widespread revulsion. And that anger will quickly focus on Joyful

Justice, which gave her the weapon. Given Joyful Justice's reputation for aiding women in avenging themselves against their exploiters, its role in this little drama is..." She pauses, her back still to me, "believable."

"How will you convince this woman to do as you ask?"

Amy pulls up a photograph of a dark-skinned woman with bruising on her face. "This was taken at the hospital after the rape." Amy pauses, her fingers lingering over the photograph, and then she drops her hand to her side and turns toward me. "We approached her, pretending to represent Joyful Justice. We've worked on her for some time now...she is ready."

"Ready?"

"Our recruitment techniques are not your concern."

But I can guess what they are...convincing someone to commit violence in the name of a cause is surprisingly easy. Inside each of us a killer lurks, waiting for the right reason to unleash pain upon our fellow man. I sigh. "Amy, you're giving me very little here. How can you expect me to work so blindly. I may want to see Natalia again, but that hasn't made me dumb."

Her smile widens. "No, but age, my dear friend, is starting to make you soft."

She brushes past me, heading to her desk, and I turn, following her with my eyes.

It's not age, *old friend,* it's Sydney Rye.

CHAPTER SIXTEEN

Sydney

There is a dead body slumped in the passenger seat, my head and upper body are in the footwell, arms up, holding a shotgun aimed at the maniac driving this van at ever increasing speeds.

Elbowing myself into a butt-down, head-up position, I look over the dashboard. *Oh great.* The van is racing up an on-ramp. We are headed onto a highway, and the driver is not checking mirrors. He's hunched over the wheel, staring straight ahead.

"Hold on, Mom!" I yell before turning the shotgun around so that the handle is facing the driver. He glances at me, and I ram it into his nose, throwing his head back and forcing cartilage into his brain, killing him instantly. His hands drop off the wheel, and I release the gun to grab it.

He's big, and I'm leaning over his belly to hold the wheel steady. I can't get near the pedals with him in the way, and I can't take my hands off the wheel because the lane we are in is ending. A horn honks as I merge into the next lane, narrowly missing the guardrail.

Keeping one hand on the wheel I try to pull the dead driver out of the seat but he's too big. "Mom, I need your help."

"Get off him or I'll shoot her." I glance over to see Dennis with the shotgun, aiming at my mother.

"He's dead, Dennis," I answer calmly, concentrating on the road again. We are coming up on another car, bearing down on its bumper. I check my mirrors. There is someone to my left, gonna have to go into the right-hand shoulder. I ease us over, the rough surface vibrating the van, pebbles ricocheting off the undercarriage. We pass the car, and I move us back onto the roadway, then make my way into the left lane.

"If you want to live, Dennis, we need to get this guy out of my way. His foot is jammed on the gas pedal."

"Phil is dead?" Dennis asks.

"Mom, can you please help me out here?"

"Don't move!" Dennis squeals. I should have killed that idiot. Lesson learned—leave no dumbasses alive. Maybe I'll needlepoint that onto a pillow for my baby's nursery.

If we survive.

A siren starts up behind us. I actually laugh out loud because this does not look good. Speeding is the least of our worries right now.

Another car is coming up, but I've got room on the right this time, so I flick the turn signal and move over, racing past the car at over 80 miles per hour now. The siren is following fast. The left lane is emptying. The cop car races past, all lights flashing. I laugh harder this time as I use my signal to get back in the left lane. The cop is clearing a path for us!

"Why are you laughing!" Dennis screams.

I don't answer him. Instead I'm working on moving Phil's leg, trying to get his foot off the accelerator. His thick thigh is pressed so close to the wheel I can't even see his foot nor can I climb onto his lap.

We reach the top of a rise and I see a traffic jam at the bottom. That's where the cop car was headed. The traffic in front of us slows, brake lights glowing ahead. "Dennis," I say, pulling at Phil's leg harder now. "We are all gonna die if you don't help me. Grab his leg while I hold the wheel."

"You're trying to trick me."

"Oh, my God."

"Son," my mom says. "You have been hurt in the past, I can see that."

Oh, my God.

"You're going to get hurt in the *very near future*," I say, giving up on Phil's leg and moving us into the left shoulder as we approach the traffic jam.

We blow by the first stopped vehicles, the carriage rattling, stones cracking against the cars we past.

"Let me help her," Mom says, her voice all quiet and calm.

"No!" Dennis yells.

I glance back at him for just a second then forward again as the road curves. I'm standing between the two front seats, leaning over Phil's body, both hands on the wheel. Dennis is out of range. I can't kick him without letting go of the wheel, and I can't get Phil's thick leg over without using both hands.

The parking brake.

No, damn, it's probably a foot pedal.

But the gear shift is right there. I grab it and shift us into neutral. We are still in a descent so our speed does not slow immediately. The road straightens out again, and I see the accident that caused the traffic jam.

Flares glow and police lights swirl where a tractor trailer is blocking all lanes of traffic...including the shoulder. Its rear end is less than a van width's away from the guard rail.

Shit. Shit. Shit.

I punch the horn, drawing the attention of the police. The speedometer reads 50 miles per hour and dropping. "Hold on! We are going to crash. Mom, dump your ID. Now!"

A uniformed officer holds up a hand like that's going to stop me. *I would if I could, officer.* I wave him away, hoping he understands I'm not doing this shit on purpose.

His eyes narrow and then broaden in recognition: *That chick is leaning over a dead guy to drive that van.*

He yells to the other officers, and they all scramble to get out of my path. We hit a flare, crunch over glass, and I hold the wheel steady, gritting my teeth, trying to thread the needle between the tractor trailer's rear end and the guard rail.

We don't fit.

The impact comes and I fly forward, the windshield shattering as I am thrown through it. I roll off the hood, landing on the pavement, face toward the sky. My vision is blurred, darkening at the edges. Footsteps crush glass, yelling, and the edges get darker. I blink and darkness takes me away.

CHAPTER SEVENTEEN

Mulberry

The air conditioner hums. The words on the screen blur. Merl spent the last two days catching me up on Joyful Justice activities. And we have only scratched the surface; I've been gone for months.

And the world went on without me.

"We've missed you," Merl says, as if he can read my thoughts.

I give him a weak smile. "You've done well without me."

"It's designed that way," Merl says in answer. "We have to be able to go on without any one of us…or more."

Because what we do is dangerous…and important.

"I know." Rubbing my face, I sit back in the squeaky chair. We are in Merl's office, just off the dojo. The subtle thud of blows against bags, along with the scent of stale sweat and orange cleaning products, infuses the space.

Merl's dogs are out in the dojo, watching the action, keeping guard. He sits behind me, looking at his phone.

"When is the next council meeting?" I ask.

"Tomorrow." Merl clears his throat and looks up at me. "Dan just messaged." The way he says it makes it sound bad.

"What?"

Merl meets my eyes. "Sydney's alias showed up at a Louisiana hospital not far from where her mother spoke last night. Dan is getting information now."

I'm standing, the chair tipped over behind me, before I even have the conscious thought to rise. "I'm going to get her."

I turn toward the door, but Merl jumps up and blocks my way. "Hold on," he says, his voice low and calm. My breathing is heavy, heart pounding. I need to get to her. "I'm not going to stop you—"

I cut him off. "Then get out of my way," I say through clenched teeth.

"Just listen for one minute before you fly out the door."

I take a deep breath and nod. "Go ahead." *Nothing you can say will stop me from going to her.*

"Please remember, when you see her, that Sydney does not like taking orders."

"She does from you," I snarl for no good reason.

He shakes his head, as if to say I'm an idiot. He doesn't do it quite as condescendingly as Robert Maxim, but they are annoyed by the same thing: stubborn, blind Mulberry. "I'm her trainer, and she will listen to me in practice but not in life. If you push too hard you'll just push her away." He takes a deep breath, holding my gaze, making sure I'm listening. "Let her lead. And you may have better results."

"As if I have a choice."

"Choose it," Merl says. "Choose her over everything, and you'll do better than if you try to make her choose you."

"More T-shirt wisdom," I say, pushing past him.

This time he lets me leave. But Merl is waiting for me when I get to the airstrip, bag over my shoulder, scowl on my face, rage in my breast pocket. He doesn't say anything, just opens his arms for a hug.

I embrace him and emotion wells up, surprising me. "Thank you," I say, though I'm not sure exactly what I'm grateful for...maybe just that Merl is still alive and still my friend. And that he, and the rest of the council, the rest of Joyful Justice, can provide a safe haven for Sydney and our child.

If she will let them.

CHAPTER EIGHTEEN

Sydney

Pain settles over me and I groan, trying to blink open my eyes. It feels like gum has glued my eyelashes together. There is the familiar beeping of a heart rate monitor.

Great.

Fear lashes through me, more powerful than the pain. *The baby.*

My eyes snap open, but my vision is fuzzy. Blinking, I bring the hospital room into focus. The heart rate monitor is speeding up as adrenaline stokes my fear into a frenzied state.

I go to pull off the blanket but can't. I'm handcuffed to the bed. *Of course.* When a woman crashes into an accident scene in a van full of dead bodies, you handcuff her to the bed. I'd do the same if I was a cop.

The door opens, and an African American woman with graying hair, wearing purple scrubs and a stethoscope strung around her neck, walks in. "You're awake," she says, coming over to check my machine.

"I'm pregnant," I say. "No meds."

She nods. "We know."

"You do? Is it…"

"We are going to take you down for an ultrasound now."

"Are you my doctor?"

She shakes her head. "I'm your nurse, Glenda." Her gaze falls on my handcuffs.

"Am I under arrest?"

"I don't know about that. But the police will want to know you're awake."

"Please, can we have the ultrasound first?" My unshackled hand falls onto my stomach. "Please," I beg.

Her lips purse, and she gives a small nod. "I'll take you down now. We'll get you checked out."

Her hand falls onto my shoulder and offers a comforting squeeze. "Do you know—have you heard anything about my dogs?" I ask.

Glenda shakes her head. "No, sorry. Were they in the accident?"

I shake my head. Blue would know how to hide. They are probably still around the parking garage. I need to get back there.

Glenda hangs my IVs on the back of the bed and pushes the curtain aside, wheeling me through the door and down the hall toward the elevator.

We go down one floor.

The wall has a jungle mural painted on it. We are in the maternity ward. A woman moans from one of the rooms. Holy crap, she's giving birth. Right here. Right now.

Glenda wheels me past an open doorway. I glance in and see a new dad in a chair holding a bundle in his arms. The pure adoration and love on his face catches my breath. He's totally absorbed and astounded by the person he helped make.

Glenda wheels me into a room with an ultrasound machine. "I'll be right back, going to check on the tech," she says before leaving.

I take the moment alone to further investigate my handcuff. It's looped around my wrist and then around the bed rail. Leaning over I try to find a way to take the bedrail off—it's held on by six screws.

Glenda returns accompanied by a woman with curly blonde hair and square glasses, whose white coat hangs off thin shoulders.

She glances up from the chart in her hands and her eyes go wide. *Oh shit. Did she just recognize me?*

"This is Samantha," Glenda says.

I give her a weak smile. Samantha clears her throat and wrestles some control over her face. "Hi," she says. "Grace Smith?"

"Yes," I say with a practiced smile. "You can call me Grace." So, they found my ID.

"Well, Grace, let's check on your little one," Samantha says, settling onto the stool next to the machine.

"I'll be back to get you in bit," Glenda says, hitting the lights on her way out leaving us in semi darkness—the glow from the ultrasound machine the only light.

Samantha pulls back the blankets to expose my stomach. "Let's see how we are doing here," Samantha says. "How far along are you?"

"About two months I guess."

She squirts goo onto my belly, and I shudder at the chill. Taking her wand out of its holder, Samantha places it against my stomach and the screen in front of her lights up in a semi circle of black and white. My heart leaps into my throat. I'm going to see my baby. Dead or alive, I'm about to see it.

Please let it be alive. *Please.*

A rapid heartbeat thumps out of the speakers and Samantha stops moving the wand, pointing to the screen with her free hand at a small curled blob wiggling on the screen. "There it is."

She pushes some buttons and lines appear around the little thing. "Looks like about 8 weeks to me. Good guess."

"It's okay?" I ask through the lump in my throat.

She moves the wand. "I'll check the placenta."

I watch her profile as she stares at the screen. She leans closer and clicks more buttons. My heart beats in my throat.

"The placenta is intact." She turns to me and smiles. "Everything looks great to me."

I release a long breath and close my eyes. "Thank you." My voice comes out scratchy with tears.

"You're welcome."

She clicks more, and I hear a printer whirl. "I'll get you a picture to take home."

Home. An image flashes behind my closed lids of a refrigerator with the ultrasound photo held to it by a magnet—maybe one in the shape of a pirate ship or some other silly memento. I can almost feel Mulberry's arms around my waist, his chest against my back, breath on my hair, as we stare at the picture together.

I need to get out of here.

Taking that fantasy and shoving it out of my mind, I open my eyes and sit up. Samantha presses more buttons, sneaking glances at me. Her hands still, and she is staring at me in a way that goes beyond professional courtesy, as if trying to figure out who "Grace Smith" really is.

With little to lose I decide to take a chance. "Do you recognize me?" I ask. Her mouth tightens and she stares at me for a long moment before giving a sharp nod. Samantha turns back to her equipment quickly, almost like she wants to disavow her agreement. "Will you help me escape?"

She goes very still before slowly returning her gaze to me. She chews on her bottom lip. "I admire everything you do, but I can't," she says. "I'd lose my job and have to answer to the police."

"We can make it look like I forced you," I say. *Because that's what I'm going to do if you don't agree.*

"How?"

"Can you get ahold of a screw driver?"

"A screwdriver?" Samantha parrots back to me. I hold up my wrist and the cufflink clinks against the bedrail. She looks at it. "Oh."

"We can remove it," I point to the big flat screws with my free hand.

"You'll still have a large metal bedrail attached to your arm."

"Better than a whole bed." I smile, acting as though this is a totally normal conversation. Samantha stares at the screws. "Please," I say. Samantha chews on her lip, not meeting my gaze. "If I stay here, I'll end up in prison. Don't make me give birth in prison."

Her eyes jump to mine, and she shakes her head. It is a horrible idea. A zing of fear rushes through me. *No fucking way.* The image of that dancing bean throbs through my mind. I'll do whatever it takes to get out of here.

Samantha takes a paper towel and wipes at my bare belly with a soft and practiced stroke. "I think there is one in the maintenance closet," she says, her voice as gentle as her touch. "Let me see if I can get it."

She's gone only a few minutes, but they drag on as I imagine days in prison might. When the door opens, Samantha is holding a large screwdriver. She turns on the overhead lights and gets to work on the bedrail. For a reluctant accomplice, she moves fast. The bedrail comes off with a clunk and I pull it close.

"What about my IV? Can you take out the needle?"

She releases me from the saline bag then helps me stand. I'm steadier than I expected after a head injury. "Give me the screwdriver." She passes it over. "This is going to hurt, but it will provide you with cover," I say.

"What—"

Raising the metal bed rail fast, I knock her on the side of the head— she falls back onto the mattress clutching her ear and lets out a low moan.

"Give me a five minute head start and then call for help," I say. Her hand still cradling her skull she nods. "Thank you."

Screw driver in one hand, bedrail attached to the other, I open the door. The hall is empty. I follow the exit signs. A cool breeze passes over my bare back as I make it to the elevators. The doors start to open, and I duck into the stairwell.

The word FIVE is painted on the wall in giant letters. Flourescent lighting reveals that I have the space to myself. I start down, my steps echoing against the cinder block walls. Where am I going?

I lean against a wall for a moment, gathering my thoughts. I need to find my mom and get us out of here. She had her ID on her. I told her to dump it, but did she listen?

Shit.

Maybe I should just run for it. Leave her behind. *Nice.*

I should at least check on her. If she did manage to trash her ID maybe we can escape without this blowing up into a media frenzy…and then maybe pigs will start flying and hell will freeze over and I'll get a job as a barista and live in a basement apartment with Mulberry and raise our child like it ain't no thang.

I close my eyes and focus my mind on my breath and the cool, hard surface against my forehead. *Breathe out anxiety and fear, breathe in calm and bravery.*

No matter what, I need to check on my mother. So I'll do that, then worry about everything else next. I open my eyes. I need to keep moving. Running around with a bed rail attached to me won't draw attention. *Nope, that's totally normal.*

I get to the first floor and keep going to the basement, assuming it will be the most deserted. I exit into a hallway with linoleum floors and scuffed white walls. Signs point to Radiation and other departments that benefit from being underground.

A map on the wall has egress points and I take note before trying to open office doors. I find an exam room that looks long deserted—empty cotton ball dispensers and a stool with a broken wheel make up the bulk of the decor, but there is a phone on the wall.

I dial nine, get an outside line, then dial the one number I've got memorized.

"Sydney." Robert sounds so damn satisfied to hear from me.

"Can you give me Dan's number?" I ask. "I've lost my phone."

He chuckles. "You want Dan's number? That's why you're calling me."

The HVAC unit clicks on, sending a fresh breeze over my bare back. I'm so not telling Robert Maxim my, ahem, *situation.* "Yes."

"You went to see your mother."

"How stalkery of you."

"You're calling from a Louisiana number. A hospital. Sydney, what have you gotten yourself into?" Again, he sounds amused, as if my exploits are those of a rascally kitten.

"If you're trying to sound like less of a stalker, you're failing."

"Let me help."

"No, thank you."

"Why not?"

"So many strings." I'm really playing this kitten thing out to the max.

"What have I ever asked of you?"

"I don't have time for this, Robert. Please, just give me Dan's number."

"I do love when you say please."

I sigh. "Never mind. I'll figure it out on my own." But I don't hang up. Because I'm mostly naked, hand cuffed to a bed rail...in Louisiana...with no other numbers to dial. *Shit.*

"Goodbye then." Robert hangs up.

Mother-freaking shit bucket.

I return the handset and stare at the phone for a second as my mind spins. Guess I'll have to get out of this one on my own.

The little dancing bean in my belly flashes across my mind. *I'm not alone.* I call the hospital operator and ask to be connected to April Madden's room.

"Just a moment," she says before patching me through.

So they have her real name. *Crap.*

"Hello?" Mom sounds tired.

"Hey."

"Where are you? The police were just here. They said you escaped."

"What did you tell them?"

"That those men tried to kidnap me and we fought them off."

We? "I can't speak with the police, Ma, you know that."

"I didn't tell them who you were!" She sounds insulted. "I said I met you at the event and we talked after, that you were walking me to my car." She is huffy. "I said I couldn't remember your name. And I described you as a grown-up Annie."

I hadn't even told her that's exactly how I describe my alias. I hate it when I'm so clearly reminded of our similarities.

"Did they handcuff you to your bed?" I ask.

"No." She sounds unsure.

"Well, they handcuffed me. So they either know who I am or are pretty clear that I'm dangerous." *Was it the van full of dead bodies I drove into the accident scene that tipped them off?* "I need to get the fuck out of here."

"Let me talk to my bodyguard. Where are you?"

"Bodyguard?"

"Yes, of course, I have protection now."

"Where were they last night?"

"I told them I wanted to be alone." Her voice is defensive. *Because I'm being a bitch.*

"Fine, they are here now?"

"Yes."

"Great. I need help." I tell her where I am. "I'll wait here."

"I'll send her down now."

We hang up, and I sit on the broken stool to wait, letting my mind wander. Is there a connection between the Incels—I'm assuming those jerks were Incels—who tried to kidnap us last night and the attempts on my life? The other would-be assassins were professional. Last night's attack was pure amateur hour. They probably came up with this plan in their basements, and the fact that they managed to even half pull it off is impressive.

If my mother had a full security detail rather than just me and the dogs, they wouldn't have gotten as far as they did. Dead in a van. So... not so far.

I allow myself a smug smile. Glancing down at the bedrail still shackled to my wrist wipes it away. I may have beaten those amateurs, but I'm still stuck in the basement of a hospital, mostly naked, my only hope my mother's bodyguard.

I send up a little prayer that she's good.

EK

My mother's bodyguard stands in the doorway. A head taller than me, she wears a cream-colored, high-necked, ankle-length robe that flows over her arms in long, wide sleeves. Her hair is hidden by an indigo blue turban. Her eyes are cat green, and her skin maplewood brown. She smells like burnt sage.

The woman belongs in front of a crystal ball.

She shuts the door behind her, seeming to almost float into the room —that flowing robe hides a powerful and trained body.

"Hi," I say.

She nods. "I am Veronica."

"Nice to meet you." I try on a smile that comes out all crooked and crazy. *Can anyone say awkward?*

"May I?" She gestures to my bound wrist, and I hold it out for her inspection. Thick gold bracelets bump into each other, releasing soft tones, as she touches the bedrail. Turning my wrist, she looks at the keyhole of the handcuffs, and then glances at the screwdriver in my other hand.

What weapons does she carry under that crazy robe?

She reaches into it now and pulls out a tool that fits neatly into the key hole and, after a few expert twists, the lock snaps open. *Well now, isn't that useful? Wonder if she has a lamp in there, Mary Poppins style.*

My wrist free, I rub at the red mark left behind. "How is April?" I ask, not wanting to expose our familial connection.

"Your mother will heal. She has a sprained ankle and some bruised ribs. But she is strong. I believe she will make a quick recovery."

"She told you?"

"That you are her daughter?" Veronica shakes her head. "No, but it is obvious. Very few people have eyes that shade of gray."

Will my child have them too?

Veronica narrows her eyes at me, and I turn away. She dresses like a fortune teller, and while I don't believe in psychics, you can't pull off a robe like that unless you're intuitive. And Veronica is living up to that robe, big time.

"You want to leave without speaking with the police?" Veronica asks in her oddly formal style, like English is not her first language.

"Yes, will you help?"

"Where will you go?"

"I need to pick up my dogs."

She nods, as if my mother told her about the animals...or she's a psychic. "Yes, but the hospital is crawling with police now. We must wait until nightfall. I have someone coming with clothing for you."

"Who?"

"They are trustworthy, do not worry."

I'm itching to leave. Hating that Blue, Nila, and Frank are some-where out there, alone. I may no longer have a bed rail attached to my arm, but I am mostly naked, so clothing would be good. But... "Won't the police eventually check down here? There must be cameras."

"Yes," Veronica agrees. "In the elevators, but not the stairwells. They are not sure which floor you are on but believe that you have not exited the building. Right now, there are still several exits without guards but they are working to cover them all. One of my team is leaving, wearing your wig and hospital gown now. So they will think you have left the building. We must make sure that you are not seen here. As your mother's guard—and with the very real threats against her life—I insisted on being informed about the security of the hospital. And have used that knowledge to our advantage. We will wait here for nightfall. Your clothing and disguise will arrive soon."

"What time is it?" I have no idea how long I was out.

"The accident was last night. You slept through to midday. The sun sets in less than two hours."

My head feels suddenly light, and Veronica reaches out, taking my elbow and leading me to the stool. "I didn't realize I was out for so long." Or that I'd have to spend hours in this basement.

Blue is out there! My brain is screaming at me. But I know Veronica is right. I can't help him by running out of here half-cocked...or half dressed.

But sitting on this broken stool for the next two hours also seems impossible. "I want to go once the clothing arrives," I say.

Veronica shakes her head. "No." She does not bother expounding on her reasons. Instead she goes to the sink and wets a handkerchief that seems to have materialized from inside her robes. She passes it to me. "Lay this across your neck," she says. "It will help. You need food as well."

Pulling a phone out, she sends off a text.

I lay the cloth across my neck. Its warmth relaxes the tension there, and I take a deep breath.

"How did you meet my mother?" I ask.

Veronica replaces the phone in her pocket before answering. "I saw the video of April's shooting and was drawn to protect her."

"I see."

She smiles at me. "I am a witch."

And I'm a demon. "A witch?"

"Yes, I practice witchcraft."

"But you're also a follower of the Her Prophet." *Lots of religion for this one.*

"Yes, there are many witches who believe in the Her Prophet. She preaches much of what we've believed for centuries."

"Right." I am half naked, holed up in a hospital basement, pregnant, hiding from the police...talking to a witch. And here, I thought my life had topped out on weirdness. "And, obviously, my mom knows you're a witch...and is cool with it?"

"Obviously."

"She has changed."

"We all evolve."

I laugh. "April Madden has certainly evolved."

Veronica pulls out her phone and checks a message. "My friend is here."

"Another witch?" I ask, almost giddy with the ridiculousness of my life.

"Yes, a member of my coven." Veronica opens the door, and I hear footsteps in the hall. She steps back, admitting a woman almost half her height, round as a dumpling, with long, purple streaked hair, wearing a similar robe to Veronica's, only hers is black. She carries a sack weighted with clothing and smelling of fresh bread. "Lacey, this is the young woman we are helping, Grace."

Lacey shifts the satchel to her shoulder so that she can take my proffered hand in both of hers. "So nice to meet you." Her voice is high and squeaky like a mouse.

"Thank you for your help." I pull my hand free, and she rummages in the satchel, pulling out...you guessed it...a robe. This one in deep ocean blue. She passes it to me, and I finger the material—a soft cotton.

"I made you a sandwich." She pulls out a bundle wrapped in wax paper. "I'd just pulled bread from the oven, and I used the persimmon jam from last year." She glances at Veronica, who smiles and nods as if she remembers this jam fondly. "And almond butter. You're not allergic to nuts are you?"

"Nope." My mouth is watering as she hands over the package. Unwrapping it, I find thick slices of a hearty bread dripping with jam and nut butter. It smells divine, and I moan as I take a bite. "Dear God, that's good," I mumble through my full mouth.

Lacey grins, clutching her satchel to her chest. She looks like a child who just won a spelling bee.

"Okay," Veronica says, getting Lacey's attention. "Let's go over the plan..."

I listen with half an ear as I finish off the sandwich and then slip off my hospital gown and pull the robe over my body. It is a bit short on me, as I'm taller than Lacey, but works about as well as any witch's robe could. Veronica helps me with the turban—it's a hat, rather than a long cloth that needs to be wrapped properly, but getting all my hair under it takes the two of us.

There are no mirrors in the room, but the metal cabinet shows me a blurry image of myself. And I look like one of three witches. It's a good disguise—and a comfortable one at that.

The hours pass with Veronica dipping in and out to check on my mother. Lacey sits on the floor, insisting I keep the stool, and lays out tarot cards, whispering to herself.

"We will have success," she tells me as she gathers the cards.

"Great."

"But we must be careful," she says, picking up the last card. "There is a powerful man waiting for us."

"Maybe it's the police?" I suggest...because, um...duh.

"No." She shakes her head. "This is a known presence. At least to you. He does not mean you harm. But..." She chews on her lip, looking at the last card. I lean over and see a male figure in a throne with a wolf at his knee. "Next to the sun," Lacey says, seemingly to herself.

"What's going on?" I ask, curiosity stirring.

She looks up at me and smiles. "He does not mean you harm. But beware the Emperor's need for control and conformity. He has ambitions, but tradition is essential for his happiness. If you are not strong, he will bend you to his will, which will leave you broken." She smiles. "Because you do not bend well."

"No," I agree. "I'm more of a bend-er than a bend-ee."

She smiles. "Yes, you are."

Veronica returns as Lacey wraps the cards in a silk handkerchief and slips them into her pocket. The robe I'm wearing has the same pockets. They are wide and long…but not quite big enough for a lamp.

"It is time," Veronica says. "Your mother is being released. I must attend to her, so let's hurry."

Relief washes over me as we step into the hall. Having the cramped, derelict room in my rearview mirror lets me breathe easier. Even if, as Lacey predicts, a controlling, traditional man waits for me in the wide world beyond.

We enter the stairwell and head to the third floor where there is a bridge to the parking structure. Lacey will drive me back to where I left my dogs while Veronica returns to my mother. The police fell for the decoy and are no longer hunting for me on hospital grounds.

As we pass the first floor, the door bangs open and a single man enters. Spotting us, he pulls up short, his eyes bouncing between us, not seeming to know where to land.

He is young, with wispy blond hair and a pale mustache that is desperately trying to come in. Contempt blooms in his eyes, and I recognize him. This guy must be related to Dennis, the Incel idiot. They have the same eyes, same hair…same hate-filled gaze.

"After you," he says, gesturing for us to go first up the stairs.

"No," Veronica says before I can. "Please, after you. We move slowly and would not want to delay you."

He hesitates for only a moment but then starts up the stairs. Veronica and I look at each other and an understanding passes between us. We follow him, Lacey pausing at the third floor for only a moment before continuing after us.

Veronica pulls her phone from her pocket and glances down at it then passes it to me. It's a text from my mother. "Mulberry called my room. He is here. I didn't tell him where to find you. He said he would wait in the parking garage." She gave a parking spot number. *A controlling, traditional man.*

Dan must have sent him when he saw my alias pop up in the hospital's computer system. He'd be monitoring the area, keeping watch over me, especially when I didn't check in.

Dennis's relation exits at my mother's floor. Veronica follows him through the door, signaling to me with a small wave that I should not. I wait in the stairs with Lacey, holding Veronica's phone and vibrating with the need to follow, yet knowing that I would only be a hindrance. Veronica can handle that pipsqueak.

But what if there are more of them?

Veronica did not ask for my help. She wants me to stay here.

"I think we should go," Lacey says. "Veronica has everything under control, I'm sure."

"I'd like to make sure April makes it out okay."

"Veronica can handle it."

She's probably right. And Mom did try to sacrifice herself to save me last time we had trouble...

I turn to Lacey. "Come on." I hurry back down the steps, and we cross into the parking lot, but instead of following Lacey to her car, I start toward the parking spot where Mulberry is apparently waiting. Time to bend a controlling, traditional man to my will.

CHAPTER NINETEEN

Robert

Declan Doyle eyes me with overt suspicion as we settle into the booth. It's off hours, and we are the only people in the dining room—the large windows look out on the upper floors of other Washington buildings, and the dark wood and leather decor reflects the wealth of those who live in the residences here.

We order our drinks from the tuxedoed waiter, and he brings a bread basket along with an assortment of cheeses—"compliments of the chef" —before Declan asks why I've invited him to join me at my apartment building's private restaurant.

"I have some information that I think will be of interest to you."

He shakes his head, a disbelieving smile twisting this lips. "You want to share intelligence with me? Out of the goodness of your heart?" He says it as though I'm a cat who's asked a mouse to perform a teeth cleaning. But Declan Doyle is no mouse, which is why I tried to hire him years ago. His integrity and trust fund kept him in public service.

"I've changed," I say with a shrug. "Become more community-minded."

Declan laughs at that one. "Sure you have."

"There is a cabal of criminal organizations plotting to destroy Joyful Justice, and I need your help to save them."

His grin fades. I take a sip of my manhattan and grimace. *Too sweet.*

"Why would I help save Joyful Justice?" Declan's tone is sober—no longer amused by or assured of my insincerity.

"It's a wide-ranging plot that involves the Incels and Her Prophet fanatics. That's why I thought it'd be of interest to you."

His brows raise. Is he surprised I know what he is working on? "I'm listening."

I outline Amy's plan to foment a massacre, leaving out her and Josh's names and thus the true identity of the organization plotting against Joyful Justice. As I talk, Declan's expression stays neutral and his drink untouched. "How do you know all this?" he asks when I finish.

"How I know it is not important. That I'm right is what you need to be paying attention to. Is there something wrong with your drink? Mine is sweet."

I gesture to the waiter, who waits on the far side of the room, well out of listening distance. He approaches. "This manhattan has too much sweet vermouth. I said a *perfect* manhattan. That means half sweet and half dry vermouth. I'd expect you to know that."

The waiter nods respectfully, mumbling an apology, before taking the drink away with a promise to bring a new one.

Declan waits for the man to be out of earshot before speaking. "Why should I believe you?"

"All of this will come to pass, and then you can follow the bread crumbs to the truth. Perhaps my warning will help lead the way. Personally"—I shrug—"I think it would be nice if we could stop the mass shooting from happening. Seems like Miami doesn't need another tragedy at the moment." I eye the cheese plate but decide against it.

The waiter returns with my drink before Declan can respond. I taste it, the smooth whiskey and aromatic dry vermouth perfectly tempered by just a hint of sweetness. I nod my approval, and the waiter leaves us again.

Declan sits forward, his drink sweating onto the table. "Is this the same group who was trying to kill Sydney?"

I raise a brow. "You heard about that?"

"She came to see me."

I know. Then she went to see her mother. And is currently in the basement of a hospital, failing to see her way out. But she will survive. She always does. "Sydney paid you a visit, how nice."

"She seemed eager to find the people who are after her." Declan is baiting me, trying to see if I've told Sydney what I know.

"Fascinating," I say, sounding bored. Declan frowns. "Do you think you can help avoid this catastrophe, or should I call someone else?"

Declan climbs out of the booth, never having tasted his drink. "Call someone else," he says. "I'm not your man, Maxim."

I let him walk away. He will look into it. Giving Declan a piece of information is like waving a fox scent under a hound's nose—he can't help but chase it down.

Back in my apartment, I call Amy. "It's done," I tell her. "But I don't think he believed me."

"That's fine. We are just planting the seed."

"When can I meet Natalia?"

"She is off the coast of Miami, waiting for you on her ship, *The Escape Plan*. Her helicopter can pick you up."

"I can be back in Miami by this evening. I'll call once I have my arrival time."

"Good luck, Robert."

It's not luck that's allowed me to survive this long. *It's always having an escape plan.*

CHAPTER TWENTY

Mulberry

"I need you to go get my dogs." Sydney is breathless and distracted, as if my presence is expected but not totally welcome.

"What?" I look up and down her body, at the strange full length robe, the swirling bruises and scratches on her neck and face. A darkening shiner circles her left eye.

"I was forced to leave them at the parking garage where my mother spoke last night. Please, go now. Blue will come to you."

"Let's go together." She looks back at the hospital and the woman waiting behind her. "Who is that?" I ask, dropping my voice.

"Look, we just saw an Incel member headed toward my mom's room. Her security, Veronica, went after him but I need to help." A pained expression passes over her features. Is it physical or emotional? "I can't just leave her."

"What can you do?" I ask. "The police will see you and arrest you. How does that help your mom?"

The strange woman approaches, her long robe brushing just above the pavement. "Veronica can take care of your mother, do not worry." She is small and round, with strong conviction in her voice.

Sydney turns to her. "Lacey—"

"He's right," Lacey says, pointing to me. *I like her more every minute.* "You're a distraction for the police. Go with him." She raises her brows. "He can keep you safe."

Sydney shakes her head. "I don't need anyone to keep me safe."

Lacey grins and it's radiant, changing her from a dowdy, odd little woman into someone glowing with warmth and power. "This is not bending; this is being smart."

"What's that mean?" I ask.

"Don't worry about it," Sydney tells me. "Lacey, I appreciate your help but—"

Lacey puts a hand on Sydney's arm and squeezes. "Go," she whispers. "Go now." Then she turns and walks away, her long robe making it look almost like she's floating.

"Let's get Blue," I go for Sydney's weak spot. "And Nila and Frank." She sighs, still watching Lacey. "Imagine the trouble that idiot is getting himself into as we speak."

Sydney turns to me and frowns. "Hold on a minute." She runs a few steps to catch up with Lacey, and they talk in low tones. I clench my fists to keep from going over there and throwing her over my shoulder. We need to get out of here. Sydney jogs back to me and relief eases the tension in my shoulders. *See, I can do this.* "Let's go," she says.

Sydney uses my phone to direct me to the venue her mother spoke at the night before. It's a big place that must seat at least a few thousand people. The parking structure is four stories, and Sydney has me drive slowly up to the top, her head out the window, calling Blue's name. He does not respond.

When we reach the roof and pull out under the night sky, it's clear the dogs are no longer here. Worry lines crease Sydney's forehead. The dark blue of the dress reflects in her eyes, turning them the color of the deepest parts of the Atlantic. "Where to next?" I ask, remembering Merl's sage advice to follow her rather than try to lead.

She focuses on my phone, zooming in on the map. "Looks like there is an alleyway with dumpsters the next building over." She holds the phone out to me. "I think it's behind a steak place." I nod, seeing the narrow passage on the satellite image.

I smile. "Blue and his pups have been dining on fine steak while you've been recuperating in the hospital. How like him."

Sydney offers a pained smile but no laugh. I clear my throat as I turn us around and start driving back down to the ground level. "So...you were in a car accident. What happened?" I ask.

She shakes her head. "Let's talk after we find Blue."

I nod. *See, following her lead.* Not exploding with frustration and demanding to know what in the eff happened to her. "But the baby?" I say, because I can't help myself.

"It's okay." Her voice is low, almost a whisper.

A tightness eases in my chest. I can wait until she's ready to give me the rest of the information.

When we reach the mouth of the alley, Sydney hops out of the rented SUV, her long robe swishing behind her as she starts down it, calling Blue's name.

I follow, leaving the car idling.

Blue leaps out from behind a dumpster and barrels down the alley, smashing into Sydney so hard she has to take a step back. She bends over, curling around Blue, whose whole body is wagging with excitement as soft whines escape him.

Frank is next, his tongue flopping out of his mouth, his aim off as he hits me in the bad leg and I lose my balance. Sydney catches me, her reflexes lightning-fast as she grabs my arm, giving me the support I need to recover my footing.

Nila trots up to us, what looks like a porterhouse bone in her mouth. They totally *were* eating high-end steak. I let out a snort-laugh and bend down to pet Frank, whose enthusiasm is likely to bowl me over again if I don't reciprocate.

Tears gleam in Sydney's eyes as she hugs Blue and reaches out a hand to pet Nila, who sighs in appreciation—but doesn't let go of the bone.

"Come on," I say. "Let's get out of here."

Sydney nods and stands, wavering a little. It's my turn to steady her.

"You okay?" She nods, but her face is pale. "Let's get going," I say again. She doesn't argue as I help her back into the SUV. Blue jumps up into her seat well, and the other dogs go in the back. "Where were you staying?" I ask.

"I didn't have a hotel yet. Came straight here. My rental is back at the venue. I've got my bag and food for the dogs."

I turn toward the venue. "I like this look," I tease. "Very fortune teller."

Sydney smiles, her eyes closed and head leaning back against the head rest. "That woman, Lacey, she said she saw you in the cards."

"What cards?"

"Tarot cards." Sydney says it like it's obvious. "Said that a controlling and traditional man waited for me."

"I'm not controlling," I say, injecting innocence into my voice.

She laughs but doesn't open her eyes. "Yeah, me either."

We both laugh at that. "I'm sure you're not the only woman with a controlling, traditional man in her life. That's how fortune tellers do it, you know—talk in vague terms that apply to almost everyone."

"I don't think our lives are like everyone else's."

I shrug. "Not in the practical ways, but we're still human, Sydney. We are driven by the same things as regular folk." I glance over to see her smiling, eyes still closed.

We stop at her rental, parked on a street near the venue, and she grabs her bag out of the back, along with a gallon of water and a bag of dog food. The dogs are thirsty but not interested in kibble—because they've been enjoying finer fare for the past twenty-four hours.

"Come on," I say as she packs up the dog bowls. "Let's get going. We can stop for food on the road. I'll call about taking care of your rental."

Sydney nods and gets back in the passenger seat, not bothering to change her clothing. She stares out the window as I get us on the highway headed east. As the wheels hum over the pavement, Sydney's breathing grows deeper and I stay quiet, letting her sleep.

My hunger gets the best of me two hours later, and I pull off the highway. Sydney wakes with a jolt as I get in line at a drive-thru fast food place. "It's okay," I tell her, placing a steadying hand on her thigh.

"Where are we going?"

"As far away from the scene of the crime as we can get. We have a council meeting this evening. I figured we'd find a hotel in a few hours and set up."

Sydney glances down at my phone and, reading a text there, smiles. "Mom is safe. That guy didn't try anything. I guess the police presence and Veronica scared him off."

"That's great."

"I should go to Miami, check on Robert's house. On Hugh and Santiago as well," she says.

"We're headed east, so that shouldn't be a problem."

She glances over at me and narrows her eyes. "You're being awfully solicitous."

We pull up in front of the speaker, and a crackling voice offers to take our order. I get myself a burger and fries, Sydney has the same plus a milkshake.

We park and Sydney offers the dogs kibble again. This time they eat it. We stand in a small patch of grass, letting them do their business.

My hand reaches out for hers, and she lets me take it. "I had an ultrasound," Sydney says, giving my fingers a squeeze.

I keep my eyes on the sky, watching the stars trying to twinkle through the light pollution, giving her space to tell me in her own time. "It's just a tiny thing. Like the size of a lima bean." There is a smile in her voice, and I can't resist turning to see it. Her eyes are unfocused as she watches the sky. "A little dancing bean."

"A little dancing bean," I echo back, wanting to feel the words in my mouth.

Her eyes come to me, and she nods. I tug on her hand, and she lets me wrap my other arm around her and kiss the top of her head. "I'm sorry I pushed you," I say. She nods against my chest but doesn't speak. "Merl said—"

"You told Merl?" she says, pulling away.

Damn. "Yes, should I not have?"

"I just—I guess. It's fine."

But she doesn't step close to me again. I'm still holding her hand as I go on, but she's looking at the dogs now…drifting away from me. "He said that he'd help keep you safe. I mean, all of them." *I'm butchering this.* I take a deep breath before continuing. "We have friends, Sydney. People who care and will help keep us safe."

She nods but doesn't respond.

Anger pushes at me. *Make her listen.*

But I shove back. *She will do the right thing.*

We return to the SUV and merge onto the highway. Sydney flicks through the radio stations. "According to the shooter's manifesto, Joyful Justice inspired her and even purchased the weapon." Sydney's hand stills on the dial. "Two victims are in critical condition, seven more stabilized, and ten deceased. We will bring you more on this story as it become available."

"What the hell?" Sydney grabs my phone and starts searching. "A mass shooting in one of the Miami refugee centers—a sports arena." She reads for a moment. "A female shooter. Says she was raped and that everyone there let it happen. So she went to Joyful Justice and they gave her an AK-47…" Sydney shakes her head. "No way."

"Definitely not," I agree. She looks over at me. "Merl caught me up. Besides, we both know that's not how we operate. We don't hand over weapons of war without training and certainly not to people so recently traumatized."

"It's a setup," Sydney says, her eyes scanning the screen. "According to her manifesto, she was also a follower of the Her Prophet. They are trying to tie Joyful Justice to the shooting and"—she scrolls some more —"possibly even to the bombing of the Incels a few months back."

"Someone is trying to make us look bad. Maybe the same someone who's been trying to kill you and Robert." I tell her briefly about what happened after she left us—the trip to the police station and the ship off the coast.

"Did Dan figure out who owns it?" she asks.

"No, shell companies upon shell companies. Robert flew out to it, but they were well-armed, and he couldn't get any information."

"Bullshit. Robert's lying. He would get the info. I know him. And there is no way he just gave up."

"You sound so sure of him." Anger is pressing at me again, just begging me to do something stupid.

"Robert knows what's going on, and he has a reason for not telling us. I'm sure of it."

"So, call him," I say, my voice betraying my anger.

Sydney ignores it. "No, this is better done face to face."

"Let's go see him then."

Sydney turns to me. "I need to go alone."

I bite the inside of my cheek so hard I taste blood. "On your own, sure."

Except she won't be alone, she'll have Blue...and our dancing bean with her. *Just not me.*

CHAPTER TWENTY-ONE

Robert

The helicopter descends slowly toward the ship. *The Escape Plan* is steady in the gentle swells. Only two weeks ago, the ocean raged like an angry beast, picking up entire neighborhoods and swirling them away—dragging detritus back into her depths, leaving a trail of destruction behind.

Entire sections of the city are gone, my own home on an island in Biscayne Bay barely standing. The wind ripped off sections of the roof, the rain beat at the interior, and the sea rose, carrying away what was left. The walls still standing are waterlogged, and I'm going to have to do a full rebuild.

My piano is the only thing of real value my people could not move in time. I have not personally seen the destruction yet, but José gave me a report. I'll head there after meeting Natalia.

An elegant Hispanic woman in her thirties greets me. "I am Seraphina." She bows slightly. "Ms. Rojas welcomes you, Mr. Maxim. She will meet you in the salon, if you'll follow me." Her accent is slight but lyrical.

She leads me through French doors into a room the width of the ship. We are on the top deck, and the view is just sea and sky. Intimate seating areas and a bar fill out the large space. The decor is beige and blues, nautical and expensive—standard yacht fair.

A barman wearing a vest with the ship's emblem embroidered on the breast offers me a drink. A seltzer with lime in hand, I lean against one of the barstools. He wipes down the bar, shining the already reflective surface and then at some unseen signal, leaves.

Alone, I even my breaths and clear my mind, the anticipation of seeing Natalia again after all these years building in my chest.

Footsteps on the stairwell raise me from my seat so that I'm standing when the top of her head appears. She is revealed one step at a time. The silky, dark hair I ran my fingers through now streaked with elegant silver, the forehead I butterflied with kisses now crisscrossed with fine lines, the eyes I fell into and out of and through...just the same. Framed in thick lashes, twinkling with intelligence and inner fire.

The nose she nuzzled along my neck, the lips I kissed with unbridled, desperate passion—turned now into a soft smile that expands into a wide grin as she stops on the top step, every inch of her small frame exposed. A ghost in all white—pressed pants and button-down blouse— elegant and timeless. She is still fit and strong, she still makes my heart race. *Still Natalia.*

"Robert," she purrs in the accent that drove me wild.

"Natalia," I answer, my own voice grating against the memories locked in my throat.

"It's been so long."

All I can do is nod and offer a shy smile. She's thrown me back to my twenty-year-old self. Puzzle pieces slide into place before my eyes. Losing her is how I learned ruthlessness. Learned that pain and sacrifice can only hurt if you let them.

And yet, here she is; and that wound, so fresh and tender at first blush, is back. I bleed for her all over again.

Natalia walks slowly toward me, hips swaying. Seeing her, aged and in civilian clothes, is surreal. She only ever wore fatigues—or nothing— when we knew each other in the jungle.

She must have changed as much as me.

Natalia takes a deep breath, looking up at me.

"It's good to see you," I say, because it is. *Achingly good.*

"You look the same, almost." She smiles, her hand raising to brush against my temple where silver grows.

I hum with the need to lean into her touch but control myself. Her hand drops to her side, though she continues to hold my gaze.

Sea birds caw, the ship rocks gently, but I'm standing in the jungle. I'm staring at the girl I loved, and I'm the boy I was then.

"I'm sorry," I say. It slips off my tongue—as planned as falling for her in the first place.

She blinks and looks down, her lashes pitch black against silky brown skin. "Me too."

"I thought you died."

"Yes." Her voice is quiet. "You sacrificed me for your freedom. I understand." She looks up at me. "I might have done the same."

"Would you have?" I sound like a frightened child who wants his mother to tell him burning the ants with the magnifying glass was normal—not the instincts of a real killer.

I am a real killer. Heartless, hungry, and concerned with no one but myself.

Natalia raises her gaze again and then steps away, perching on one of the bar stools. I sit next to her. She rests her hands in her lap—nails long and painted a soft pink. In the jungle she kept them short with her buck knife.

"It was so long ago now." She looks past me out to the sea.

"You're angry with me still, though," I say. *You've been trying to assassinate me.*

She shakes her head and smiles. "I am not."

"Then why," I am careful with each word. "Are you trying to kill me?"

She shakes her head. "I'm not."

I let the words hang between us, hoping that she will continue—explain why the helicopter from her yacht shot at me on the beach. Why a group of mercenaries ambushed my home.

Footsteps on the stairs interrupt our conversation. I stand, muscles tensing, as I watch another figure appear from below.

Dark hair, just like Natalia's when we met, but on a man. A forehead smooth with youth, green-blue eyes that stop my breath. A nose I have not seen since my father's death. Natalia's lips formed into a tight line of anger.

He is my height.

He has my father's nose, my eyes, and Natalia's lips.

"Hi Dad." His voice is dripping with sarcasm and...hate.

I have a son. And he's been trying to kill me.

CHAPTER TWENTY-TWO

Sydney

"I'm going to go to Miami to talk with Robert," I announce to the rest of the council. Mulberry and I are in a hotel room, still a day's drive away from Miami. The council members are up on my computer screen.

Dan sits alone in his office on the island. Anita is mid-flight, en route to Miami for damage control. Lenox sits in the sun somewhere on the Mediterranean. Merl is in his office off the dojo.

"You think he's lying that he doesn't know anything about the ship?" Dan says. I nod. Dan shrugs. "I never trust him."

"Do you think he is in some way involved with this shooting?" Anita asks.

"I don't think he's behind it, but he probably knows something about it. He knows everything."

"The man's not omnipresent," Mulberry grumbles.

I ignore him. "Face to face, I can tell when he's lying."

Lenox cocks his head. "Do you think he will confess the truth to you?"

"I don't know, but I'll know if he is trying to kill me."

"Because he will actually try to kill you." Anger sharpens Mulberry's tone. "I think I should go with her," he says, turning to the computer.

"I'm sitting right here," I snap.

He purses his lips. "Sorry."

"Robert isn't going to talk to me if you're there. You two will probably just end up trying to beat each other up, *again*."

Mulberry's neck flushes red. I put a hand on his thigh, under the small desk so the rest of the council can't see. I want to reassure him that I care about him. Even if I don't always listen to his advice.

"Obviously, someone is trying to set us up," I say. "This is designed to turn public opinion against Joyful Justice and the Her Prophet—and to put even more pressure on the government to destroy us."

Dan nods in agreement. "The Incels are talking about ramping up the *war*." He shakes his head. "They are all riled up online. I wouldn't be surprised to see more violence from their side soon."

Anita chews on her lip for a moment. "I'm going to do my best to get out in front of this, but obviously a lot of damage has been done."

"Isn't it dangerous for you to come stateside?" I ask.

Dan makes a hand gesture that implies Anita and he already had this argument.

"I need to find the person who duped that poor woman into thinking they represented Joyful Justice."

"I doubt they are just sitting around waiting for you in Miami," Dan says.

Anita narrows her eyes. "Trust me, will you? I'm also going to speak with reporters off the record. I still have a lot of contacts."

Chastised, Dan slumps in his chair and gives a small nod.

"Sydney," Anita says. "Your mother is headed to Miami as well."

"What? Why?"

"To speak. She wants to make the public case that this slaughter does not represent the Her Prophet. She does not preach violence against the innocent."

"Great."

Mulberry puts his hand over mine on his thigh, offering his support.

"I'll go to Miami with you," he says. "You can see Robert alone, but I'll be there if you need me."

"Thanks." I look over at him and he smiles, lifting his chin, urging me to tell the council about my pregnancy. We discussed it on our drive to the hotel, after I told him about what happened with the van full of Incel would-be assassins. Mulberry didn't push for me to tell the council, but he urged me...*they are our friends*.

I turn back to the council. "There is something I should tell you. Well, Dan and Merl already know."

"What?" Anita asks, frowning.

"I'm pregnant."

She looks stunned—her face frozen, mouth slightly open, eyes wide. Lenox nods slowly. "Congratulations," he says.

"Thank you," Mulberry answers, making it clear he is the father.

Anita clears her throat and smiles. "Yes," she says. "Congratulations."

"This doesn't change anything right now," I say. Mulberry doesn't argue. "Let's deal with this crisis, and then we can talk about it more."

Lenox nods again, his movements regal. "Of course," he says.

"Any news on Ian?" I ask desperate to change the topic.

"We've isolated him," Lenox says. "Petra has brought most of his establishments under our umbrella, and we are in the process of talking with each sex worker to make sure they are happy in their position."

"What do you do with the ones who aren't?" I ask.

"They are free to leave with a small severance or a ticket home."

"That's not much of a choice."

Lenox frowns, there are new deeper grooves around his mouth—this is taking a toll on him. "I agree. But all we can offer them is their freedom. We cannot change their history. Many of them were sold by their families; those that were kidnapped want to go home. The ones sold... they are—" He shakes his head. "Most of them cannot imagine any other kind of life. That is something I'd like to change. But I don't know how."

Silence descends on all of us. We can fight with our fists, with weapons, but we can't climb inside the minds of traumatized victims and convince them that their lives are worth living.

"What about offering them training?" Merl asks. "Here. What if we could turn them into fighters?"

Lenox sits forward. "That's interesting."

"They could become instructors or operatives." Merl goes on. "If nothing else, we could instill some confidence in them."

"I'm not sure it's so simple," Anita says. "They need therapy. What they've been through isn't something you can just get over. Not without help."

"Fighting helps," I say.

Anita gives a small smile. "If we want to do this, we need to bring in some professional mental health help."

"Agreed," Merl says.

Dan turns to another monitor on his desk and starts typing. "Let me see who I can find in our membership."

"Very good," Lenox says, his voice hopeful.

Our meeting done, Mulberry and I get into our separate queen-sized beds. Frank jumps up on his, and Blue on mine. Nila sleeps with her back against the door.

Despite my exhaustion, I can't sleep. Lying awake, I stare at the ceiling, my brain a mouse on a wheel.

Can we really help those women by training them?

Will Robert tell me the truth?

Is he behind this shooting?

Will he help me?

Does he still want me?

Or will he try to kill me?

I slip into dreams of shadows and mist—I'm being hunted but can't see the beast on my heels. I run, my heart hammering, feet sucking into mud. I fall forward, and the monster jumps on my back, pushing me into the ground, sinking me deep into the earth...I can't breathe.

"Sydney!" Mulberry is shaking my shoulders. I gasp for air. His eyes are glittering in the dark hotel room. "It's just a dream," he says, his voice quieter.

A sob escapes, and his arms come around me, hard and strong. "You're safe," he promises. "You're safe."

But I'm not. And I never will be.

We can't win this war. It will never end. Justice is always under assault. Evil is a many-headed beast, and when you cut off one, another grows in its place. All we can do is keep fighting.

I wrap my arms around Mulberry and bury my face against his neck.

Death is inevitable.

But so is new life.

CHAPTER TWENTY-THREE

Robert

The piano, folded up on itself like an accordion, is hunkered in a corner of what used to be my living room. I lay my hand on the buckled wood, warm from the sun streaming in through the open ceiling, and a sigh slips free.

My mother taught me to play on this instrument. I close my eyes and hear her voice, gentle and loving, as she guides me through the scales.

Pressure behind my eyes pulses. I rest my head in my hands but do not cry.

"Robert?"

My head snaps up at her voice. Sydney Rye stands at the top of the steps leading down into the living room, Blue by her side. She wears rubber boots and jeans—the uniform of those filtering through the rubble of their lives.

But Sydney left nothing here. She came to my house with just her dogs and she took them away, too. Her memories are not crushed, waterlogged, or destroyed. She owns nothing so has nothing to lose... except for the ones she loves.

I owned many objects and loved no one for so long. And for good reason.

Love crushes you as easily as a storm surge crumples a piano. I learned that lesson in the jungle, and I held onto it for the decades that followed, but somehow Sydney Rye pried it from my grip, leaving me exposed and in danger.

"Are you okay?" She steps down into the room, picking her way through the piles of debris.

"What are you doing here?" I ask.

"I wanted to see it...and you." She pauses in her trek to me and surveys the damage. "I'm so sorry."

"Just objects," I say dismissively. "Easily replaced." She returns her attention to me. She knows I'm lying. "I see you extracted yourself from the basement of the hospital."

"Yes, with the help of some witches." She smiles.

"And you're in Miami now to gawk at the ruination."

"That's not the only reason." She frowns at my unkind words. She's forgotten how cruel I am. How strong. *Because she makes me weak.*

"The shooting," I suggest.

"You know it had nothing to do with Joyful Justice. We wouldn't just hand a powerful weapon over to a distressed woman."

"I know," I say, looking back at the piano.

My mother died before I truly became a man. She passed while I was stuck in the jungle—a prisoner in love with his captor. *A cliché.*

Sydney's hand touches my arm, and I jump, not realizing she'd come so close. "You sure you're all right?" she asks.

"You care?" I sneer.

Her mouth firms into a line of discontent. "Of course I do. We're friends."

I bark out a laugh. "We most certainly are not."

Her hand drops from me, and I miss its warmth. I step away, creating more distance between us. "It's not safe for Blue here." I gesture to the destruction. "There are all sorts of things that could cut his paws."

"I know." Sydney is watching me, her silver eyes glinting in the sunlight. "That's why he's wearing booties." Blue stands next to her—his paws covered in rubber slippers that tighten at his ankles. "You're acting really weird," Sydney says.

I take a deep breath and look out to the bay, calm and sparkling but thick with debris. "I'm a father," I confess.

"What?"

"That's who was trying to kill us...me. My son."

I blink against the glare coming off the water and see spots in my vision.

"You have a son?"

I nod, once. It doesn't feel real. Nothing that happened on that ship feels real. But there is no denying the resemblance, the age...he is mine.

"Who's the mother?" Sydney asks.

"A woman I loved..." I turn to Sydney. She is standing next to the ruined piano, a fading bruise around her left eye and a healing cut on her cheekbone. "I thought she died." Clearing my throat, I go on. "I believed her death was my fault."

"But she's not dead?" Sydney says. I nod. "And she is the mother of your...son?" I nod again. "Who has been trying to kill you."

"That sums it up."

"But why?"

"Ah." I look down at the floor. There is a doll, one eye missing, the other open wide. *Where did it come from?* "He is angry—his mother recently told him about me. And he, understandably, is upset that I abandoned her to die."

"You met him?" I nod, the movement mechanical. "And is he still trying to kill you?"

I shake my head. "I promised to fight for him and his mother. To help destroy Joyful Justice, which is trying to change their way of doing...business."

"Fatherhood has apparently made you more honest."

I look over at her, at the only other woman I've ever loved. *I'm a fool.* It's a shocking realization. To go so long believing that I could control myself, my environment, and those around me. It was all a lie. A lie I told myself—a comfort, just as the ruined doll at my feet must have been to some child. My will protected me as well as the doll protected its charge: not at all.

Sydney approaches, her eyes sympathetic. She places a hand on my bicep then steps closer and gives me a hug. I stand there like a statue, arms tight to my sides, her warmth pressed against me. "It's going to be okay," she says.

I don't respond. She feels like a comfort. Like if I did wrap my arms around her and confess all—that I love her, that I want her and her baby, that I'd die for her. If I told her all that and more—if I let the truth out into the air—it would save me. *More lies.*

I've given her the power to destroy me, just like this storm ruined my home. If I tell her the truth and she does not feel the same...I know she does not feel the same. I don't have to tell her anything to know that she does not love me. Not like I love her.

In time, I may change her mind. With patience and perseverance, I once believed that she would be mine, as I am hers.

But now it feels as if time has taken a distorted turn and that there isn't any left.

My son gave me an ultimatum: help destroy Joyful Justice, protect him and his mother, or die.

He is arrogant and young—foolish with youth and pride. As I was before they took me into the jungle and showed me how vulnerable, how human, I am. The real ultimatum was to help him or kill him.

I will not murder my own flesh and blood.

"Robert?" Sydney's voice interrupts my thoughts and brings me back to the present.

"Yes?" I look down at her, my arms still by my sides even as she continues to hold me around the waist. She is chewing on her lip. It makes me want to kiss her. I must rebuild my defenses. Brick by brick, Sydney Rye has exposed me. Exposed the soft, tender part of me.

She will suffer for it.

Did I not warn her? For all that she has accomplished and suffered, is she so foolish not to recognize what happens when you play with a man like me?

Sydney is strong. But I am stronger. She has weakened me. But I will come back.

And she will pay.

Yes. She will.

CHAPTER TWENTY-FOUR

Sydney

"Robert wouldn't tell me anything useful—well, that's not totally true." Anita watches me with patient eyes. "He admitted that there is someone trying to destroy Joyful Justice, and that he knows who it is. But he won't tell me any more than that."

She picks up her mug and finishes the final sip. "Let's take a walk," she stands, leaving cash to pay the bill. We leave the hotel lobby, entering the garden. A plane rumbles above us; the airport is only a few miles away.

I crane my neck to watch its path, wondering for a moment about the lives it contains. Where are they going?

"We know there is a cabal of organizations working to destroy us," Anita's voice pulls me back to the garden, and I turn to look at her. Her long, dark hair is up in a high ponytail. Her short kurta is a vibrant pink, and her jeans a light wash. "Our enemies are wide ranging—Joyful Justice fights for justice around the globe. And now these criminal organizations are coming together to defeat us."

"Obviously, killing Ian's brothers and crippling his sex trafficking enterprise has not discouraged the rest of the group from coming after us—they've just changed tactics," I say.

"Yes, this is smarter. Ian and his brothers tried to turn our own people against us using blackmail—which may hurt us but could never destroy us. Trying to attack us physically makes as much sense as trying to kill a religion—you can't murder beliefs. But you can taint prophets." She gives me a small smile.

"Joyful Justice isn't a religion." I point out, my words forceful. It's important to me that our members not treat the organization as gospel —they need to question us, guide us. The only way Joyful Justice works is if its grassroots are strong.

"No," Anita agrees, pausing in front of a fountain. The nude female figure is missing an arm. Probably lost during the storm. This hotel suffered minimal damage, being of new construction and far from the ocean. "We are not a religion, but we are susceptible to the same folly. And attacks. If people believe that we are dangerous, foolish, not to be trusted, they won't come to us for help. And law enforcement agencies will be more interested in taking us down."

"They should be after the people who are after us." I sound like a petulant child. *I should be allowed to go to bed whenever I want and eat ice cream all the time.*

Anita reaches out and squeezes my shoulder. "Of course. But we also have a job to do. We must protect ourselves. Defend our honor, as it were."

"And kill the fuckers who are trying to destroy us."

Her hand drops from me, and she shrugs. "First, let's deal with this mess."

"Have you had any luck finding the 'contact' who gave the shooter her weapon?"

"I'm running down some leads. I've got a friend, a reporter for the Miami Herald. He's good at what he does. He has copies of the email messages between the two—probably got them from the shooter's defense lawyer. We are meeting later. He's agreed to show them to me before going public with them."

"That's good of him."

"Yes. Like I said, he's a friend." She turns and continues down the path. It winds between tropical foliage before opening up to a view of the airport.

"Let me know what I can do to help, since Robert's been a dead end."

Anita nods. "Do you think it's worth speaking to him again?"

I shake my head, chewing on my lip. *He hates me.* I saw it in his eyes. I hurt him.

"What?" Anita asks.

I meet her gaze. "I think a part of me loved...loves him."

She raises both brows. "I'm not shocked to hear that but still surprised. What about Mulberry?"

I let out a weary sigh that turns into a laugh. "I don't know. I mean, I know I love him. And have for a long time. But I feel like Robert is right, that we are alike in a lot of ways."

"You two have a connection."

"Yes."

Anita gestures to a bench facing the airport, and we sit. "I know you want to help deal with this present crisis and then face all the issues around your impending motherhood, and that's fine—as long as you realize there will be another crisis after this one."

We can't ever end this war.

"I know."

"When we met," Anita says, "you were running from your life." I look at her, but she's watching the planes taking off and landing—morning sun glinting off their metal bodies. "You couldn't avoid confronting injustice for long." She turns to me, her eyes serious and sympathetic. "You're like a magnet for it." She offers a soft smile.

"You're telling me. I'm terrified."

"Are you going to run away again?" Anita reaches out and takes my hand, lacing her fingers through mine. In the webbing of her thumb is a dark, circular scar—from a cigarette seared into her skin when her journalistic pursuits nearly cost her her life in India.

"Isn't it the safest thing to do?" I ask.

She sighs, her breath sweet, scented with cardamon and black tea. "I don't know." She gives my hand a squeeze. "I can't, you know? Get pregnant."

I raise my eyes to meet hers—warm brown ringed in dark charcoal. "I didn't know that. I'm sorry."

She gives me a sad half smile, but her eyes are dry. "Thank you. I've come to peace with it."

"Children don't really go with our lifestyle," I point out.

Her smile is full this time. "No." She shakes her head. "But I don't know anyone who is prepared for a baby. Not really. From what I understand, they change everything." She's grinning now, teasing me.

"Right," I agree. "But if you're a normal person, one with a regular job that doesn't involve killing people or being hunted down by criminals, then you're in a little better position to take on the challenge." By the time I finish the sentence my voice has gone mousy and terribly pathetic.

Anita bumps her shoulder against mine. "You don't think we can keep you safe?"

"I don't want to be kept safe. I want to *be* safe."

Anita laughs at my dreams. "That's not a thing, Sydney. Even if you were this imaginary normal person with their normal job and their normal commute, danger is everywhere...and nowhere. Car accidents, cancer, random acts of violence. You know how easy it is to die."

"Are you trying to make me feel better? Because it's not working..."

"No," Anita shakes her head. "I'm trying to make you see that you're not the only woman to fear for her safety while pregnant. To want a perfect life for their child."

"But it's not possible."

"It's never possible." She sounds exasperated. "I'm sure your mother wanted to keep you safe. To make sure nothing bad ever happened to you. But that couldn't prevent your father's illness. Your own instincts to help others no matter the cost—"

I cut her off. "This is a price I'm not willing to pay." I'm cradling my belly. "I can't risk..." I can't even say it without tearing up.

"I know." Anita puts her other hand on top of our laced fingers. She looks out to the sky—robin's egg blue criss-crossed with aircraft trails. "We will do everything we can to keep you safe."

"But," I swallow the lump in my throat. "Isn't it possible, we'd be safer away from…all of this? A new name, a new life…?"

Anita shrugs. "You've tried that before. I don't know the future. But you'll need help, Sydney. And you've got people who care about you, love you even." Anita looks over at me. "I think you should stay. I think you owe it to yourself and your baby to be surrounded by the family you've created."

"Where could I go, anyway?" Hiding from Dan seems impossible.

"I'd help you."

My brows raise. "But you just said…"

Anita's brow contracts into a stern frown. "I wouldn't force you to take my advice, Sydney." Her eyes shine with emotion. "You saved me in more ways than one." The memory of Anita strangling her captor with the chain linking her bound wrists flashes across my vision.

"You saved yourself," I remind her quietly.

"I'll always help you in any way I can. And I'm not the only one. Which is why I think you're safer with us than without."

"What about the fact that everyone I love dies?" I try to laugh, but it comes out all distorted and weird.

"I'm still here," Anita says. "So is Merl and Dan. Even Mulberry is still limping along." She smiles, teasing me even as I reveal my darkest, deepest, most painful fears. "Isn't it possible that people you loved have died, but it's not because of you? It's life. It ends, Sydney. For all of us."

"You're just a ray of sunshine."

Anita laughs, putting her arm around my shoulders and pulling me close. "I try."

We sit like that for a long time, watching the planes taking off and landing.

"Do you think this incident could really hurt Joyful Justice?" I ask. "Will people really think Joyful Justice would be so irresponsible and stupid?"

Anita sighs. "Those who already hate us will believe, and those who love us won't. The people in the middle may barely take notice."

"So why bother?" I ask. "Why risk yourself coming all this way?"

Anita sits back and looks at me, her head cocked. "I had to defend us."

I nod, knowing what she means.

Just because a battle can't be won doesn't mean it isn't worth fighting.

CHAPTER TWENTY-FIVE

Sydney

Hugh and Santiago's house is still standing. Rain and wind ripped off palm fronds and tore shingles from their roof, but there are no stains from receded flood waters. The destructive, toxic waters that picked up homes in other neighborhoods, swirling them around—moving refrigerators and couches as easily as wind blows dust—did not reach this street.

I pull the Jeep into their circular driveway and spot Santiago in the yard, shirtless and raking up branches.

He mops at his brows with the sweatband at his wrist and squints as I climb out of the rental. Recognizing me, Santiago grins, his smile lighting up the whole block.

He drops his rake, and in a few long strides, picks me up and spins me around. I laugh and hug him back—he's sweaty and smells of soil and plants.

"You are a sight for sore eyes," he says, putting me down. "Hugh will be so happy to see you."

Blue gives a bark and wags his tail, excited to see Santiago as well. I left Nila and Frank back at the hotel with Mulberry.

"Sorry I didn't check in earlier," I say as Santiago bends down to give Blue a good petting.

"Oh, honey, we've all been busy." He smiles up at me.

"I lost my phone," I shrug.

Santiago raises one brow. "Uh-huh."

Hugh and Santiago know who I am, they know what I do, and are smart enough not to ask questions that, if answered honestly, could threaten their safety.

"Sydney!"

Santiago and I both turn to the house—Hugh stands on the front steps. It's a one-story bungalow built in the twenties and has that era's romance and charm.

Hugh, wearing jean shorts and a T-shirt streaked with dirt, gives me a hug almost as enthusiastic as his husband's. We grin at each other. "Good to see you," I say.

"Can you believe this?" Hugh asks, releasing me so he can greet Blue.

"Your neighborhood survived well," I say. The other homes that line the street seem to have fared about the same as Hugh and Santiago's. Whirring generators can be heard up and down the block—people here were prepared.

"It's one reason I said we should buy in this neighborhood," Santiago says, his voice sad, as if he wished he hadn't been right.

"How's the restaurant?" I ask. Hugh and Santiago own *James*, one of the most beloved restaurants in Miami, and it sits on much lower ground. Named after my brother, it took me a long time to get comfortable going there, but it's become one of my favorite places in the city.

Santiago shakes his head, but it's Hugh who answers me. "We can rebuild."

"I'm sorry." And I am. They put so much work into that space, filled it with love and hospitality. It was more than a restaurant.

"Thanks," Hugh puts his arm around my shoulder and pulls me close. "But we are both healthy. And we have our home. Really, we're the lucky ones." I lean into him, taking a deep breath and enjoying his gratitude. "Robert's house must be…"

"It's fucked," I say, bluntly.

Santiago frowns. "I'm sorry, honey."

I shrug. "Hey, we are all healthy, like Hugh said. It's just stuff." Robert's strange mood comes back to me. *He's a father.* That would be enough to throw anyone off. But Robert's eyes seemed different. He looked at me differently—like a wolf watches a bunny before the kill.

I am no bunny.

"Come inside," Hugh says, pulling me forward and out of my thoughts. "Let's catch up."

We eat peanut butter sandwiches and drink bottled water. "Something is going on with you?" Santiago says, his eyes narrowed, as I lick the last of the peanut butter from my fingers.

Hugh cocks his head. "Yeah...but I can't put my finger on it."

"She ate that sandwich too fast," Santiago says.

"And she didn't ask for a beer," Hugh continues.

"Do her boobs look bigger?" Santiago drops his gaze to my chest.

"Hey!"

"They do," Hugh nods.

"She's pregnant!" Santiago yells, pointing at me.

A flush ignites at his accusation. "She is!" Hugh agrees, watching the color infuse my cheeks. "Oh my God!"

"Who is the father?" Santiago asks.

"Santiago," Hugh hisses, putting a hand on his husband's shoulder.

"What?" Santiago can't seem to imagine why that question is awkward, which makes me laugh.

"Mulberry," I admit.

"But when?" Santiago's brow furrows. "When did you see him?"

"Right before your wedding," I pick at crumbs on the table, so I don't have to meet their eyes.

"Two months ago, at Robert's house?" Santiago says. "How is Robert taking it?"

"We've never been romantically involved." I sound defensive.

"If you say so," Santiago smiles.

Hugh raises his brows at his husband in a *shut up* message.

"It's okay," I sigh. "You're right, it's such a mess." I have an urge to lay my head on the table.

"Honey." Hugh reaches out and covers my hand with his, offering me a warm, accepting smile. "I'm so happy for you. This is wonderful."

"You sound like my mother."

Hugh cocks his head. "Words I thought I'd never hear." My mother and Hugh don't get along—she refused to acknowledge his relationship with my brother, acted as if he didn't deserve to mourn him, didn't deserve to love him. A memory of her face, pinched with anger, telling me that James's sins barred him from heaven flashes across my mind and exhaustion settles more firmly onto my shoulders.

"Sorry," I say.

"I know she's changed," Hugh says. "I'm glad your mom is happy for you."

"When are you due?" Santiago asks.

"I'm not sure."

"Oh, we can figure it out." Santiago pulls out his phone. "When did you and Mulberry..." He clears his throat and waggles his eyebrows.

"Personal much?" I joke. Santiago blows me a kiss, and I tell him.

Santiago plugs it into his phone and then announces the date. My eyes jump to Hugh—he's staring at me, too.

"What?"

"That's James's birthday," Hugh answers, keeping his eyes on me.

"That's...weird," I say. "Right, that's just bizarre. Am I crazy?"

"Oh for sure you're nuts," Santiago says with a laugh. "But you're right, that is strange." My hand covers my stomach. "Have you read *Many Lives, Many Masters*?" I shake my head. "It's wild, all about past lives. How we travel in soul pods. Maybe James is coming back."

I cringe at the words. *There is no coming back.*

The alarm on their oven dings, and Santiago jumps up, pulling two trays of food from the oven. The scent of lemon chicken reaches me, and my stomach growls. "Someone's still hungry," Santiago says as he pulls another two trays from their second oven.

"Why do you have so much food?" I ask.

"We are taking it over to a local shelter. So many people lost their homes. The least we can do is feed them."

"That's so nice of you."

Hugh shakes it off. "It was all food from the restaurant. What should we do? Let it sit in our freezer when there are hungry people who've lost everything?"

"Let me help you." I push back my chair to stand. I'm suddenly wobbly on my feet, and Hugh notices immediately.

"You need to rest," he decrees. "Take a nap. You're pregnant."

Santiago spoons a few pieces of chicken onto a plate and leaves it on the counter. "Eat that before or after your rest. Preggers's choice," he says with a grin.

"I'm fine." They both ignore me. "Really," I press. Blue comes out from under the table and looks at me like he agrees with Hugh and Santiago. *Traitor.*

"You know where the guest room is." Santiago finishes packing up the food and carries it toward the door.

"We'll see you in a bit." Hugh stops to kiss my forehead and ruffle Blue's ears, before following his husband out.

Bastards.

The guest room windows are open, and I drift to sleep on a soft breeze. When I wake the sun is below the horizon and the sky a deep blue. I reach for my new phone and discover that it's almost nine.

I only have one number memorized and I dial it, sitting on the edge of the bed while I listen to it ring. Robert doesn't pick up. That's not like him. Not like him at all.

He's acting very strange.

Blue follows me out to the kitchen. I write a quick note to Hugh and Santiago while eating the plate of food they left me. I give Blue some kibble and then head out to my SUV.

Getting back to Star Island takes an hour, and the sky is dark by the time I get there. Stars twinkle above—clearer than I've ever seen them in the city. With so much of the metropolis without power, the night sky shines down on the ruins.

A guard I recognize sits in a chair at the entrance to Star Island—a shotgun across his lap. He stands when my headlights hit him. "Harry," I say, rolling down my window.

"Sydney," he says with a smile. "What are you doing here so late?"

"Forgot something when I was here earlier."

He shakes his head, gesturing to the destruction around us. "So sad."

"It is. How is your family?"

His lips firm. "We survived. And will rebuild."

"Good to hear, Harry."

"José is still there." Harry points with his chin onto the island.

"Great, I look forward to seeing him. Robert left, though?"

"Right when I came on shift."

I ignore the disappointment that tries to weigh me down. My tires bump over debris as I pull up to Robert's house. The garden is totally denuded, exposing the single-story building.

I pick my way through the wreckage and go in the open front door. Blue taps my hip as we enter. *Something is off.*

I turn on my flashlight and rake the beam over the entryway—soggy bits and pieces of Robert's house, and those of his neighbors, lay in drifts.

"Hello!" I call out.

A mumbled reply comes from the living room. I move cautiously toward the sound, my body tense. Blue trots ahead of me and gives a loud bark.

José, bound and gagged lies on the ground—his feet and hands held by zip ties and attached to each other with a third. He squints against the flashlight beam when it hits his face.

Blue gets to him first.

I pull the knife from my ankle holster and approach slowly, keeping my senses alert. But from Blue's reaction, I'm assured we are alone.

I cut the zip tie connecting José's wrists and ankles, and he groans through his gag as his legs flop to the ground. I release his hands and then his feet. José sits up and works on the duct tape covering his lips.

His eyes are wide with fear, and he is pulling at the tape with desperation. That's when I notice the package taped to his chest—a clear plastic bag with a piece of paper in it.

José follows my gaze and pulls it free, holding it out to me. When I take it, he starts on the duct tape again.

Printed in black ink, the note reads: *José will die in twenty four hours if you can't get him the antidote. Come to the refugee center at sunrise if you want him to survive.*

"Did they leave this for Robert?" I ask.

José shrugs, taking the paper from me. His face pales, and his eyes roll. I catch him as he tips to the side. José tries to take in a deep breath, the tape suctioning to his open mouth. "Breath through your nose," I remind him. "Put your head between your knees." I help him get his head down.

A puncture wound on the side of his neck catches my attention.

I rub José's back. "Stay here," I say. "I've got to get something from my car." José nods but does not lift his head. "Blue, stay with him."

I go back to the SUV and get the jar of coconut oil I use as a moisturizer out of my bag. José is sitting where I left him when I come back, his breath even. "Oil helps with the tape," I tell him.

I work the oil on the edge of tape where it binds to his skin and pull slowly, applying more oil as I go. It takes almost twenty minutes to free his lips, and the tape leaves a red swath of irritated skin in its wake.

"Water." José's voice comes out cracked and dry.

"Hold on, I have some in the car."

Leaving Blue with José again, I get a gallon of water from the trunk. He drinks deeply and winces when he wipes a sleeve over his wet lips.

"It will hurt for a while," I say.

"What does that note mean?" he asks.

"You know more than me. What happened?"

"I'm not sure." José takes another sip of water. "I met Mr. Maxim here. We were going over what was lost and discussing the rebuild. He left me here, and the last thing I remember is writing a note about..." José looks around and, spotting a leather notebook, grabs it and pulls it close. "The gun safe."

"What about it?"

"It is still in place," José says, looking at his notes. "But the flood water damaged it, so Mr. Maxim wanted us to order another." He glances at me.

"Was there anything in it?"

José shrugs. "I don't thinks so. Mr. Maxim didn't open it. I just was putting down the dimensions."

"I'll check the safe." Standing, I head toward Robert's bedroom—the wall of glass is gone, opening the room to the elements. The four-poster bed is in pieces and scattered around the room. I can't see the floor for all the sand and crap on top of it. I make my way to the closet, which no longer has a door.

Taller than me, and four feet wide, the safe is set into the wall, which was once painted an elegant gray and is now stained a muddy brown to my shoulder height. Putting in the code, I open the heavy door.

Inside is damp, but the top shelf remained dry. On it are two plastic cases I recognize as the cases for Robert's dart guns. He designed them last year. They can hold six cartridges and deliver them with impeccable accuracy at short distances. He's still working on a sniper version, but the weight of the cartridge and the liquid inside makes it more difficult. I pull the plastic cases out and open them. There they are, nestled in their foam. Extra cartridges next to them. None are missing.

I take the two cases with me and return to José.

"So, Robert left, and then you just…"

"Don't remember. I should call Mr. Maxim."

"Yes," I agree.

He tries Robert, but there is no answer. José leaves a message, reading the note. "It must be for him," José says to me. "The same people who tried to kill you in Cartagena, right?"

"I don't know."

There are tears in José's eyes. "Will I?"

"No," I grab his hand. "I'll go if we can't get ahold of Robert. Don't worry. We will get you that antidote."

"Should I go to the police, or a hospital?"

"The police are a bad idea—they will want to stake out the meeting point and could scare off whoever has the antidote. A hospital might help, but they'd call the police. Let me make some calls and see if there are any doctors in town that we can trust to be discreet. Where are you staying?"

"With friends," he says.

"Let me drive you there. I'll make some calls and figure something out. And we will probably get ahold of Robert soon. He's never out of touch long."

"Right," José nods.

I help him up and we get back to my SUV. Leaving José's scooter at the house, I give him a ride to where he is staying. Robert still hasn't called by the time I've dropped him off but I get ahold of Dan, who starts the hunt for a doctor.

I call Anita as I drive back toward our hotel. "I need your help," I say.

"What's going on?"

"We need to go to the refugee center at dawn tomorrow." I lay out what happened briefly.

"Let me make some calls."

Next I try Robert again. He's still not picking up. Unease settles in my stomach as I navigate to the hotel. *Where is he?*

CHAPTER TWENTY-SIX

Robert

There are lies we tell ourselves and by telling them we make them truth.

Natalia joins me on the bench, sitting close enough that if I move but a bare inch, our thighs will touch. "I love this spot," she says, her accented voice whispering over my skin.

Being showered and in clean clothing, sitting on her deck, feels a whole lot better than being dirty and climbing around in the destruction of my home. "Will you rebuild?" she asks about my house.

"If I live." I turn and smile at her.

She shakes her head. "Come now, Robert. I know that Fernando is…"

"Young." I finish for her.

"Yes," she nods. "And mouthy." Natalia gives a small shrug. "You used to be mouthy."

"I learned the hard way how to hide my true intentions." There is bitterness in my voice, but I do not regret the lessons that molded me.

"I think it is the only way to learn," Natalia looks up at me. Is there a plea in her gaze? She knows I will not bend to my son as easily as he thinks. She's told him as much…is she now hoping that I can teach him without killing him?

It's a fine line.

"I did the best I could." Natalia turns to the sea again. "He is a good man, really," she smiles. "He reminds me of you—your confidence, intelligence, cunning. All the things I loved about you once."

"Once?" I say. "I don't think I ever stopped loving you." She doesn't turn to look at me but her jaw clenches. I reach out and take her hand from where it rests in her lap and pull it to my chest. "Why, Natalia? Why didn't you tell me?"

When she meets my gaze, there is fire in her eyes. "You left me to die."

"I thought you were dead." My voice is quiet, her hand still held to my heart.

"You used me to escape…"

"You were holding me prisoner."

She laughs. "My reasons are clear."

"Not to me."

She pulls her hand free and stands. "I would have been beholden to you, Robert. You would have felt obliged to care for me, to absorb me into your world and to make it impossible for me to forge my own path in life." Her eyes hold mine. "You are not a partner Robert, you are a predator."

I stay seated, allowing her to feel taller than me—bigger. Stronger. "So instead you hid from me for the last two-and-a-half decades. Because this wasn't just avoidance, Natalia." I wave at the ship. "Our paths must have crossed countless times. You hid from me. You hid Fernando from me."

"Yes," she says it simply. "I did not wish for you to control me."

I laugh, because it's the same thing Sydney says to me. Will I ever tire of trying to control women who do not wish to be? What stroke of fate will teach me that lesson? Because obviously words are not enough.

"Why are you laughing?" Her voice is tight.

"Sorry," I wave a hand. "I am. Truly sorry." The mirth dies from my voice. "If I'd known you were alive, I would have come back for you."

"No, you wouldn't have."

I meet her eyes, so dark and angry. "You doubt how I felt?"

She sneers. "You do not know what love is."

"I loved you." I link my fingers in my lap, holding them steady. "The pain of losing you changed me." I clear my throat. "In many ways, it made me who I am." I hold her gaze. "Losing you broke a part of me. And the sharp edges left behind allowed me to find the success I so desired."

"Then thank me for hiding. If I'd revealed myself, what would have become of you?" There is disdain in her voice.

"Who knows what would have become of us—who knows how my ambitions in life might have changed?"

Natalia shakes her head. "You wouldn't have changed."

"I did. We all do." I hold her eyes with mine, refusing to be the one who breaks the connection. I won't turn my back on her again.

I won't make the same mistake twice.

Natalia turns away, walking to the edge of the deck and holding the rail.

"How do you know Sydney Rye will go back to your house?" Natalia changes the subject.

I stay seated on the bench, watching Natalia's hair blow in the wind. "I just do." She can't stay away from me as much as I can't stay away from her. That's why my plan to make her mine would have worked—and why this one will too.

"You're so sure of yourself?" Natalia looks over her shoulder at me. "Whatever broke in you has served you well."

I nod, agreeing again that I have fared well. That I have taken everything I wanted.

And that's not going to change.

I smile at Natalia. "Don't worry," I say, my voice a deep and comforting baritone. "Everything will work out just fine."

She doesn't smile back, just raises one brow. "Yes," she agrees. "It will."

My escape that day must have broken something in her, too. "How did you survive?" I ask.

She does smile now. "I always had an escape plan, Robert. You should have trusted me." Before I can ask any more details, the door opens and Fernando steps onto the deck. Natalia's eyes light when they land on him. *That is true love.*

"Mother, Seraphina is looking for you."

"Thank you." She places a kiss on Fernando's cheek before stepping inside...leaving me alone with my son.

I wait in silence—anger wafts off him, as pungent as the briny sea air. "My mother has forgiven you," he says.

I glance at him. "Has she?" I stay seated, letting him be taller... believe he is bigger, stronger, wiser.

"She's had my entire life time. I just learned you lived a few months ago." His accent is not as strong as Natalia's, and it's different. Her voice holds the remnants of a childhood in the mountains, his the sophisticated lilt of an international education. *He's spoiled.*

"And I've known of your existence for a day."

His expression does not soften. "That's no excuse."

A smile slips across my lips. "You want me dead?"

Fernando shifts his weight from one foot to the other. A tell. But of what? His eyes meet mine, clashing blue and green. Anger. "I wanted you scared."

He's still a child.

I raise one brow. "You did not succeed." There will be no trophies for trying hard in this relationship.

Fernando takes a step toward me and stops short. I don't flinch. In a physical fight we are well matched—he has the strength and speed of youth, but I the skill and mental fortitude of experience. "I don't want to fight you," I say. "I think we can work together. Amy and Josh came to me some time ago asking for help with destroying Joyful Justice."

"You refused them."

"Yes. Like I said"—I wave a hand toward him—"I only just learned that you existed. I loved your mother very much."

His face twists into a sneer. "You left her to die in the jungle."

"She let me rot in a cage." I shrug. "There is a lot that a cage can teach you. My point is that I do not want to be your enemy, Fernando." I pause, as if gathering my thoughts. "I'd like us to begin to build a relationship." A flicker in his eyes, just the hint of hope hiding behind those glittering jewels. "Let me tell you my plan, and then you can decide."

He nods, and comes closer.

Yes, son, step into the trap…learn from the cage.

EK

Mulberry

Frank lies on his side, front legs crossed, snoring like a steam engine at the foot of the bed. Nila, curled into a ball, rests with her back against the door, a low growl emanating from her chest every time someone passes by our hotel room.

Sydney left this morning and hasn't returned. She did text that she planned to stop by Hugh and Santiago's house—I'd like to see them too, but she didn't invite me, and I'm desperately trying to follow Merl's advice and not push.

Anita is out meeting with her press contacts, trying to change the narrative that Joyful Justice provided the means and inspiration for a mass shooting where innocent people died. I've got the TV on, flicking through the channels, doing fuck all about jack shit. The new story of my freaking life.

Nila stands up but doesn't growl. Sydney must be back. I'll wait for her to knock. Maybe she's just headed into the adjoining room to take a shower, leaving me as her dog sitter until she's ready—a knock at the door interrupts that bitter train of thought.

Nila gives a low woof of greeting and turns to look at me. *What is taking you so long?* Even dogs are judging me now, great.

Frank wakes up as I stand. He rolls over and flops onto the floor in a tangle of long legs and giant paws. Righting himself, Frank barks as if someone pushed him off the bed. "You did that to yourself," I tell him as I open the door.

"Who did what to themselves?" Sydney asks, walking in with Blue by her side. She's carrying two plastic gun cases.

"Frank is an idiot."

She grins. "I love that about him."

Nila and Frank both greet Sydney and Blue with unabashed enthusiasm. No one has ever been that excited to see me in my life.

My heart gives a quick thud—my child will be. Memories of meeting my father at the door when he got home from work flood my mind. His strong arms lifting me up, the scent of cigarettes and his cologne engulfing me...how my heart burst with love for him. I *needed* him.

"Thanks for watching them," Sydney says.

I blink away the memories, the scent of my dad somehow lingering as I bring Sydney into focus. "Sure, they're easy. How did it go?"

Sydney lets out a weary sigh. "Not great." She sits on the bed, and Nila and Frank each lean against a leg. Blue pushes his head against my hand, and I rub his ears.

"Did you find Robert at his house?"

"Yes, but he didn't tell me anything about the shooting."

"What about the yacht?"

Sydney looks down at Frank. "Robert knows something, but he's not sharing." I hide a smug smile. She was wrong about him—he wouldn't give her information like she'd hoped. "So I went to Hugh and Santiago's. They're doing well." Sydney glances at me and smiles.

"That's good news."

"I rested at their place for a while and tried calling Robert but he didn't pick up, which is strange."

"Is it?"

She drops her gaze again. "In the past he's always answered my calls. Anyway, I went back to his house, and José was there."

"Who's José?"

"Robert's chef—he runs the house."

"That's nice." I can't keep the sarcasm out of my voice.

Sydney stands and paces to the window. "Not so nice for José. He was tied up with this note around his neck." She reaches into the back pocket of her jeans and pulls out a folded piece of paper, holding it out to me.

"This was meant for Robert?" I ask after reading it.

"I'd guess so."

"Robert cares about his chef enough to risk his life for him?" I ask, meeting Sydney's gaze.

Her lips press together. "I don't think so. I don't know anyone Robert would risk his life for…"

"No," I agree, holding out the paper. "I don't think there is anybody he loves more than himself."

Sydney takes back the note with one hand, the other touching her stomach. She turns to the window. A plane takes off, headlights cutting through the night and wing lights flashing. She turns to me. "I'm going to go at dawn."

"Sydney," I take a step toward her. "The note isn't even for you. What makes you think they will give you the antidote?"

"I have to try." Her eyes narrow. "I'm not going to just let him die."

I shake my head. "Fine, let me go, then."

"Anita already agreed to go with me; she can get me into the refugee center with one of her press contacts. Can you take the dogs again?"

"At least let me come with you."

"We need someone here who knows where we went in case something goes wrong."

"We can tell Dan."

"I already spoke with him." Sydney pauses, not making eye contact. "I don't want to put anyone else at risk."

"Please," I step forward and take her hand. "Let me go instead of you." She won't meet my gaze, but she doesn't say no either. "Please," I say again.

She shakes her head. "I have to go."

"Why?" The question comes out angrier than I wanted it to. *Crap.*

Sydney's gray eyes flash with annoyance. "If Robert is there, I don't want you two trying to kill each other."

"Fine." I grit my teeth and step back, giving her space. "Whatever you want."

"Thank you. I'll bring Nila and Frank by before I go." She points to the gun cases on the bed. "Those are dart guns—I got them from

Robert's gun case. I'm not going to be able to take any weapons in with me, so I'll leave them with you."

"Fine," I say again, refusing to look at her as she and the dogs leave.

I flop back onto the bed and start flipping through stations, but that doesn't last long. Restless energy forces me onto my feet. I'm staring at the door that connects our rooms when my phone rings.

Robert Maxim wants to talk.

CHAPTER TWENTY-SEVEN

Sydney

The tall façade of the sports arena looms into the morning sky, part of its roof missing, the entire structure battered and slumped. For as bad as it looks, it smells worse—a rancid mix of urine, feces, and rot. A shelter of last resort.

Several camouflage-painted National Guard trucks with canvas bed covers are parked near the main entrance. Armed soldiers blanket the area. To maintain order inside or to keep the wrong people out?

"The shooting was the last straw," Anita says. "There had already been one murder, multiple sexual assaults, and a suicide. Not to mention the gang activity and drug dealing. They didn't have enough food or water. The city just wasn't prepared."

"How many people are sheltered here?" We cross the parking lot toward the fortified entrance. Anita had parked next to a black Mustang she recognized as her contact's ride, a good distance from the armed men. *Give them plenty of time to see us coming.*

"At the height there were 20,000—I think about half that sheltered during the storm, and afterwards they brought a lot of people who were rescued here. I'm sure you saw footage of people on their roofs." I nod.

"There were about 5,000 remaining when the shooting took place. Now there are only about a hundred left. They had already started moving people before the shooting but after…"

Barbed wire surrounds the trucks and entrance, creating a protected area. Following my gaze Anita answers my unasked question. "The National Guard is separating themselves from the citizens—a guardsman was murdered even before the mass shooting."

"Terrible." There is a heaviness in my chest. I left this city in a luxurious, private helicopter while people fought to survive in such desperate conditions. The world just might be totally fucked.

I grip the handle of Blue's harness as he moves forward. Dark sunglasses shield my eyes, and I've got on a baseball cap. I appear blind to the casual observer. This alias is my least favorite—pretending to be blind goes way past tasteless—but also the most effective.

A man in a baseball cap with a press pass around his neck steps away from where he is talking with one of the soldiers and comes to us.

"Good to see you." He smiles at Anita.

"Jack," Anita greets him. "This is my friend, Sarah." She introduces me. I put out a hand and Jack takes it, glancing down at Blue.

"This is my dog, Champion," I say.

"Nice to meet you. Anita tells me you are considering donating to our site. I'm happy to hear it." I'm pretending to be a wealthy heiress looking to support his investigative journalism website—specifically to cover the aftermath of the hurricane.

"Yes, the work you're doing is so important—independent journalism is crucial to the survival of our democracy."

Jack nods and then flushes—this happens a lot when I'm pretending to be Sarah. Jack assumes I can't see him nod and is embarrassed by his inability to clearly communicate. Humans use body language almost as much as dogs—our bodies communicate in ways that are more trustworthy than our words. Same as dogs can be trusted more than most people.

"I agree," Jack says, suddenly talking fast to make up for the nod. "The major networks left when most of the hurricane refugees cleared out. Those left behind are mostly poor, many of them undocumented.

I've also heard from a source, though it's not confirmed yet, that there are some men they didn't want to move—gang members ." His focus shifts behind me. "My photographer is here."

I don't turn, keeping up the facade of sightlessness. An African American man in jeans and a T-shirt, carrying a camera around his neck and a backpack, joins us. Jack introduces us and we move to the security checkpoint.

The guardsmen who checks my ID wears body armor. The AK-47 strapped to his chest is the same make as the one used in the shooting. A name tag over his heart reads Private Unrath. He chews gum, his stubble-lined jaw working hard. Unrath glances at my face with tired eyes but does not linger… or ask me to remove my sunglasses. He hands back my ID and waves me through.

As we step into the lobby of the sports arena the scent hits harder —it's revolting. Main doors leading to the arena floor and its surrounding stands are flanked by guardsmen but Jack points us upstairs. "We can get a good picture of the whole situation from the balcony."

We follow Jack to the top of the stands and look out onto a wide open space littered with trash about thirty feet below us. A small group of people—men, women and some children—crowd together at one side, separated from the guards by barbed wire. "The smell is so strong," I say.

"There is a canal on the other side of the building that flooded part of the first floor," Jack says. "The water, as I'm sure you've heard, is a toxic mix of bacteria, waste, chemicals and petroleum." He clears his throat and glances at Anita before returning his attention to me. "Would you like me to explain what we can see from up here?"

"Yes, thank you."

He describes the scene for the sightless Sarah and then continues. "The remaining refugees are supposed to be moved out today or tomorrow."

"Where will they be taken?" I ask.

"I'm still trying to get that information," Jack answers. "Have you heard of April Madden?" I cock my head, acting as if I'm not sure. "She's a big Her Prophet figure. Goes around the country preaching her gospel."

"Oh, right," I nod. "I've heard the name."

"She is coming today, wants to make a point that she does not condone violence—is bringing supplies and donations."

Fantastic, my mom is on her way. Just what this shit-show needs.

I step to the edge of the balcony, and keeping my head straight up so I don't appear to be looking, scan the crowd below. There is something invasive about being so close but above them—like we are observing animals in a zoo from a safe distance.

"So there is no way in or out except through the guardsmen and their barbed-wire enclosure?" I ask. "That sounds like a prison."

"There are other exits and entrances," Anita tells me. "The National Guardsmen are protecting themselves, not imprisoning the people here. The people are staying because they have nowhere else to go."

Louie, the photographer, is snapping pictures. He pauses to switch a lens. My eyes catch on a man below—at first I think it's Robert Maxim. But he's much younger...he smiles at me. I suck in an involuntary breath of surprise.

It must be Robert Maxim's son, Fernando.

"You okay?" Anita asks.

Fernando ducks his head, a hat covering his face. He begins to move through the crowd, stopping at a clump of young men to speak for a moment and then disappearing under the balcony beneath us.

"You said something about gangs?" I ask.

"Yes," Jack answers, but before he can elaborate, the clump of men Fernando spoke with begin to move toward the fencing at the main entrance, catching his attention. Tension spreads through the crowd like a gas. The powder keg is about to ignite, and Fernando threw the match.

Like father, like son.

Jack is looking down at the crowd, his face set in lines of concentration.

The men begin to pump their arms as they reach the fencing. "Be Brave!" they chant. Hearing the Joyful Justice slogan yelled with such anger and aggression sends a chill down my spine. They are trying to destroy everything we stand for…smart.

Families separate themselves from the chanting group, moving away; children cling to their parents, men wrap arms around women. "What's happening?" I ask as Louie switches to video on his camera.

The guardsmen line up along the fence—their shoulders tense, weapons held tight.

"You should get out of here," Jack says, turning to Anita.

I need to go after Fernando.

I pull on Blue's harness and he turns us around. Anita takes my elbow and we start toward the stairs as the chanting grows louder. "Follow me," I tell her when we enter the stairwell.

The sound of a gunshot freezes us both. Screams echo in the building. I start down the steps, taking them two at a time.

"Where are we going?" Anita asks as I burst out the emergency exit leading out the back of the building. The canal is straight ahead, almost a football field's length away. There are two figures arguing on the edge of it.

"I just saw Robert's son."

"He has a son? What!" I start to run—Blue pulling me forward. Anita moves with me, her stride long and even. "Sydney, what is going on?" Anita huffs.

I should have told her about Fernando… but it seemed personal, like I'd be betraying Robert somehow.

The two men look up—the resemblance is staggering and disturbing. Robert must have gotten my messages. He came for José. Or is this a trap?

My feet slow at the thought. Robert frowns deeply. Anita is breathing heavily next to me. "What the hell is going on?" she whispers.

"Not sure," I answer.

Robert says something to Fernando and then jogs the last 20 yards to us. He's wearing a suit—the jacket buttoned, as if he's walking into a business meeting. It probably costs more than the families we just left behind collectively have in the entire world. My teeth grit with the injustice of it.

"Take this," Robert says, stepping in front of me, as if blocking me from his son, and pushing a pill bottle into my hand. "It's the antidote."

I glance down at it. "Why can't you take it to him?" I ask, standing on my tiptoes to see behind him. A speedboat bobs in the canal's putrid waters.

"I have to go with him."

"He wants to kill you," I point out, calm as can be.

Robert touches my cheek with gentle fingers, drawing my attention. "I'm not so easy to kill. Now go." His voice is low and velvety soft.

"Sydney," Anita says. I glance at her. She points to a bus pulling up to the entrance we ran out of...it has a giant picture of my mother on the side and the words "Release the Wolf #IAmHer" printed in bright red ink.

Great. My mom's here.

EK

Mulberry

I shift my weight, the tarp under me crinkling as I turn my attention away from the video on my tablet back to the scope on the sniper rifle. *The one-legged assassin.*

I'm a decent marksman, but never considered myself an expert. I don't need to be for this task, though.

The national guard's radio communication crackles—they are not prepared for this kind of revolt from the refugees. And why should they be? They're supposed to be on the same side. But the soldiers are tired, angry, and scared.

Frank sits next to me, his nose in the air, sniffing the breeze coming through the broken window. Nila, her booties crunching over broken glass, circles the abandoned office space, checking for threats among the overturned desks and waterlogged carpeting.

Sun glints off the canal as I steady my crosshairs on Robert. This office building gives me the perfect view. Scanning the area, I see Fernando come out the back exit and start running toward his father.

"Be brave! Be brave!" The chanting of the crowd draws my focus back to the tablet. They are pushing up against the fence. A shot is fired; I'm not sure which side. "They are firing on us," a voice announces.

My stomach clenches.

"Hold your fire!" a command comes back.

There are only two cameras still working on the building—one on the outside, which is how I saw Sydney enter, and another in the interior. It's high up and angled toward the fencing, so I can see the skirmish line but not the rest of the cavernous space. There are bodies pressed up against the fence. I stare at the grainy feed, trying to make out if anyone is hurt.

"Fuck Joyful Justice," a guardsman says over the radio. More shots are fired, and the crowd at the fence surges back. I pray the guardsmen are firing into the air to scare them.

Sydney and Anita come out the same door as Fernando and start running across the pavement toward the canal. Sydney's hat is low over her face, and Blue runs next to her, Anita struggling to keep up. I lick my lips, fear tingling down my spine. I'm trusting Robert Maxim, that she won't be hurt. That this will help her in the end.

"We've got a bus incoming," a guardsmen says over the radio.

"Get them out of here!"

I glance at the tablet—April Madden's bus is getting waved away from the entrance. Instead of turning around to leave, they pull around to the back of the building. *Why aren't they leaving? What the hell is she doing? That woman is as bad as her daughter.*

Sydney is talking with Robert. He's giving her the pills. Telling her to go. I breathe slow and steady. I can't see Sydney's face so don't know how it's going. All I can hope is that Robert's plan works.

My gaze flicks back to the bus—April Madden climbs out, a tall woman in a long robe follows and grabs her arm. I recognize the outfit; she must be the witch Sydney told me about, Veronica.

I focus my scope on them to get a better look. It looks like Veronica is trying to convince April to get back on the bus. *Good luck, lady.*

April shakes her head vehemently and, turning to the bus, yells something. Women start flowing off, carrying supplies.

April pushes past Veronica and runs toward Sydney. The witch races with her. *Shit.*

I focus through the scope again—Robert and Sydney are watching her mother's approach.

"Another vehicle is incoming," I hear over the radio. "Unmarked bus."

A smaller bus pulls around back and men start to pour off of it, one holding a flag with the male symbol on it. *Fucking Incels.*

They rush toward the Her Prophet followers. The two sides crash into each other like waves caught in cross currents.

Robert made this happen, and I agreed to help.

EK

Sydney

The Her Prophet followers and Incels attack each other with the ferocity of fundamentalists. Inarticulate yelling and the solid thunks of hand to hand combat fills the air.

The men's rights activists carry clubs and tire irons. The Her profit followers, mostly women, have nothing but the supplies they brought the hurricane victims.

I stare at the melee, as my mother and Veronica run toward me— Mom in the lead, the younger woman following, her body a shield from the violence.

"Go," Robert's lips brush my cheek—the light kiss surprising but not unwelcome. *This feels like goodbye.* "I'll catch up with you. Get your mother somewhere safe."

"What did he want for this?" I hold up the bottle of pills.

"There's no time to explain now." His eyes are soft, the green warm and the blue bright—like looking up into a tree in spring, the new leaves dappled with sky.

The thwapping of helicopter blades cuts through the noise of the brawl.

"Oh shit," Anita says, drawing my attention. I follow her gaze to where a helicopter thunders between two of the skyscrapers. "That's media," she says. "CNN, looks like."

I can just make out the logo on the side of the helicopter.

"Sydney!" Mom grabs my arm and pulls me into a hug—the earthy scent of sage and a floral perfume breaking through the rot of the canal for a second. I break free of her. *There is no time for this.*

"Mom, what are you doing here?"

"Robert?" She's looking past me to where he stands—Fernando and his speed boat ten feet behind him in the canal.

"April," Robert's voice is low and calm, as if there isn't a massive brawl happening across the parking lot, or a media crew capturing it all. As if there are not people inside the stadium pretending to be members of Joyful Justice, causing a riot. As if this is a cocktail party and he's greeting my mother over canapés.

"I've got to run." Robert gives my elbow a light squeeze before he turns and walks to the canal's edge.

"We need to get out of here," Veronica says.

I nod, but don't move, holding onto the bottle of pills, watching Robert...sensing that something is very off.

Fernando climbs into the boat and starts the engine. Robert stops and turns back to me. He raises a hand to wave goodbye.

Blood explodes from Robert's chest and his eyes go wide as the echo of a gunshot ricochets off the surrounding buildings. He teeters for a moment on the canal's edge.

I lurch forward.

He falls back into the water—the dark, putrid liquid splashing up, slapping against the boat and spraying over the bank.

Robert disappears into its murky depths.

In three strides, I'm feet from the canal, when a strong hand grabs my bicep and yanks me back. I twist to see Veronica gripping me, her dark eyes brilliant in the bright sunshine.

"You can't go in there." It comes out as a command.

"Let go of me," I demand. Blue growls, warning her that I am not defenseless.

"Sydney," my mom says. "That water is toxic. Think of the baby."

The rev of the boat engine interrupts us. Fernando pushes the throttle and zooms down the canal, the dark brown water turning copper in his wake.

Robert doesn't surface. I can't even see any bubbles.

"We can't just let him drown!"

"We are not letting him drown," Veronica says. "Someone shot him in the chest. He was dead when he hit the water."

"We need to get out of here now, " Anita says.

Veronica lets go of me and takes my mother's arm instead, leading her along the canal, away from the brawl and the refugee center.

Blue barks a warning; the bus that the Incels arrived in is speeding across the pavement toward us. Veronica sees it the same time that I do. Blue barks again and taps his nose to my hip, nipping at my shirt, trying to herd me away from the oncoming vehicle.

It's not coming for me.

The bus chases down my mom and Veronica. The younger woman pushes Mom to the side, taking the full impact.

Her body flies ten feet, skidding to a stop, the white of her robe stained with dirt and blood. She doesn't move. Smoke plumes from the bus' engine.

A horrible scream tears through the air as my mother runs to Veronica's slumped form. A man gets out of the driver's seat and starts toward my mom. Reaching down I pull the knife free from my ankle holster and move to intercept him.

"Sydney," Anita's voice fades as I close in on my prey.

Enough is enough.

EK

Mulberry

The water takes Robert's body, as if it's been waiting for it. Veronica stops Sydney from going in after him—I expected it to be Anita or Blue, but this works.

The helicopter circles above, capturing it all on film. I sit back, Nila coming to stand by my shoulder, her nose sniffing at the air. *I make a better one-legged assassin than a follower.*

Frank's booted paws crunch on glass as he paces behind me.

I may have just killed any chance of a future with Sydney, but I hope I've secured her safety—at least for a time.

Robert involved me in this drama to destroy my relationship with Sydney, knowing I'd do anything for her. I trust him in this matter only because I know how he feels. But I also know that Sydney will never forgive me once she finds out what happened here today. I've betrayed Joyful Justice, lied to her, and our friends. *It is unforgivable.*

But I agree with Robert Maxim.

We have to keep her safe, no matter the cost. If she thinks it's better for Joyful Justice to hide, then she will and the only way to make her believe is to make it true.

I close the clasps on the gun case, roll up the tarp, and, carrying both, head for the stairs.

CHAPTER TWENTY-EIGHT

Robert

My back hits the water as I take in one more breath. The weight of my clothing helps to sink me deeper, faster. With my lips and eyes pressed closed I reach out blindly with my hands. The water is oily—burning my skin where it isn't covered by the wetsuit hidden under my clothing. Debris bumps against me, disorienting me in the dark quiet.

My fingers brush the slimy wooden side of the canal and I kick toward it, diving deeper, feeling along the beams until I hit the hard metal of the oxygen tank. I clear the mouthpiece, my lungs throbbing, then lay it over my lips and take in a breath. I find the mask and fit it over my head.

The engine of the speedboat throbs to life above me. My face-mask in place, I look up to see Fernando's craft churning the water as it speeds away.

I kick off my shoes and put the flippers on. Settling the oxygen tank straps over my shoulders I swim forward, navigating through the murky water.

It takes fifteen minutes to reach my exit point. When I surface, Declan reaches out and helps haul me up onto the bank. Dr. Smith immediately begins spraying me down with cleansing water as Declan helps me out of my clothing, taking the fake blood packs and bulletproof vest off and then unzipping the wet suit.

The toxic water washed away, the doctor injects me with a shot of antibiotics before putting cream on my face and hands where the water left chemical burns. I dress quickly in dry, clean clothes, my stomach unsettled but my mind clear. My hands are red and blistered, and I can feel the same where my mask and mouthpiece didn't protect me—it's painful but not unbearable. "Keep the burns well lubricated and they should clear up in the next two weeks," Dr. Smith tells me.

No one but Declan, Dr. Smith, and Brock will see me anytime soon, so there is no need for vanity.

By the time I come back to life the burns will be healed, and my plan almost complete.

EK

Sydney

"Please," Mom grips my hands, blood from the now-motionless Incel bus driver sticky between us. "If not for you then for the baby."

I grit my teeth. "I can't just leave." My eyes jump to Veronica, she's breathing but for how much longer. *She needs an ambulance.*

"Please," Mom says again, her eyes wide and pleading.

"We need to go," Anita says. "That helicopter is getting everything." They are centered over the brawl so right now we are off camera but if I run over there…

"I know you want to help," Mom says. "It's your nature. Always has been. But, you must take care of yourself and the baby—don't make the same mistakes I made."

Oh Lord, here we go.

"Mom—" It comes out almost like I'm whining.

"Take care of yourself so that you can care for your child. *Go.*"

My eyes flick behind her where the Incels are overwhelming her followers. There are women on the ground, men standing over them, blows raining down.

"Sorry, Mom," I break free from her. "I can't." The bus driver lies dead at my feet, his tire iron next to his limp hand. I wipe my blade off on my jeans and slip it back into my ankle holster, then scooping up the tire iron, I run toward the fight. Blue taps my hip; he is with me.

"Sydney!" Anita yells as she runs behind me.

A red-headed guy in his early twenties is kicking a women in the fetal position—his hair flopping over his forehead, a grin distorting his face into a bizarre mask. He looks up at the sound of my approaching footfalls. His eyes land on mine and the grin falls. I swing the tire iron, he stumbles back, tripping over his victim and splaying on the ground.

Blue leaps onto him, and Red Head screams, his voice high and terrified, sending a shiver down my spine. Movement in my peripheral vision makes me pivot. A man, blood streaming from a cut on his cheek, is running toward me like a bull seeing red.

I steady myself, the tire iron cocked on my shoulder, ready to play t-ball with this dumb fuck's head when he grabs at his neck. His eyes roll into his head and he drops to his knees, then keels over onto the pavement—a dart sticking out of his neck. What the—?

"Sydney!" Mulberry is jogging toward me, Nila and Frank with him, one of Robert's dart guns in his hand. He's wearing cargo pants, a black T-shirt, and a baseball cap tugged low over his eyes. His gait is lopsided but steady.

Sirens wail in the distance. "We have to go," Mulberry says, gesturing to where an SUV idles behind him.

"I've been saying the same thing," Anita pants, catching up with us.

"Give me the dart gun." I hold out my hand.

He passes it over without question, pulling another from a holster at his lower back.

Red Head is lying still, Blue's teeth around his neck. "Off," I tell Blue, then shoot Red Head. His body goes limp.

"Come on," Mulberry says.

"First we need to put down more of these fuckers." I still have four darts left in this clip. And Mulberry has six. "How many cartridges did you bring?"

"All of them."

And this is why I love this guy. A radio on Mulberry's belt crackles as I aim at the closest Incel member—he's straddling a woman on the ground, trying to press a tire iron against her throat. Her legs kick, and she's got both hands wrapped around the weapon, arms shaking with the effort of holding it at bay. I shoot him in the shoulder, and he slumps over.

"The riot inside is under control," Mulberry tells me, holding the radio to his ear.

I shoot another Incel member. His face hits the pavement. *That's going to leave a mark.*

"How do you know it's contained?" I ask.

"I'm tapped into the National Guard's radio. There are ambulances en route." *Good.*

The helicopter buzzes overhead. I don't look up at it, my baseball cap still shielding my face. Mulberry shoots a man to our right.

I take out another Incel member.

"Why are these guys here?" I ask no one in particular, glancing down at Red Head.

"Dan says they put a call out online. Figured this would be a good place to ambush your mom, considering the lack of police."

"But what about the National Guardsmen?"

"Somehow they knew they'd be occupied," Anita guesses.

"Bingo," Mulberry says, firing again.

Mulberry's radio crackles again. "The guardsmen are coming now," he says, grabbing my arm. There are only a few Incels left and the Her Prophet followers are circling them so we can't get a clear shot anyway. I let Mulberry lead me away, Anita and the dogs coming with us.

We get into his SUV, and he peels out of the parking lot. The helicopter continues to circle over the scene like a giant vulture.

Adrenaline fades from my system. The image of Robert sinking beneath the water flashes back. It's impossible that he is gone. I just don't believe it. My throat tightens. *What if I'm wrong?*

EK

An explanation for the sharpshooter comes that evening. I'm sitting with José at his friend's house, his eyes are red and swollen. "His own son," José sniffles. "He lured him there and then shot him. It's terrible."

Is it true?

I hold the note that was inside the bottle of pills. A warning to Joyful Justice. If we don't back off, we will all die. Robert is just the first. They promise assassinations of all kinds.

The house is modest but comfortable, the owners Cuban immigrants like José. Mulberry stands by the door, his hat still on, head bowed so that I can only see his jaw—it's clenched tight and covered in a day's worth of stubble. Frank leans against his leg, tongue lolling out. Blue sits on José's foot, resting his head on his knee. Nila waits by the door, her ears swirling.

We left Anita at the hotel, her brow furrowed as she furiously typed on her computer, trying to sort out what is going on.

As we head back to meet her, Mulberry clears his throat. "Are you okay?"

I turn to him. "Sure."

"I know you and Robert were close."

"Yes," I agree.

He glances at me and then returns his attention to the road ahead. There isn't much traffic. "You don't seem that upset."

"I don't think he's dead."

"What are you talking about? Anita said you guys saw him get shot, fall in the water, and not come back. He's dead, Sydney."

I shrug. "Doubt it."

"Then what do you think is going on?"

"I think people are trying to destroy Joyful Justice—Robert's son included. They are smart and ruthless and know that killing individuals does little to stop a movement like ours. We are an ideal—justice for all. You can't kill that. But you can tarnish our reputation, make us out to be corrupt, reckless, addicted to violence. You can't do that by creating martyrs. Look what happened when I tried to kill off Joy Humbolt. She became even more popular, a bigger influence. And this group that's going after us, they're not dumb. They're just on the wrong side."

Mulberry stays quiet for a long time. "Is it possible they plan on both —tarnishing our reputation and killing people?"

I shrug. "Sure."

"And do you really think Robert is somehow part of this plot, that he would turn against you?"

Is it better if he's dead or has betrayed me? "I don't know. I'll deal with it if he turns up. One thing at a time." My phone buzzes—a text from my mother. "Veronica is in stable condition," I tell Mulberry.

"Good," he says. We spend the rest of the drive back to the hotel in silence.

Anita knocks on my door as I'm getting out of the shower. I let her in and then dress quickly in the bathroom. She's standing at the window, holding a glass of cognac and watching the airline traffic, when I come out.

"Long day," I say.

She huffs a small laugh and turns to me. "I want to ask a favor."

"Okay…"

She puts her drink down on a side table and clasps her hands in front of her.

"There is more footage of you, from today. People are piecing it together—it doesn't look good for us. Convincing the world that we had nothing to do with that riot is hard when there is video footage of you in the middle of that fight." I nod but don't respond. She hasn't asked for anything yet. "You're a liability. Please lay low. Stop fighting for a while."

"How can I?" my voice is quiet, genuine. "They are trying to destroy us."

"What you resist will persist, Sydney. They will succeed if you refuse to work with us and instead act as a lone wolf." Anita takes a deep breath. "I'm sorry, but you need to hide for a while. Go to the island or Costa Rica. Let me deal with this—this, Sydney, is a PR situation. The more we fight, the faster we sink."

I sit on the bed, lips pressed tight. *She's right but I hate to admit it.*

Anita sits next to me and takes my hand, lacing her fingers with mine. "Motherhood will make you strong. Stronger than you've ever been, but in new ways. Please." She isn't pleading, just asking gently. "Acknowledge this change and work with me. You're better off away from all this."

I'm exposed and vulnerable. My hand comes up and rests on my belly. Blue taps his wet nose to my elbow.

"Okay," I say, my voice low.

"Thank you." Anita lets out a long breath. "Thank you," she says again. Then she smiles and squeezes my hand. "Don't worry, you're going to have plenty of time to fight, but right now you can take comfort from your friends—let us take care of you for a while."

I nod my agreement.

Alone, in the dark, the curtains pulled aside, I watch planes take off and land. Blue lays on the bed with me, his back pressed to my spine. Frank snores at my feet and Nila is curled in the bend of my knees. My hand rests on my stomach.

Determination hardens in my gut. I will survive. My child will survive. Joyful Justice will not be destroyed by rumors or lies. We will fight this war until the end of time.

I'm pulled from my sleep by another knock on my door.

Blue is waiting by it, his tail still, his eyes trained on the wood. Frank is still snoring and Nila waits by the bed. I cross to the door and look through the peep hole. *Impossible.*

Mercury gray eyes stare back at me. I fumble to remove the chain, my mind reeling...I must be dreaming but oh what a beautiful dream.

I get the door open and stare. "James?"

He opens his arms, and I fall into them. This is impossible. He's dead. There is no coming back. But his breath on my shoulder feels real, the press of his arms around me, the scent of him. It all feels so real.

"Hey, Sis," he says into my hair.

I'm crying, sobbing...elated and terrified. If this is a dream I don't want it to end.

EK

Turn the page to read an excerpt from
Blind Vigilance, A Sydney Rye Mystery Book 13 or purchase it now
and continue reading Sydney's next adventure:
emilykimelman.com/BV

* * *

Sign up for my newsletter and stay up to date on new releases, free
books, and giveaways:
emilykimelman.com/News

SNEAK PEEK
BLIND VIGILANCE, SYDNEY RYE MYSTERIES BOOK 13

Chapter One

Dan

Blood. It's blood. The dark stain circling Sydney is *blood.*

Fuck. Fuck. Fuck. I grab my phone, unlock it, navigate to favorites, and touch Mulberry's name without even fully registering the thought.

It rings. *How am I going to explain knowing Sydney Rye needs help?*

I'm thousands of miles away, stationed on a private island in the middle of the fucking Pacific. And yet—

"Hello?" Mulberry's voice, gravelly with sleep, cuts through my thoughts.

"Sydney is bleeding."

My phone beeps. I'm getting another call.

"What?" Mulberry's voice clears as sheets rustle in the background.

A dog barks. I focus on the monitor with the live feed of Sydney's room. Blue is up and going wild. *Shit.*

I didn't even need to call. The dogs would have alerted Mulberry. *Foolish. Careless. Shit.*

"What's going on, Dan?"

I don't answer.

The door between Mulberry and Sydney's rooms flies open—I watch it on the screen and hear the hinges swoosh over the phone line. Reaching out, I slide my finger along the stylus bar to raise the volume. Mulberry stumbles into Sydney's room, unsteady on just his one leg.

She didn't lock the door. That isn't like her. Except it was Mulberry on the other side. A subtle invitation?

"Fuck!" Mulberry's voice echoes between the phone and computer speakers. He lunges toward the bed.

Sydney lies on her back, a dark stain spreading around her hips. Mulberry drops the phone when he grabs her shoulders.

I swivel to a different monitor and bring up Mulberry's phone screen. I dial 911. Someone has to. I can always be counted on to do what needs doing. Overstepping saves lives.

"What's your emergency?" the Miami 911 operator asks.

I clench my fist on the glass surface of my desk. *Answer her, you asshole.* Mulberry doesn't follow my mental command. *Fine.* I take full control of the phone. "My wife is pregnant and bleeding. We're at the airport Marriott, room 523," I say, my voice even and clear. I say it like it's my baby. Like it's my life. Not something I'm watching on a screen. My eyes flick back to the live feed of her room. "I can't wake her."

Dear Jesus. Mulberry sits on the edge of the bed, face tear streaked.

Sydney isn't moving.

She isn't moving.

Don't let her die.

EK

Sydney

"It's time to wake up, Joy." James smiles at me, his hand warm in mine.

"Wake up?" I ask. He nods. "Wait." Tears thicken my voice. "This isn't real?"

He shrugs, eyes sad. "It is, but you're sleeping. And now you have to wake up." James smiles; it's subtle, not like the grins he used to offer so freely. There is a film of sorrow around him now. We didn't understand the price of joy or it's fleeting nature.

"I'm so sorry you're dead," I say. The words are like glass in my throat, leaving behind a thirst that a million gallons of water will never quench.

His smile widens, and he reaches up to swipe a tear from my cheek. "Me too, me too...."

I awaken from the dream in a wash of confusion. Blue's nose is wet against my hand. Mulberry looms over me, his fingers digging into my shoulders. "Get off." I raise my arms to push him away. They are heavy... too heavy.

I'm cold.

This is shock.

"Sydney!" Mulberry is yelling.

"What?" My mouth is full of cotton, that raging thirst still there.

"You're bleeding."

He swings his arm down to indicate my lower half. I struggle to lift my head. There's a red stain around my hips. *The baby.*

Panic seizes my chest. "Mulberry," I eke out.

He's holding his phone now. "She's awake," he says. "She's lost a lot of blood."

Blue whines softly next to me, and I meet his eyes. "I'm okay," I promise him, my speech slurred. I must have lost a lot of blood. My eyes slip closed, and the darkness takes me again. But this time, I'm alone. James is gone.

Really gone.

Sharp pain strikes through my chest like a lightning bolt, and I hear the sizzle of the electric current, feel it writhe through me. Love will destroy us if we let it.

EK

Dan

They take Sydney out on a stretcher. Mulberry has the presence of mind to close the hotel room door, locking the dogs inside. He forgets to grab Sydney's phone, computer, and bag. *That won't blind me though.*

Blue sniffs at the bloody sheets before herding his puppies into Mulberry's room through the still-open connecting door.

I watch Mulberry's text scroll across the screen—he's letting Anita know they are on the way to the hospital. I use my app on Anita's phone to turn on the cameras and microphone. Her face fills one box and her rumpled sheets the other.

Dark brown eyes flanked by thick black lashes read the text. Her lips part, and the wrinkle she gets between her brows when she's upset appears. Anita clamps her teeth down on her bottom lip, worrying it as she responds to Mulberry's text. *I'll meet you at the hospital.*

His phone is in his pocket, but the siren wails through the speakers. I'm leaving the sound up in case the paramedics say anything important.

Anita takes her phone with her into the bathroom and puts it on the counter so that one camera darkens and the other shows the light fixture and mirror.

I silence Anita's phone and turn away from the screen, offering her some privacy. On a different monitor, I shoot Anita a quick text to remind her to take Sydney her phone and computer—I'm sure she'll want it. I'm being thoughtful.

My phone chimes to remind me I have a message. *My mom.* I glance at the transcription. *Hi honey, just calling to check in. Call me back when you can. I know how busy you are, so don't feel any pressure. There is something kind of (unintelligible) so call.*

The siren turns off, and there is motion in Mulberry's pocket. Anita throws her phone into her bag. I turn up the volume on Mulberry's device, straining to make out what is being said. I grab my headphones and slip them on.

Sorry, Mom, you'll have to wait.

Sydney

"She's going to be fine, sir."

My eyes are glued shut, but it's bright out there.

"What about the baby?" Mulberry's voice—edged with anxiety—asks.

"We'll know soon."

I want to speak, but I can't. I want to scream, but I have no voice. I want to sit up, run out of there, be away from all of this... but I can't move.

I hear James's voice. *Relax, everything is okay. Rest.*

And I slip back into darkness.

EK

"Hey." Mulberry leans over the bed, his face coming into view. "You're awake."

I blink. He turns and grabs a cup of water, offering me the straw. I suck, my head feeling light and my body weak. The water slips down, soothing my burning thirst.

Lying back against the pillows, I close my eyes. "The baby?" I ask.

"It's fine," Mulberry says. Relief hits me like a ray of sunlight bursting through cloud cover. "Hold on, I'll get the doctor."

He leaves, and I cradle my stomach, gratitude welling inside me. Tears burn my eyes, and I let them flow, don't even try to stop their slow march down my cheeks.

Mulberry comes back with a doctor. "This is Dr. Hope," Mulberry introduces the tall, graying man. The doctor smiles like he's heard everything one might say about an OBGYN named Hope so there is no need to add to the repertoire. Mulberry returns to the chair next to my bed, and I rub at my eyes, pulling myself together.

"The baby is fine for now, " Dr Hope says from the end of the bed. "You've had a subchorionic hemorrhage, so we need to take some precautions."

Mulberry squeezes my hand so hard I wince and pull away. He looks at me and then down at our hands. "Sorry," he mumbles and lets go.

"I'd like to keep you overnight, and then bed rest for the next few weeks while we keep an eye on this."

"Can we move her out of the city?" Mulberry asks.

Dr. Hope nods slowly. "Yes, she should be fine to leave the hospital tomorrow, just no carrying any heavy bags. Did you lose your home in the storm?" His brow furrows as he references the hurricane that recently tore through Miami, leaving it devastated.

"Yes," Mulberry lies easily. We didn't have a home here. The only thing we share is a fraught history and the new life growing inside of me. "What does bed rest mean exactly, like how much movement?"

"She doesn't need a bedpan or anything but restrict movement as much as possible."

Mulberry nods, mulling this over with a furrowed brow. "So, she should get a wheelchair at the airport. And she should stay still. But a couch is okay?"

"Yes, that's fine."

"I'm right here," I point out. Mulberry turns to me, all male confusion. "You two are talking about me like I'm not here." I switch focus to the doctor. "What is a subchorionic hemorrhage?"

He clears his throat. "A hemorrhage that forms between the placenta and uterine wall. You had a medium-size hemorrhage. Lots of women go on to have healthy pregnancies, but the blood loss is frightening for the patient."

"Why didn't she wake up?" Mulberry asks. "It took a lot to get her to come to."

"Again," I say, my voice tight, "I'm *right* here."

"Sorry." Mulberry sighs. "I'm upset."

"That doesn't give you the right to stop treating me like a person."

His lips thin, and color raises into his cheeks. "I'm worried about *you.* I am very aware *you* are a person."

"Good. Feel free to use my name."

A tight smile tugs at his lips, and he raises one brow. *Which name?* his expression questions. I return my attention to the doctor who seems used to couples squabbling. "Why bed rest?" I ask.

Mulberry stiffens next to me. Dr. Hope cocks his head, surprised that I'm questioning his prescription. "We want to avoid this happening again."

"Are the hemorrhages caused by movement?"

"We don't fully know what causes them, but rest is important during the early months of pregnancy."

"Exercise is almost always a good thing," I say.

"Are you really arguing with him?" Mulberry asks, his voice growing louder.

I glare at him, and his eyes narrow to mere slits of anger and frustration. "It's *my* body."

"It's *our* baby."

I may punch him in front of the doctor. I don't want to, but I might have to. "I'll let you two discuss," Dr. Hope says, removing himself from the room posthaste. *Smart man.*

"I will go insane sitting around for months, Mulberry; you know that."

"I guess you'll have to dig deep."

I bark out a laugh, and the tension around his eyes lessens. He reaches out for my hand, and I let him take it.

I take a deep breath. "Here's the deal. I'm going to do my own research. But from everything I know about my body, being still isn't good for it."

"Maybe this is its way of saying it wants you to slow down." Mulberry drops his gaze to our linked hands. "Your body may need something different than it ever needed before."

Hold up. What are we talking about?

He looks up at me. Yellow bands of color radiated from his pupils, carving a path through the green irises. I drop my gaze. He wants things I can't give him.

The door opens, and a nurse enters. "Hello, Tara," she says, using my alias. "I'm Maud. I'll be your nurse for the next twelve hours. How are you feeling?" She walks up to the machine next to me and checks the IV.

"Fine," I say.

She looks at her watch and then across to Mulberry. "Visiting hours are over in fifteen minutes. Just a heads-up."

"I'm her husband," Mulberry says.

The nurse shakes her head. "Not according to my paperwork, honey." She smiles but isn't falling for anything.

"We're engaged," he says. *Damn, he's good at lying. When did he get so good at that?* Maybe always and I just never noticed.

"Don't lie to me," the nurse says, not falling for any of it. "I've got five kids."

"Five?" I sputter out.

She pats my hand. "It gets easier," she says before returning her attention to Mulberry. "Tara needs to rest, and while you two might be having a baby, it seems you're also having some disagreements." Mulberry's cheeks brighten. Oh my God, she's making him blush. This woman is my hero. "So get ready to hit the road, son."

With that she leaves the room. I'm grinning. "I'll be back first thing in the morning," Mulberry promises. "I'll take care of the dogs; you don't need to worry about them."

"Thanks."

He stands, looking down at me. I tilt my chin to maintain eye contact. "You scared me." His words hit me right in the chest.

"I'm sorry."

He nods then turns toward the door but pauses when he reaches it, refocusing on me. "I'll see you tomorrow."

I nod.

He opens the door and leaves. I reach for my phone, grateful that Anita thought to bring it for me. Time to turn to Dr. Google....

Chapter Two

Lenox

A unicorn stands with its head bent, the mythical creature's horn directing the viewers' focus to a gangly foal at her feet. Mountains in gold and green rise up behind the new mother. Intricate flowers, each petal shimmering in pale pink, create a border around the central image of the tapestry.

I cross my arms. "$23,257," I offer, a specific and final amount.

The salesman doesn't respond immediately; he wants more. *Doesn't everybody?* But my voice leaves no room for bargaining. We've gone back and forth over several cups of tea—the mint scents the air, along with the wool rugs. Fiber dust motes drift in the shafts of sunlight that filter through the stained skylights.

One of my first regular clients, a rug salesman's wife, liked to get fucked on her husband's stock. The scent of this showroom brings the sweet perfume of her to my nose, reminding me that I, too, was once stock to be bargained over and sold.

The dealer and I have reached the end of negotiation. He must decide: should he sell to me or wait for another offer?

A low thud vibrates through the room. Someone in the market dropped something heavy. And though only a few feet separate us from the busy passageways beyond, the tapestries on the walls and rugs layered on the floor keep the sales room suspended in near silence.

"That is a good deal," Petra says, her heels quiet on the rugs as she moves across the room.

She stares at me with an intensity that sends shivers down my spine. Now that Petra no longer pays me, it's as if her gaze has become that much more riveting. She has me, yet her longing grows.

Petra has never claimed to love me. And while I spent a brief moment in my youth thinking I loved her, my heart is my own again. It sits to the left of my spine and beats with the will of a warrior, the tenacity of a street dog, and the ice-cold certainty of a vigilante. It is mine, and so it shall remain. It is the only sure way to survive.

"You drive a hard bargain," the salesman says.

"You have no idea," Petra purrs, circling behind me and running a hand up my spine. Her nails scratch through the layers of coat, sports jacket, and shirt to leave a trail of heat. "He is very hard."

I suppress a laugh as Petra stalks to the salesman. "Leave us," she says.

The merchant glances at me, and I keep my face unreadable. He looks back at Petra—whose back is to me so I can't see her expression—but it makes the man leave his own shop.

Petra stands in a band of sunlight. The black knee-length cashmere coat absorbs the light, but the sheer stockings reflect it. Her green eyes, catlike in shape and temperament, smile.

Petra is good at smiling with just her eyes. The stern line of those luscious lips—painted harlot red—tighten my stomach. "I want you," she says, her voice even. The woman never plays coy, never acts shy.

I let a smile twitch across my lips.

"I don't want much." She takes a step toward me, showing the flash of red from the bottom of her black pump that matches her lips. "Just a kiss."

Her lip trembles as if she is afraid I'll refuse her, and she bites down on it with white teeth, her eyes turning soft. But not pleading. She won't beg... yet.

Petra needs to be on the absolute edge to beg.

I glance at my watch—a gold Rolex gifted to me by another client—and then back to the rugs. I could have her there in six minutes, but to do it right, to *really* make her scream, would take seventeen.

I only have fifteen. I'll make it work.

I always make it work. I'll have Petra on a lovely vintage Oushak rug and, before we leave, I'll have the tapestry too.

EK

Petra's arm rests in the crook of mine as we leave the restaurant. A fine mist thickens the air and sparkles in the streetlight's glow. A cool breeze blasts down the street, and Petra grips my arm, her hair whipping around her shoulders.

We make our way to the Paris Hotel—one of the oldest and grandest in Istanbul. We've come to see Yusuf Polat, who keeps a suite here. The doorman bows to us as he opens the door.

Water shimmers in Petra's chestnut hair like dew in a spiderweb. She smiles at a bellboy, and he blushes. *Poor thing.*

"Good evening," the front desk attendant greets us. "We are expecting you, please." She waves a graceful arm to another bellboy. "Mustafa will show you up." Mustafa bows and takes us up in the elevator.

To think there was a time when people could not operate elevators on their own. During that period, people of my skin color would not have been welcome in this hotel unless as an employee. Now I enter as an honored guest. We shall see if I make it out with such auspicious reverence.

EK

Yusuf reminds me of the *Star Wars* character, Jabba the Hutt. Except the beautiful young woman attending him is not held by a literal chain around her neck but rather the invisible economic bonds of class, birth, and sex.

I watched *Return of The Jedi* mostly naked in a British tourist's hotel room, the curtains drawn tight against the bright beach sun trying to blast into the dark, intimate world we'd created. *Marigold.* Lovely in her fifties, she told me I was beautiful enough to be on film. Her skin smelled of sunscreen and the hotel's jasmine-scented soap. She ate her toast dry with black coffee and laughed easily. Marigold remained a client for years.

A weight swings from my heart at the memory of that day, of her, of the me I used to be. When I see a young woman forced into the same profession, flashes of my past work life evoke a mix of nostalgia and relief. I *chose* to sell my body to climb out of poverty. I held on to my dignity, creating a strong and thriving identity that still serves me today.

This girl, with her sallow skin, dark circles, and slumped shoulders, teeters on the edge of total destruction. If the drugs don't swallow her, then that viscous inner voice will tear her to pieces. Princess Leia knew she didn't belong in chains. This girl looks as if she believes she was born to wear them.

I inhale slowly through my nose, taking my gaze from the ornamental whore to the beast of a man sitting on the love seat beside her. His pudgy fingers, decorated with fat gold rings, dig into her thin thigh hard enough to leave fresh bruises. They will match the ones on her arms that she's covered in makeup but still shine through.

"Petra." Yusuf smiles broadly and stands. His silk Versace shirt, patterned with gold lengths of twining rope, gapes open to his stomach —tan, hairy, and shiny, as if he is sweating or had just rubbed on oil.

Petra shrugs out of her coat, and one of Yusuf's guards, a mountain of a man in a sharkskin suit, steps forward to help her. Mountain's diminutive counterpart—the physical opposite but wearing the same suit with its bulging sidearm—stands just behind us with his hands loose at his side. Ready to kill.

Yusuf takes Petra's hand, and they kiss cheeks. Petra turns to me. "This is my partner, Lenox Gold," Petra says. I bow my head as Mountain moves behind me, a silent request for my overcoat.

I slip it off my shoulders and let the man take it, acting as though the weight of it, the extra layer between me and the scum in this room, wasn't a slight comfort. Yusuf holds out his hand, and I meet it with my own, placing a subtle smile on my lips and bringing a light of vague interest into my eyes, ignoring the slick feel of him.

The best whores are the best actors.

"Please," Yusuf says, "what can I get you to drink?"

"Red wine," Petra says. I nod that I'll have the same.

Yusuf waves a hand at Tiny, and he stalks to a bar, his suit glinting with each step. Yusuf returns to his seat, not bothering to introduce the woman next to him. She doesn't meet our eyes, just stares down at her hands lying limp against her bare thighs. The dress she's wearing is black and clingy as a bathing suit.

"Sit," Yusuf invites, gesturing to the two armchairs that face the love seat. I wait for Petra to settle into the gaudy gold and red thing before taking my place beside her.

"Chivalrous," Yusuf comments. "Did you learn that as a gigolo?"

He says it as if to elicit shame. *Sorry to disappoint, Jabba.* "My mother always taught me to respect women, treat them with delicacy, while also recognizing their incredible strength. They are creators, after all, Yusuf. We merely provide the seed."

"But without the seed, a plant cannot grow."

"Without the soil and sun, it will never survive." I smile.

Yusuf barks out a laugh. "I like him." He flings an arm around the nameless creator next to him.

Mountain hands us our wine, and Yusuf's grin slowly fades. "I like you." He says it to me this time instead of addressing Petra. "But I don't like you coming into my city and doing what you're doing."

"Yusuf." Petra uses that purr of hers, the one that raises the hairs on men's arms… and other parts as well. "I've worked in this city for a decade, and you never had a problem with me before. I still pay my dues."

He blinks slowly, the fat around his eyes tightening as he stares at her. "Ian is very upset about his brothers." Murdering a man's family does often upset them.

"Business." Petra shrugs. "You understand." She raises one brow, as though they share knowledge of past deeds done.

"What you're doing isn't business. It's charity."

My voice catches in my throat, holding it in, not letting my own beliefs and emotions into this moment. Yusuf runs this city's under-world, and if we want to survive not just tonight but the years ahead, we either have to negotiate with him… or end him.

"Yusuf," Petra uses his name again. "Charity?" She shakes her head. "Happy whores make happy customers. Also, better working conditions allow us to have a higher level of entertainment. And—" She sips her wine. "—keeps Joyful Justice off our backs."

Yusuf sucks at his teeth. "I don't like it." He frowns. "You used to work with the McCain brothers. Now you turn on them." The lines around his mouth deepen. "You start letting girls out of contracts." The girl next to him flicks her gaze up to Petra just for a second, but Yusuf senses it. His hand grips her shoulder, and she curls deeper into herself. She won't be safe anywhere until this man is dead.

"You worked with Omer for many years," Petra says, her voice light but edged with warning. "And that did not stop you from moving up."

Yusuf shifts in his seat, leaning further back, feigning a relaxed and powerful pose, but the man does not like having his inglorious past put in front of his face. *Petra, be careful. A puppy will let you rub its nose in its mistakes, but a full-grown pit bull will not.*

"You have higher ambitions then?" Yusuf asks, the warning in his tone absolute—*do not answer wrong, or I will kill you now.*

Mountain and Tiny are still behind us. They have not moved, but they don't have far to go for their weapons.

237

"I only wish to make the most money that I can with the least amount of hassle," Petra answers. "As always."

Yusuf shifts his gaze to me. "And what about you, Lenox Gold? Do you have ambitions?"

"Of course. I am a man."

Yusuf bares his teeth in a grin. "What do you want?"

"I wish to create a profitable business and healthy work environment for my employees."

Yusuf coughs a derisive laugh, his belly shaking from the sound. "Employees." He sits forward, putting his elbows on his knees. "Call them what they are, Mr. Gold. They are whores." He says the word as if it is a wine he wants to fully get the taste of, swirling it around in his mouth, enjoying the subtle flavors. I offer him a friendly smile. His eyes narrow. "You don't like women?"

I allow a flash of a grin, a hint of my true wolfish nature to peek from behind the blinds. He will trust a man who likes to fuck because he believes that none of us can control our inner beast. What men like Yusuf never learn is that leashing the beast heightens its appetite and pleasure.

"I enjoy consensual sex with women," I answer, cool as a sunset cocktail on the bow of a yacht. "Very much so." My voice drops an octave to a velvety, dark place that every sensual being knows and desires.

Yusuf laughs. "Consensual. You are very modern, aren't you, Mr. Gold?" He grips the girl's leg again but maintains eye contact with me, daring me to challenge him. To see which of our wolves can tear out the other's throat first.

I sip my wine, my expression once again that gentle friendliness that has served me so well. Yusuf shifts his attention to Petra again. "I will need a higher royalty," he announces. "You're hurting business all over the city, starting to get whores talking about rights." He says *rights* like it's a foul-tasting oyster he has to spit out or risk infection.

"But, Yusuf," Petra keeps her voice friendly, "we already pay you 10 percent. With overhead, you leave us so little," she pouts.

"What do I care?" Yusuf drops the words like stones into the bottom of a well—deep, big plops. At least we know there is water down there.

"You see no reason to care," I mirror his language.

"That's right. Your business margins are not my problem."

"Not your problem."

He nods, enjoying the mirroring. So many men do. I wait in silence, knowing he'll speak again. "I don't like what you are doing or the way you are doing it."

"Our methods are not to your liking."

He nods, agreeing with me... himself. "It does not make sense to treat them so well."

"Why should we treat them so well?" I smile gently. *I hear you.* That's all anyone wants... to be heard. Understood. Empathized with. If you give a man empathy, you earn his soul. The devil is so good at bargaining because he knows what his victims truly want. The key to any good negotiation is to find out what your counterpart wants, empathize with them, then show them how giving *you* what you want can better fulfill their needs.

"Exactly! Letting whores out of their contracts, that looks bad for all of us."

"Bad for everyone."

His nostrils flare. "It riles up the workers."

"Riles up the workers."

"Makes them think they are important and can stand against us."

"Gives them a false sense of importance."

"That's right!" Yusuf glances at the girl next to him. "Take Anna here." The girl flinches as if someone might actually *take* her. "She's a good girl. But what if she worked at one of your places? Would you treat her right, keep her in her place? Or let her cry and beg off?"

I nod slowly. "It seems like you want to make sure that your business practices won't be undermined by the changes we've implemented."

"Right!" I wait, letting time slip by, letting silence work its magic. "Giving into Joyful Justice is no way to defeat them."

"We can't defeat Joyful Justice by giving into them."

His mouth spreads into a cat-who-ate-the-canary smile. "You've got it." He glances at Petra. "Your man here knows what he's talking about."

Petra sips her wine and offers a friendly smile. *We just want to find a way to live together in this crazy world.* "It seems like you want to destroy Joyful Justice," Petra says.

"Of course I do." His eyes narrow. "Don't you?"

I shrug. "They have backed off since the McCain brothers left Petra's organization."

Yusuf laughs. "You are a slick one, aren't you, Lenox Gold?"

"You seem to think I'm trying to trick you."

"No." His brow furrows as his ego rebels.

"Sorry." I raise my free hand. "I just said it seemed that way. I must have misread the situation."

"That's right. You did." He calms.

"It looks like what you want isn't a bigger percentage of our business but for your business to remain the same. You want the status quo to be maintained."

"What if I want both?" He leans back again, putting a fat arm around Anna.

"You want us to return to standardized practices and give you a larger percentage?"

"That sounds good to me."

"Our business is a problem for you."

"It's *a* problem. Giving into Joyful Justice's demands is dangerous and shortsighted."

"Dangerous and shortsighted," I mirror.

"Exactly! Next thing you know, they'll be demanding that we shut down altogether."

"It seems like you're concerned about future problems with Joyful Justice."

He leans forward then, faster than a man of his girth should be able to move. "I don't worry, Mr. Gold. I prepare."

I nod, using my imagination to try to slip into his skin. *If I was Yusuf, ran illegal trade in Istanbul and environs....* "You are always prepared."

"Yes, always." A bead of sweat slips from his hairline down the side of his face. "So you will give me my 20 percent and stop letting whores out of agreements. Then maybe, *maybe,* I will let you continue to work in *my* city."

"How are we supposed to do that?" *Ask a calibrated question when a demand is made.*

He raises both brows. "Not my problem."

"There are other services in the city that have rules similar to ours."

"High-end escort services. That is very different."

"How is it different?"

His nostrils flare again, and he shakes his head. "I'm done with this conversation."

"What if we could help with Joyful Justice?"

He raises his brows, a sneaky smile cresting his lips. "I have that in hand. You don't need to worry about them."

"We will need to think about all this," Petra says, standing. "Thank you for your time."

"Come back with your new percentage, or don't come back," Yusuf warns, also standing. Anna and I are the only two still sitting. Our eyes meet for a brief moment, but hers dart away quickly.

"How much for her?" I ask, cursing myself but knowing I can't leave without her.

"Who?" Yusuf sounds genuinely confused.

I look up at him. "Anna."

He glances at her. Yusuf shakes his head. "She's not for sale."

I smile. "Yusuf, everyone has a price."

He likes that—the idea that people and morals can be bought and sold. "Make me an offer."

I stay seated, letting him feel bigger than me. "$1,000." I start with a low, round number.

He snorts and turns away, pacing toward his armed guards. "Not even close," he throws over his shoulder.

"What if I promise to treat her 'right'?"

Petra catches my eye but gives nothing away. She won't undermine me in front of Yusuf, but her heart does not bleed like mine. This is foolish.

I stand and join Petra. Yusuf looms behind the love seat, his hands on Anna's shoulders. She stares glassy-eyed at her lap. "She is one of my favorites," Yusuf says. "Never knew a man before me."

"You are lucky," I say.

"I am powerful, and I take what I want."

"Yes," I agree. "Very powerful."

He straightens, relinquishing the girl. "I will give her to you, a gift." He smiles. "A thank-you for the increase in profit sharing and return to normalcy at your establishments."

"Thank you," Petra says before I can speak. "Come," she says to Anna. The girl looks up at Petra, her eyes wide with astonishment and fear. She doesn't trust this turn of events. None of us do.

Continue reading *Blind Vigilance*: emilykimelman.com/BV

AUTHOR'S NOTE

I hope you enjoyed *Savage Grace*! I'm guessing you did since you've gotten all the way to this note. I'd love to hear your thoughts about the *Savage Grace*—and I'm not the only one. Reviews help other readers make decisions.

I appreciate you giving me a chance and am grateful to every reader who takes the time to read my books.

Let people know what you thought about *Savage Grace* on your favorite ebook retailer.

Thank you,

Emily

ABOUT THE AUTHOR

I write because I love to read...but I have specific tastes. I love to spend time in fictional worlds where justice is exacted with a vengeance. Give me raw stories with a protagonist who feels like a friend, heroic pets, plots that come together with a BANG, and long series so the adventure can continue. If you got this far in my book then I'm assuming you feel the same...

Sign up for my newsletter and
never miss a new release or sale:
emilykimelman.com/News

I also have an exclusive Facebook group just for my readers! Join *Emily Kimelman's Insatiable Readers* to stay up to date on sales and releases, have exclusive giveaways, and hang out with your fellow book addicts: emilykimelman.com/EKIR.

If you've read my work and want to get in touch please do! I loves hearing from
readers.
www.emilykimelman.com
emily@emilykimelman.com

[f] facebook.com/EmilyKimelman
[o] instagram.com/emilykimelman

EMILY'S BOOKSHELF

Visit www.emilykimelman.com to purchase your next adventure.

EMILY KIMELMAN
MYSTERIES & THRILLERS

Sydney Rye Mysteries

Unleashed

Death in the Dark

Insatiable

Strings of Glass

Devil's Breath

Inviting Fire

Shadow Harvest

Girl with the Gun

In Sheep's Clothing

Flock of Wolves

Betray the Lie

Savage Grace

Blind Vigilance

Fatal Breach

Undefeated

Relentless

Coming Winter 2023

Starstruck Thrillers

A Spy Is Born

EMILY REED

URBAN FANTASY

Kiss Chronicles

Lost Secret

Dark Secret

Stolen Secret

Buried Secret

Coming 2023

Lost Wolf Legends

Butterfly Bones

Coming 2023

Made in the USA
Middletown, DE
22 September 2022

10667529R00149